Richard James was born in 1965 in Buckinghamshire, studied French and German at St Andrews University, and worked in the wine business in London and Manchester for ten years before going freelance five years ago. He is a writer, journalist and tutor specialising in wine, food and travel. He currently lives in Manchester, but plans to move to the Mediterranean. *Red* is his first novel.

Red

RICHARD JAMES

Thanks to Faber & Faber Ltd (UK and Commonwealth)
and Grove/Atlantic Inc (North America) for permission
to quote lines from *Krapp's Last Tape* by Samuel Beckett.

First published 2002 by GMP (Gay Men's Press),
PO Box 3220, Brighton BN2 5AU

GMP is an imprint of Millivres Prowler Limited,
part of the Millivres Prowler Group,
Spectrum House, 32-34 Gordon House Road,
London NW5 1LP UK

www.gaymenspress.co.uk

A CIP catalogue record for this book is available from the British Library

ISBN 1-902852-41-9

Printed and bound in Finland by WS Bookwell

Distributed in the UK and Europe by Airlift Book Company,
8 The Arena, Mollison Avenue,
Enfield, Middlesex EN3 7NJ
Telephone: 020 8804 0400
Distributed in North America by Consortium,
1045 Westgate Drive, St Paul, MN 55114-1065
Telephone: 1 800 283 3572
Distributed in Australia by Bulldog Books,
PO Box 300, Beaconsfield, NSW 2014

Part I

Pictures of Cities

BEGINNING, DREAM, BAR

I woke up unfiltered, camera still rolling in my head, from a disturbing but probably meaningful dream. It seemed very bright, what was I doing in bed? Clock 10.34, duvet thrown against the wall, waterfall of piss Barnes Wallising into the toilet then gushing as if poured from a jug. Steaming hot shower, the mirror condensated, my face dissolved into it. The dream started on what appeared to be the moon or maybe just a distant desert, and I was sitting talking to a man I didn't know who slowly turned to reveal he had no face. We were chatting for a long time; the subject eluded me now, perhaps about perceptions of oneself or the high price of bottled imported beers. He suddenly pulled out two silver automatic handguns and blew me away. I looked up, his face now clear; it was mine. I woke up; it wasn't the first time I'd had this dream.

Fast forward to later. I was slouching in an overcrowded trendy bar in Manchester drinking an overpriced imported bottle of beer. Quite good though, nice balance of rich maltiness and tangy hoppiness. Where the fuck is Ben? My watch was usually fast, so my eyes cut to the station-large clock on the wall: 9.50. Day? Date? Of little interest to me but it might help, so I'll pluck 1997 out of the air. Better? My head then scanned and quickly edited the people in the bar: old one-eye to the left sporting a purple patch, a fashion accessory rather than ophthalmic, I thought; two 'pretty' boys over there, all androgynous make-up and Adidas T-shirts. The music was Radiohead, morose but moving. He looks nervous – is he out on his own or has he

3

been stood up? Beautiful dark eyes, deep-set in his face causing mystery-laden shadows around them; can't quite see his soul. Smart short formerly blond hair, subtle earring, drinking perhaps Australian Chardonnay: certainly a golden colour anyway. Black-ish jeans, bold red shirt, slim, in his 20s... maybe 30s: one of those who appeared (or dolled up) younger than they were. Enough of him; Ben obviously wasn't coming. My mind raced, a combination of free-fall thoughts, too many beers and that strong dope Bob and I had smoked earlier. I couldn't stop staring at red-shirt, not just that I found him attractive but he reminded me of somebody from the past; several people in fact. I dissolved into my glass of beer.

PARIS, JEAN-LUC, SHIRAZ

I refocused on a glass of red wine, a terrific Chinon if I remember correctly, but definitely don't remember the name of the vineyard.

Paris was the first stop in my road movie to rediscover myself – well, London was actually but that didn't really count as I'd lived there in the past. It was...how many years ago? Ach, doesn't matter; anyway, not allowed to tell you yet. It was a sombre but dry March day, I think, and I sat outside an outrageously Parisian-look-ing café sipping red wine and purposefully scoffing olives – heav-ily marinated in tarragon, rosemary and chilli, juicy yet pruney. I was reading a critical article on David Cronenberg's latest film, which concluded it was immoral or some such crap. Probably had-n't even seen it. Sorry – I'm the one talking crap, mixing up my Paris stories. I was outside a café eating olives, but it was more like July; it was hot, I remember now. In fact I was reading Joyce's *Dubliners* as I recall finishing it the following day. Glad that was clear. A... yes, handsome man was parked across from me flicking through a newspaper. Deepest of dark eyes, reminded me of somebody.

I spent about two months in Paris at that time, rightly deemed a magnificent city: my mind picked out and conjured dramatic shots of the ferric-clad Eiffel Tower, exposed arteries of the Centre Pompidou, Arc de Triomphe resting in imperial arrogance, Place de la Concorde in traffic gridlock. Apart from it being the first stage in my journey, I was there for another reason. I wasn't consciously aware of what that reason was when I arrived in the fair city, but did after I became acquainted with mystery man displayed opposite me outside that catalysing café.

I stayed at the comfortable but not too expensive Hotel Éluard located near the École Militaire. It vaunted its attractive early 1900s design: windows like dining tables, decorative rusted iron balconies, lots of red flowers, grey slate roof. I managed to relax well there and in Paris generally, avoiding the busy day-to-day routine of normal mortals. I met this guy again three days later – his name was Jean-Luc – who was eating in the same restaurant as me on Avenue de Suffren, both alone. Perhaps he lived around here? He obviously remembered me from the bar the other day, as the waiter approached:

"The gentleman over there would like to buy you a glass of wine, would you care to join him?" I accepted and moved tables. I'd already ordered asparagus salad with red peppers, goat's cheese and basil dressing, followed by tuna steak in a rich tomato sauce. He then ordered the soup – seafood bisque perhaps, or it could have been creamed tomato with garlic and herbs. No, that was the soup we both enjoyed the following night at la Folie. His main was vegetable and bean *cassoulet*. He offered me a glass of excellent Menetou-Salon; old vines, I thought as I tasted, concentrated and crisp. Went well with the salad. He was impressed by my keen interest in wine, I was impressed by his job – a television producer.

"I'm working on a programme about European film funding,

comparing the progressive attitude of the French and Italians to the lukewarm British government and private sector." He caught himself and joked, "but that's boring work and I sound like a news presenter!"

"No, it's OK, it's interesting; I'm a big film fan."

I was also bowled over by his snazzy apartment on Rue Desaix close to the Eiffel Tower: clean, spacious, virtually empty. He hadn't got around to buying much furniture apart from the focus of attention displayed in the centre of the dining room – a silver steel table the size of a bridge bulging with bolts and struts with a thick glass top. One chair stood awkwardly by its side. I'd also ordered red wine earlier but unfortunately knocked it over, staining his designer-label trousers, which he peeled off and chucked into the washing machine. Double clumsy – almost ruined my chances and arguably the best Aussie Shiraz you could find in Paris.

MANCHESTER, BAR, BEN

My mind returned to Ben arriving at Malloy. Clock: 10.14.

"I'm really sorry, had a bus-mare."

"*C'est pas grave*," I shrugged. Ben glanced over to red-shirt and back to me.

"Anyway, I see you've had something to keep yourself occupied with."

He ordered a Czech beer, I had a Bitburger.

"Get some crisps as well, but not those disgusting lamb ones," my voice followed him to the bar.

We talked about nothing in particular – Ben was quite good at that, a refreshing change from the usual arseholes in here. He was another one who belonged to me, although not just yet; he wasn't ready at that time. Actually we were in Charlie's Bar, not Malloy; that was the previous night. We enjoyed a binding mutual relationship: I drew and thrived on his vitality, his energy; he felt he needed my respect, interest in him, company, physical presence. Ben used to get very lonely, very directionless.

"Yeah, I did." He confirmed he'd seen the programme on Prokofiev last night. "The music was tops."

"Stirring," I agreed.

He created a face, taking the piss out of my pretension, and went on... "But not as funny as Paul Merton on *Have I Got News For You* afterwards!"

He was on a roll on that particular show, I had to admit, even if it was a repeated repeat of an old one. So we decided to go and see *Romeo and Juliet* at the Palace next week; we'd recently seen, and had our socks utterly knocked off by, the loud, gorgeous and furiously paced Baz Luhrmann film. I noticed my beer was only 5% alcohol – I assumed it was stronger for some reason – as I peeled the label off the empty bottle and gave it the last rites. Then I ordered a bottle of red wine, probably Spanish from the aroma, and toasted Ben's health. The deep liquid clung to the glass as I held it up. I drank and savoured. My eyes instinctively wandered across to red-shirt, still alone, looking very bored. I decided to invite him to join us, because he reminded me of somebody I used to know. In fact no, I didn't ask him until about two hours later and to come with us to a different bar. The Navarra Reserva was dark and smoky.

BARCELONA, ALEX, CAESAR

Club 8 Degrees West was dark and smoky. I was staring at my drink, a seen-better-days Rioja. I'd ended up here, very trendy apparently, having flowed with friends down Carrer de Santaló.

"Are you alright?" Fernando seemed concerned, but probably only because his girlfriend Mercedes had gone to the toilet. That was unfair, I was fond of Fernando and we became good friends in that glorious year I spent in Barcelona, Spain's sexiest city. I was probably just bored because I hadn't scored. Yet.

"Yeah I'm grand, just a bit pissed." I could smell the garlic on my breath – it seemed likely to stay with me for several years – derived from the world's strongest dressing on a Caesar salad consumed earlier in Los Inmortales, a restaurant over the other side of Muntaner, I think. It was delicious, though. Fernando and Mercedes had lobster – a little extravagant I thought, then again he was paying. The fish I ate with gusto was exquisite: perfectly cooked, very fresh, delicate herbs, lots of lemon juice. I couldn't remember which particular fish, yet another Spanish word I didn't know and Fernando had no idea of the English. It didn't matter, I preferred to speak Spanish – Castilian mostly, which annoyed the locals – took me a while to suss out Catalan. Besides, I could live with the mystery fish. On another note, why was I steaming *and* disturbed that night? Half-cut I could cope with, not both; I felt tired, drained of energy. Mercedes unexpectedly dragged me onto the dance floor; I hadn't noticed her return. She was a scream, always determined to have a good time and make sure everyone else did as well. Nice little nothing you're almost wearing, as Sean once said in an earlier Bond, back when they could just about get away with it. I suddenly felt refreshed to the anthemic crescendos of *Encore une fois*. It was tropical-hot and humid-sweaty on the floor, and I felt trapped in slow motion. That young man does keep bumping into me, it's not just me? Gorgeous dark eyes; looked almost North African, so black magic and alluring. So I flirted a little, we danced a while longer. His name was Alex; he was actually Portuguese but had lived in Barcelona for a few years. He was an actor but surprisingly seemed a touch nervous and, reluctantly leaving, said: "I'm with friends. I should see where they are."

"Come over later and have a glass of wine with us," I suggested. His situation seemed somewhat unclear, as I discovered on going to the toilet ten minutes later. Alex was there arguing with somebody, presumably one of his friends – a jealous boyfriend or an overprotective best mate? I wasn't interested – I knew he'd already decided to join me.

The following evening was still and breathless yet buzzing and manic with cars and people. Alex and I ducked off the main flow on la Rambla – a solid sea of bobbing heads and loitering heels lined by locals selling birds in cages and touristy shite – heading to a restaurant in the Barri Gòtic. I never remember the name of the restaurant, strangely, as we ate there often, but I could vividly recall the menu and wine list. Something like Nación Morena. The bottle of seriously chilled Cava didn't last long, although the mousse on the wine did. Like atoms, a thin layer of bubbles rested on the surface, a constant stream of little glass balls rising to replace the balloons that had burst, disappearing with their aroma into the air. I sniffed and approved of the yeasty, fruity and slightly earthy smell and watched the bubbles and Alex's reflection in them.

MANCHESTER, BEN, MARK

The rain fizzed outside on Canal Street. I topped up Ben's glass, finishing off the bottle; the purple liquid oozed pensively then quickly, then trickled, then died.

Earlier we had met his father and uncle to discuss some business. Ben's father was Chinese, actually from Hong Kong, and had settled in London in the 60s with his brother's family. He had then moved to Manchester to expand the growing empire and married, controversially at the time, a pretty young Welsh girl. He and his brother owned or controlled more than ten restaurants in London, Manchester and Dublin and had other interests, such as dealing in art, like myself. Ben worked for them, I helped out with 'special projects'. We'd talked about an exhibition we were hoping to sponsor and had arranged to 'meet' a local rival later, somebody who'd done a disservice to his uncle in London six months or so ago.

Back in Charlie's Bar, I motioned my head towards red-shirt: "I'll ask him if he wants to come with us to Dark Nation."

"Yeah cool," Ben replied vacuously.

He would like to join us; *he* was Mark.

The sky was Manchester-orange, a moody reflection of red brick buildings and amber streetlights glaring on dense grey cloud. It loomed and dominated, making the people on Canal Street seem tiny and insignificant. It was busy out now – the rain had pressed pause and it was moderately warm. We strolled and chatted; Mark was nervous, still looked younger than he was, a little self-conscious. Like me a few years ago.

"I'm assistant manager in a restaurant. Fusion, on..." he was explaining.

"I know it. Not bad food, needs a decent chef." I interrupted like a knife. He agreed.

My head tilted to the sign Dark Nation above the door and back to Ben's neck as I followed him in. Fairly full, bizarrely there was a live jazz band playing that night – usually they were into not-too-noisy techno. However, the music put its arms around us, laid back yet uncontrolled. I persuaded a group of four people that they were just leaving, without them being aware that they were. No free tables, they left. Ben ordered more wine, as the Alsace Pinot Gris we'd just guzzled looked unhappily empty – we'd already been here for about forty minutes – and the waitress duly delivered a bottle of the "same again please". Mark also liked wine; that was fine, it meant he was already ours. I tasted it: ab fab, that spicy, honeyed aroma helped me melt into the past.

PARIS, GALLERY, JEAN-LUC

I had been impressed by the Musée d'Orsay the first time I'd visited it several years earlier. I'm afraid I can't tell you the date; that would give too much away. Let's just say it was a while ago. The French showed natural talent for this sort of thing – creating an art gallery out of a disused station – cultural genius: wonderful natural light, high ceilings, lots of smaller rooms off the main huge hall. Jean-Luc and I had come here a fair bit over the last few weeks; it was necessary to acquaint ourselves with the precise layout and security measures. These things were important if you intend to steal a painting. Jean-Luc had suggested it back in July, as a joke I think, but I thought it was an interesting idea, suited my purpose. It was now September. We'd studied all the plans and security details I managed to acquire; you don't want to know how I got hold of these.

Rewind your minds to my hotel. Ear-splitting explosion of fireworks, sun-bright flashes intermittently illuminating the room like a strobe light. The 14th of July. I was dressing after a vigorous shower and shave; black jeans, sexy red shirt. Jean-Luc was already sitting in the bar downstairs reading yesterday's paper. I joined him.

"Glass of champagne? It's your favourite, Charlie Heidsieck."

"*Bien sûr.*"

We sipped and enjoyed. A bowl of cashew nuts, not too salty, was an excellent accompaniment.

"That bastard de Casanove really has gone too far this time. Outrageous, blatant anti-Semitism." He was referring to a story on page 6; France's delightful Deputy Minister of Culture had put his large foot in it again. In fact, for the last time – he resigned a week later. A stray comment on a new synagogue, which went a little beyond the architectural style. Jean-Luc's grandfather was a

Jewish-German émigré who'd been high up in the Résistance; he'd been tortured to death by the SS.

The champagne bottle was empty and we had to leave. We were meeting a friend of a friend of Jean-Luc, who was the gallery manager of the Musée d'Orsay. What a coincidence. He'd booked a table at le Chat qui Fume in Les Halles; well, it was the 14th of July after all, no chance of just turning up. I'd eaten here once before – quality food, impressive wine list (more cosmopolitan than most in Paris). A passer-by witnessed the fast motion blur of our taxi across her eyes, before it neatly turned the corner and stopped at the restaurant. Let's skip a bit of time – the three of us half-way through the main courses: I had a delicious traditional Coq au Vin, Jean-Luc a seafood lasagne, I don't remember what our guest was eating – looked like some kind of bean, vegetable and cheese Mexican thing. We had two different wines, as the red (a rich, oaky, single-estate Côtes du Roussillon) didn't go with Jean-Luc's dish; he chose a California Sauvignon Blanc. The gallery manager, a pleasant enough bloke I had to admit (let's call him Joe), handed me the plans we needed over coffee and Calvados (*Pays d'Auge* of course). Cost us a lot of money – the plans rather than the Calva, although this place certainly knew how to charge – but it didn't matter, I knew we would get it back. Very mysterious, the disappearance of the Orsay's most valued employee. His body was found three weeks later in the Seine, not far from the Pont Neuf. The official verdict was accidental death; traces of high levels of alcohol were found in his liver and kidneys. However, the coroner couldn't account for the odd, frozen expression on his face – you might've said terror, maybe surprise. Yet blank at the same time, as if he'd been emptied into the river, sucked dry.

The night rolled on, us with it. The restaurant had a timeless quality to it: the decor, the way the staff were dressed, their twenty-something going on fifty superior attitude. It all came to a bizarre climax, which just passed me by. An old woman entered, obviously known by the proprietor who seemed delighted to see her, judging by the number of glancing kisses exchanged. She was hugely overdressed in days-gone-by, music hall cabaret costume, enormous inverted volcano hat and feathers and dead animal draped around her shoulders. She could've made up three times over, her face was very pale apart from big red blush cheeks and Mae West sofa lipstick. I overheard somebody say something about *"une grande dame"* singer in the 40s. She burst into the most passionate recital of *la Vie en Rose*, unaccompanied by instrument or other voices. She held, playfully in her hand, the attention of the now silent, admiring and perhaps startled crowd for the whole song; she could've done the whole album without interruption. The scene was very moving, laughably kitsch and dumbstriking all at once. An ethereal French time warp. As Jean-Luc joined in the rapturous applause, I had to leave and stand outside; I felt slightly dizzy and emotionally confused. The woman passed by me majestically as she departed; she'd just come to sing, busking was not what she did. The waft of her heady perfume threw me against the wall; I leaned there for a few minutes and breathed slowly.

Run away from me, off-balance and unfocused, back to the gallery. We contemplated further but didn't want to hang around for too long – even dozing museum staff would notice after a while. And anyway, I was tiring of walking in Monet's pretty garden, high on the scent of lilies and willows. We left; a bar around the corner found us, not uncommon in whimsical Paris. The two 1664s didn't last long; we had more. I watched the golden liquid as it was poured: thick, frothy head. I dived into the glass.

MORE PINOT GRIS, BEN, MARK

"This really is good Pinot Gris. I always knew the '88s would show their potential; excellent vineyard site."

"Yeah, I can taste it," Ben replied sarcastically whilst swirling the fermented grape around the glass, "just drink it."

I smiled, Mark laughed. I gave him my card – I knew he would ring fairly soon. He was framed in a picture, reading the card; I looked close up on his face, holding the barman in the background, a vodka bottle protruding from his head. He also looked familiar: he could've been Mark's brother. My eyes switched back to Mark.

"Consultant?" he asked, interested.

"Consultant of life. I advise people on how to get the most out of life, for a long time." He laughed but didn't really understand the joke. Or at least he thought it was a joke. "Restaurants, wine, art exhibitions, paintings, other stuff as well," I added to make him feel more comfortable.

Mark gradually became very chatty, seemed to enjoy talking. To see him now compared to the twitchy loner earlier was encouraging, uplifting even. Our presence, return of conversation seemed to bring him alive. We could all relish a little solitude from time to time but also needed confirmation; a mirror wasn't enough. He continued to tell us the story about a school days' experience; I listened and sipped succulently...

"I dismissed it at the time but wish I hadn't. A classmate and I had become good friends, but he gave me more and more attention. I sort of flirted with him, I suppose, but wasn't aware that was what I was doing; we exchanged glances in the changing rooms, I told him to stop staring, denying to myself I got a kick out of being looked at. One night we were celebrating another friend's birthday and got pissed and crashed at his father's flat. We groped each other drunkenly but affectionately, semi-conscious. In the morning I asked him if he was gay: 'I don't know.' Of course, I refused to ask myself the same question. Time passed, I dated a few women, got engaged then broke it off. Why was I pretending? I didn't want to hurt her either. I had an amusing, horny encounter with a waiter which finally made me accept, although not funny at the time, quite nerve racking..."

"But amusing now, looking back!" Ben laughed in sympathy, although in reality the last thing he wanted to hear was another heart-felt coming-out saga. Mark told us his waiter episode on a different night, or was that my memory? I'll enlighten you about that one some other time, maybe.

MEETING, CHINATOWN, KUNG FU

Leaving Mark in the bar curious about where we were going, Ben and I marched purposefully through the aimless swarms of partied people, parting the waves like religious prodigies. A homeless guy sat on the pavement muttering, and I gave him a fiver knowing it wouldn't really make any difference, but at least the queen smiled at him. We continued across the road, homing in on the neon and noise around the square formed by George, Faulkner and Charlotte Streets. The din from cars, voices, laughter hovered in the air; so did the sullen fumes and garlic smell of food. We climbed the steps to the Golden Dragon, Ben greeted the owner Rosie in Cantonese, I shook her hand and offered idle chat. We sat with her briefly; she pointed out the bloke we were to meet. He was with a strikingly attractive woman, very black hair – more Japanese than Chinese, I guessed. Rosie left us, familiar amiable beam attached to her lower face, and ordered us some assorted light dishes to nibble at. She sent over champagne too, bless her, which the waiter nearly dropped thanks to the slippery ice bucket and clumsily fished out the bottle from the melting ice.

"Leave it, I'll open it thanks." Ben smirked at my disapproving expression. We were on our second glass when the garlic-ginger-coriander perfumed prawns were placed on the table. I cut to a vivid flashback to Soho (London), to my favourite Szechuan restaurant there, the same intense combination of ginger and coriander: very fresh. They were delicious but not as good as the simple, seaweed-stuffed pancakes that followed: very crisp, very chilli.

His name was Hong Kar-Wei but he didn't know he was meeting with us tonight. We waited, watched, ate, drunk. Ben commented on the much improved wine list.

"I know, I chose them," but of course he knew that anyway; he'd just forgotten.

Hong's companion departed and he paid the bill ten minutes later, giving us time to finish the refreshing aromatic tea. We followed him outside like prowling panthers; he didn't seem to notice. I grabbed his left arm, subtly, and persuaded him to talk with us in a nearby back street. Ben mentioned his uncle in London...

"You're making a mistake trying to get involved in our business, here or in London. I'm not afraid of you or your gangster friends or the outcome of this, erm, *situation*."

"But *you* should be," I added. I think he appreciated Ben's conviction, especially after I cut off the middle finger from his left hand with one delicate slice.

The scene became complicated and urgent, as a car in dark glasses pulled up in slow motion. Three men I didn't recognise jumped out with vigour in their limbs: colleagues of Hong, I presumed. One reached for a gun from inside his jacket, but not quickly enough; Ben swiftly kicked it out of his hand and cracked him on the chin with the outer edge of his boot. I pounced in slow motion, like a whirlwind, a firm roundhouse kick followed by lightening-quick blows. The Kung Fu movie clip ended abruptly; we melted away from the scene. The men remaining probably understood our sincerity; the meeting seemed to have gone successfully without too much fuss.

Ben and I arrived at my flat, now calmed down a little. He fell asleep quickly; he usually did. I followed huddled next to him; rapid eye movement ensued.

DREAM

I'm back on the moon again, or maybe that elusive desert, and talking to the guy I don't know. He still has no face. He is just talking, talking non-stop; I don't utter a word, yet we seem to be communicating. The conversation is more familiar this time, but his words are a garbled stream, no real recognisable sentences – they all merge, without punctuation or pause, no change of intonation or drawing in of breath. However, I understand and respond without speaking. I seem to have been here for a very long time, maybe ten years, when he suddenly reaches into his pockets. This time he doesn't shoot and hands me the guns; it's important I don't lose them; they are dangerous and powerful. He tells me I must return in the distant future to this place and give him back the guns. We drink a glass of red wine; it's good for you, he explains.

I'm now falling, falling quickly, plunging downwards to a distant planet. My descent slows, I'm now floating and observing lots of people crammed on the streets of a city; it could be any city. They don't seem to know where they're going, just milling around. I fall amongst them but don't harm myself on the ground. I walk for a while, watching everybody. There are men, women and children, all different races, shapes and sizes. But they have something in common – each person's face and shoulders are melted like wax on a candle, the flesh dripping. The people all seem lost yet they begin to follow me as I gently lead them off the dreary street. "The sky's gone out," someone sings in my ear. That was the last time I had this particular dream.

LONDON, SERGE, BOB, ESSEX-BOY

I woke up, lightly cleansed, in London in a large room in the Griffin Hotel at the top of Tottenham Court Road. The traffic hummed outside, surprisingly not too unbearable. My head panned slowly to the clock – 8.59 – the alarm went off as it turned 9. I spent a few idle weeks in London on my way to Paris and I couldn't resist visiting some of the old haunts. I'd lived here for a few years in the past – difficult to remember now how long exactly – London was frustratingly love-hate, I found. The very things that repulsed you from it also excited – the mad, constant business, throngs of people and cars, 24-hour high if you wanted it. Also peaceful areas, although still surrounded by traffic in the distance. Crazy city. Not as crazy as LA though, but that was another story.

The scene jumped to Covent Garden: imagine a wide-angle close-up of the roof of the restaurant on the Opera Terrace, then track back to me standing in the crowd. Although the surrounding areas appealed to me, I hated the so-called Plaza itself. All the blind tourists seemed to flock here, as if it represented everything there was to see around. However, I was meeting two friends for lunch Chez Jeanne on the Terrace. One was an old pal – Bob who lived in Manchester now – the other was Serge, the deputy manager of the Griffin, who I'd slept with the other night. It was his day off; really cute, soft-spoken sexy Arabic-French accent.

We greeted one another in the European style, I asked for the wine list. The set lunch sounded ideal and reasonable, as I read it in my head. So I ordered a bottle of Mosel Riesling Kabinett '95 to get the juices flowing. The sprightly waiter brought some appetisers; we weren't in any hurry to order. I insisted on keeping the wine list – we were bound (contractually) to have more. It was rapidly turning into one of those lazy days, therefore get pissed at lunchtime. Bob and Serge seemed up for it. The manager approached, asked how I was; she was an old friend:

"Haven't seen you here for a while..."

"Just passing through, on a trip of discovery," I explained in the tongue-in-cheek fashion. "This is Bob, old university pal, and Serge... blah blah..." I translated blah blah for Serge later.

The Riesling lasted through the first savoury courses; the second bottle of it did anyway. I perused the list; 'gutsy red' Bob had ventured in conversation. Duly noted and requested – 1990 *Amarone* big enough for you, Bob? "Nice one," I think he muttered but I didn't hear him properly: something strange happened. I was considering a Provence red, *Domaine des Am...*, but it seemed to have vanished from the list. Did I imagine it was there, having drifted to another occasion? No matter; Serge took the list, interested if they sold dessert wines by the glass for later. I pictured sticky golden Sauternes dribbling down his milk-chocolate stomach and licking it up. Sweet could be sexy. Perhaps he read my thoughts as he smiled at me then chuckled childishly.

The demolished main dishes were cleared. I drained the last drop of *Amarone*; it began to kick me in the head. Bob looked flushed, Serge was hyperactive; he ordered three glasses of Muscat de Rivesaltes. They appeared, accompanied by two desserts we shared: rich and chocolatey, light and fruity were the flavours; the names escaped me. We talked about love-hate London – Serge had been working here for three years but wanted to return to Paris. He did actually, as we would meet up there just as I was about to leave for Berlin. In fact, he came with me but more of that another time.

Bob had had a strange and amusing encounter a week ago: "I was walking along the Strand with some guys from work, when this top quality nutter bumped into us. He was ranting all sorts of stuff and gibberish, complaining about the government, the hoax of the moon landing in 1969, which was apparently brilliantly staged in a warehouse in Arizona. He was raving, on a roll, dressed like John Cleese in the Ministry of Silly Walks sketch; remember that? Pin-stripe suit, bowler, umbrella. I stayed for a while to listen, I was intrigued..." So were we; then Serge and I parted company from him outside the restaurant. He had to see a man about some South American tobacco substitute. We would meet him later to indulge.

"*Putain*," Serge shouted at the taxi that had almost flattened him on Bedford Street. My gaze chased the back of the cab; it turned the corner, but I could hear the crunch of crashing metal and plastic glass. Fast forward to me at the bar in Kajoz paying for two more espressos.

"Shall we have a bit of a cruise around, up Charing Cross Road, then over to Soho?" Serge agreed with a minor movement of the head. We installed ourselves by the window, watching the passing folk, reading the flyers scattered on the table, talked about Paris.

A while later. We were randomly crossing Clapham Common in the dark, heading for Serge's house on the Southside. He had to work the following day but not until the afternoon; I could also go back to the hotel then. Chris staggered beside us, even more pissed than we were, counting the blades of grass. Who he? Youthful but not particularly young, brown-blond, slim, horny, I guessed, judging by the way he'd flirted with both of us in the club. He said he lived near Southend somewhere (Essex-boy night on the town), missed the last train home. That's okay, there was plenty of room *chez* Serge. I sensed I'd feel well tomorrow, stronger. Would this one make it home? We shall see. (He did, actually, although a changed man. I imagine he wouldn't have believed that he'd develop a passion for red wine in sociable SW4. Probably his most eventful trip to London). For me, London was always like this. Would be forever.

The Eurostar gently eased out of Waterloo, like shedding a favourite pair of jeans. Images of lurid London began to run into one another through the window and merged with my own. Paris conjured itself up in my head; I pictured swigging glorious champagne on the 14th of July. But who with? Difficult: "always emotion is the future," Yoda reminded me. I sipped from my glass of champagne (tasted like Bolly) and closed my eyes.

BARCELONA, GAUDÍ, ALEX, PICASSO

A well-thumbed guidebook of Barcelona flicked its pages through my mind, imprinting dizzyingly fast and washed-out coloured images of Gaudí architecture: Sagrada Familia, Palau Güell, Casa Batlló and twisted chimneys on La Pedrera. Looming, gothic, modern, bizarre. At night the Casa Batlló – the ultimate *Modernista* designer apartment block – was even more amazing lit up. Balconies like skull masks, pretty patterned splash of floral Déco glass, caves and skeletons, giant cloverleaf on a single turret.

I could hear animated loud Spanish conversation all around me and refocused on the glass of Cava in my hand. Nación was very busy now, not surprising as Barcelona only really came to life at this late hour (late being a subjective term). Barcelona was the third stop in my road movie after Berlin; I drove here leisurely across Germany, Switzerland and France. What a trip that was – enjoyable when you had a fast car and no time limit – but more of that later. Alex was talking to a smooth-shaped friend of his (he had potential too); the music and conversation became so deafening that I no longer heard it. In this isolated peace my eyes zoomed to a picture on the wall: Picasso's Las Meninas. I'd seen it before, I don't remember where. Odd and intriguing – one of several versions he painted based on a Velazquez picture. I couldn't help focusing particularly on the shadowy character framed in the light shining through a doorway at the back of the picture. I stared and watched. I followed him through the door beyond the canvas.

1957: it was boiling hot in Cannes. I had stepped into the artist's studio overlooking the Côte d'Azur. The impossibly blue sea was planed flat and glistening gold; the stillness and sunshine warmed my soul. My head slowly panned around to take in the various canvasses scattered here and there, mostly unfinished. The vivid colours of some of the pictures and the bright summer's day clashed with the black and white of the painting, which rested in the centre of the room on a broken easel. I asked the artist about his apparent obsession with Las Meninas, told him of the intriguing attraction it had for me and many others. We chatted for a long time in a mixture of French and Spanish; he kept lapsing into Catalan, which didn't help my incomplete understanding of his very personal vision. He told me of his love of the south of France, the vitality he felt here compared to Paris. We consumed a bottle of inappropriately dry and strong Côtes du Rhône Villages, which made us thirsty and hungry. He suggested we went to his favourite bar for a beer and a snack. Details have faded from my mind now (it was over forty years ago, after all) but the bar wasn't far. We walked side by side in the quiet streets; I laughed to myself about how this place would change. I watched the drip of condensation, as it slowly dribbled down the bottle of ice-cold beer.

I wiped the salty tear from my eye and blinked: we were in the Museu Picasso, Barcelona. Step back from the door in the background of the picture; the figure whispered goodbye. I was standing staring at Las Meninas; I wiped a tear from my eye. Alex nudged me and whispered "Time to leave now." I was surprised when he told me we'd been there for two hours – it seemed like only a few minutes. On the other hand, it could have been days; it wasn't clear anymore. It was, however, the fourth time that I'd been to the gallery. The fourth time with Alex anyway. I felt I'd been there with others; don't remember their names just now.

"I'm hungry, let's go and eat." I couldn't disagree, I hadn't eaten since last night and 1pm was nearly upon us. The energy of the red wine had faded and I felt weak. As we idled up Via Laietana, we cruised past a team of *Bombers* (firemen) who had stopped their colourful wagon and stood around on alert, although they didn't look especially concerned. I peered up the long straight road to the hill in the distance, pot-marked by a building with a wacky pointed *Modernista* tower. Then suddenly I heard the rumbling stomach of the Metro below; or perhaps it was mine. We crossed over the edge of Plaça d'Antoni Maura towards the imposing but dull, neo-classical-ish Caixa de Catalunya offices, bypassing the cathedral behind us and to the left. This landmark elderly cathedral looked in better condition than we did: the ancient stone walls were being restored, but this couldn't detract from its Thunderbird spire with gigantic corkscrew. We then cut across down Carrer de Julià Portet, leading to Carrer de Montsió. Skip to Alex shoving a too-large piece of *tortilla* into his mouth.

"Pig," I offered. He smiled cheekily, having chewed and swallowed, although not entirely successfully as the odd strand of omelette dangled grossly from his oniony teeth. The *pimientos* were particularly succulent today: the texture was perfect, still firm and slightly spicy, yet softened and sweet by marinating in olive oil and quickly fried or grilled. I took in the serene atmosphere outside *Els 4 Gats* – busy people criss-crossing, probably unaware they were being watched by still old buildings; and by me of course. Otherwise this narrow paved street was very quiet; around us stood mostly apartments, a few bars, an old fashioned barber, one or two posh shops and what looked like a church to the left, but probably wasn't. Inside it was equally quiet although two-thirds full; the restaurant was almost as slender as the waiter's hips, simple with basic wooden tables. At the back I could make out pretty blue tiles behind the bar: more Portuguese than Catalan, I would have thought. Alex agreed.

My mission in Barcelona would be completed in the near future, but he didn't know this yet. We were to spend just a few more months together.

"*Hola*," Mercedes breathed in my ear, as she had crept up behind me. Fernando and she joined us for lunch. So Alex ordered more food and sparkling mineral water – I think even he had had too much wine last night. They lived in (the) desirable Eixample (area) off Passeig de Gràcia – Fernando had been at home all morning, trying to complete the article he was writing on two new local rock bands. He did tell me the names of them: Casablanca and something like Mision, as Alex reiterated to me later at his flat ("I wish you'd listen to people!"). Fernando was a freelance writer on music and cinema; Mercedes was also a journalist but a reporter for *El Periodico*. She told us she'd been interviewing an allegedly corrupt local councillor.

"He didn't want to talk at first, but I soon turned everything on its head and got some of the info I suspected and wanted for the story..." She was good at that; I laughed.

"It wasn't funny at the time, he was hard work." No matter, a fascinating story was to appear in the paper two days later: front-page shocker. Not Mercedes' article; that followed on the next page. Excellent coincidence, cutting edge journalism. The front page carried a dodgy picture of the official and the bold headline: "Bizarre suicide... blah blah..." The man was found smashed on the ground below La Sagrada Familia.

Said cathedral presented itself in my thoughts: I stood below it looking straight up. The wide-angle lens on the video camera gave a strange distorted view, exaggerated the mad genius of Gaudí's style – somehow so modern and abstract, yet classically gothic (if that's possible) and spiritually religious. The view from Plaça de Ramon Berenguer el Gran revealed its more run down side, combining dirty stone with new where they were rebuilding the little subdued turret. Started by someone else, uncompleted on Gaudí's death – and will probably always be being finished – this masterpiece and wonder was a mish-mash of styles, peppered with sculptures of animals and people starring in the bible, plants and flowers and dead babies slaughtered by a knight. All melted and smoothed together into liquid waves of sand (I should've written a travel guide). One side appeared more conventional than the other, which was also under construction and had two platforms underneath stalk leg prongs. This gleaming white stone section featured grape clusters on pointy supports and trademark skeletal windows. And not leaving out those giant, corn on the cob spires: four sets of two spike sunflowers with balls on top like the weirdest kind of dildo. I adored this church, certainly like no other – on this planet at least.

Alex grabbed the camera from my hands. "Let's film from the top."

"Good idea; you're the actor."

"We could re-enact a great film overlooking Spain's fabbest city, or just play around with it if you want."

I wanted to film him, actually, to keep his image forever, that charming young actor. Those dark eyes, that smile.

"Shit; look, the queue for the lift's really long."

"Fuck that. Let's take the stairs!"

We did but it proved too far to the top, for Alex at least. Up on one of the viewing platforms/pulpits, I spun the camera around quickly catching a set of images all together: scaffolding, cranes, people, the towers and the rest of the view inwards. Then I slowly revolved to a stop, focusing just on out of breath Alex, who, having recovered after a few deep breaths, talked to the camera, to me, to the audience. He recited dramatically some of the dialogue from Beckett's *Krapp's Last Tape*, in which he was to perform shortly in Madrid (clever git).

"Just been listening to that stupid bastard I took myself for thirty years ago, hard to believe I was ever as bad as that. Thank God that's all done with anyway. The eyes she had! Everything there, everything, all the... (he paused)... everything there, everything on this old muckball, all the light and dark and famine and feasting of the ages..." He stopped. I was mesmerised: he was very good. I continued to film, capturing Alex, his physical expression and beauty and the pain of the character; Alex's very being was imprisoned forever on film. He dissolved into the celluloid, like Krapp's memories on the tape. I stopped filming and looked over to where Alex stood. Was standing. I circled around; he was nowhere to be seen. Then I stepped forward and peered down to the building site below.

MANCHESTER, MARK, THE CITY

I was craning my neck looking up from the street at the two-thirds-naked person standing in a large window a few floors up in the Royal Hotel. He looked familiar but couldn't place him. The hotel's appearance was even better, even more bizarre at night: the ridiculously out of place tower, a huge phallus, totally out of proportion to the rest of the magnificent building, waiting for the countdown; dirty red brick to match the grubby orange sky above. It was now a luxury hotel, the latest incarnation, in the past the Refuge Assurance building amongst other disguises it had worn. The red neon Royal illuminated the tower on all four sides, the final touch to its oddity, a modern signature as incongruous as the building itself with the surroundings. The sky was as orange as the rosé Mark was sipping in the Boxhouse bar behind me.

He tapped impatiently on the glass, looking perplexed. A bored queuer at the bus stop opposite glanced through the window at us both sitting at a table drinking Navarra Rosado, although it could have been anything from where he was positioned. I wanted to see the film showing at 8.30, the new Coen Brothers', but Mark wasn't keen: "I didn't really like *The Big Lebowski.*"

I could go off you, I thought, and said: "OK, but I don't fancy the Italian film in 3 and I've seen the other one."

"Let's just go for a wander, take in the city!"

"Nice night for a walk..." I interrupted in my best Arnold S accent.

"Besides," he continued, determined to finish despite my childish movie-buffism, "the new David Lynch movie, what's it called – *Dune 2: Fall of Atredis*? – starts next week. We can go and see that."

Good suggestion on both counts; maybe there was something up there after all. We drained our glasses dry ("I'm not leaving a single drop at that price," Mark had countered to my excessive mimicking of his actions) and said *adieu* to the intelligent (degree in Art History; you could tell from the way he poured) blond-ish (chemically enhanced) barman with the small nose. We crossed Whitworth Street West, avoiding death by bus, heading up Oxford Street, but then ducked off to the left down the steps to the canal. The water (you could perhaps just about call it that, despite the colour) level was unusually high, almost lapping at our feet, and it smelt damp and musty under the first bridge; presumably the path had flooded recently.

"You know, you must get a real thrill travelling down the canal on a barge, the high speed causing the breeze to whistle through your hair," Mark commented sarcastically pointing at the suspicious water, where no boats sailed past. "Pissing about for days waiting for locks to fill and empty every 200 metres. You can walk faster!"

He had a point. The tops of distinctive and distinguished buildings waved as they passed by on the right. Chepstow House, an elegant Victorian orange brick and grey slate flat complex, built by Samuel Mendel (textile merchant and patron of the arts) in 1874, now a slice of the past converted to form part of chic post-post-industrial Manchester, for those who could afford it. An eye-catching landmark on the eclectic skyline, crowned with a huge chimney and an odd castle turret at either end – I lived there, by the way – but not as dominant or isolated as it used to be. It was now shadowed by the Bridgewater Hall, stalking it: a triumph of 90s design made of gleaming metal, glass and marble forming a kind of sharp oyster shell peak on top. At night blue, green or red lines of light (or combinations) illuminated the structure and the wacky tubey, spiral bits of silver metal. 'Prince' Charles (destined to be just Charles) probably didn't like it, but he didn't have any taste. New apartments had also sprouted up from an empty space by the canal, not as tacky as the initial 'artist's impression' implied, but still no doubt modern shoe boxes masquerading as 'warehouse-style flats in the heart of the City Centre etc'. Beyond that wobbled the unmistakable metal curves of the roof on the G-Mex: needed little introduction, a splendid Manc landmark and home to plenty more of those ubiquitous orange(ish) bricks. Nice car park, too.

Enough of the guided tour; fast forward ten minutes to Cerba, trendy bar-restaurant in Castlefield. We'd emerged like grateful amphibians at Dukes Lock 92 and crossed the stone bridge into Catalan Square. It felt quite European-city around here but still quintessentially northwestern, now another newly fashionable residential and office district. Cerba was busy; we sat outside. I faced the bouncy bridge over the canal because I liked the design: lop-sided high metal curve painted very white.

"They should put the price of the drinks up, they're too cheap," Mark quipped. I liked his sharp wit; what else was in that mind, I wondered.

"Pop stars and restaurateurs like to be kept in style, give or take the odd million."

Mark's blank face registered no understanding of my remark. The cashew nuts crunched and cracked, having no choice in the matter, as he ground a mouthful between his taut teeth, then washed them down with Pils. Good combination. I contemplated the remains of the average Spanish house white in my hand, as much information as I could glean from the average bar person.

"They've done a reasonable job though," Mark commented on the design of the restaurant on the floor above the bar; the whole built into an arch under the old railway bridge. "You get the scent of Barcelona and the vibe of cool Manchester," he added, affecting the tone of a backslapping PR release.

"Especially when a train passes over to mix the salad dressing," I threw in to conclude.

"Ever been to Barcelona?" he asked.

"Yeah, top city. You?"

"No. I'd love to go."

Mark was talking to somebody I didn't recognise, but probably guessed who he might be, as I returned from the toilet. He was gone by the time I reached the table. "Who was that?"

"Don't know, but he left this message. It's in Chinese, I think. What does it mean?"

"You don't want to know," I replied not looking up from the card.

"I do," he insisted.

"Basically, you're a dead man, leaving out the embellishments."

"Isn't it about time you told me more about yourself, what you do exactly?"

My piercing stare gave him the message; he didn't need an answer. Not yet.

Jump to half-an-hour later; my eyes focused on the grubby number plate of a passing Peugeot, as I watched it through the window of Cosmos bar. The digits almost formed the postcode of my address in Edinburgh, when I'd lived there... again precise dates escaped me but the vivid images didn't. Cosmos was also slotted into a railway arch (how 90s Manchester) next to Deansgate station, one of the first of its breed. I liked the super-large windows at the front, plenty of space to gaze. Contrasted with the geriatric brickwork and strange motif above: was it a lion sleeping or was that my eyesight? I sharpened my focus without much effort and held the close-up for a handful of seconds. I still wasn't sure what it was but couldn't blame my eyes; I'd forgotten my sight had improved enormously over the past few years. Inside: large minimalist, fashionable mixed crowd, wood and metal.

"I will tell you more about myself, at some point..."

"I just wish you wouldn't be so fucking mysterious, that's all. Anyway it doesn't really matter. You don't know much about me either..." I indulged him; I was interested in learning more. Maybe he would say something that confirmed what I thought I knew – that we'd met before but not here, not in this time. Or did he remind me of Gordon or someone Gordon had known, someone from his adventures?

Mark was actually born in Manchester (his accent twanged back in as he drank more – definitely north Manchester) but his family had moved to Hertfordshire when he was young. He came back to university here and, like many, stayed. He played golf when he could; no, he said tennis, or was it squash? I'm afraid I wasn't really listening. Well, not to his words but to his thoughts. The lips were moving, but these words were not truly what he wanted to say. He was hiding something. "Could he be the one? He shall know your ways." A mystical scene from a Lynch film forced itself through my consciousness, probably as Mark had brought up the subject. His familiarity and casualness made it feel like I'd known him all my life. There was a powerful voice towering over the music playing in the background; it was part of the song yet so superior to it. It helped to pass on to the next day.

I didn't hear the buzzer at my door as I had Beethoven's *Ninth* playing very loudly on CD. Digitally re-mastered to annoy the neighbours. It had reached the shattering choral climax with all voices and instruments soaring to an emotional high. However, I turned it down so I could hear the buzzer the third time. Mark didn't complain about having to wait – he understood the importance of playing such music at top volume. You needed the entire orchestra in the room, in the kitchen, in the fridge and in the bedroom above all. We drank too much strong, bitter black coffee before leaving – it seemed to make sense. I enjoyed talking for a while – Mark had some ideas to improve his restaurant's wine list and asked for my recommendations. His boss had finally conceded that he knew nothing about wine nor had any interest in it and let Mark take over, including an overhaul of the design and layout of the list. I was impressed by his vision to distribute more wine to the thirsty masses.

"What's that?" he remarked, having a close-up look at the pendant which dangled freely on my naked throat and chest.

"A gift; a memory of a special friend," I replied, momentarily dipping into my waveless emotional swimming pool.

"I've never seen anything like it; it's hypnotic."

"It's antique, made by a Navajo Indian." Mark furrowed his brow in ignorance, so I allowed him a few more secrets, just a gem or two. "You know, the North American tribe. Never seen any Westerns?!" He laughed; I continued. "It's supposed to hold the souls of lost loved ones." We snuggled close together on the settee while listening to the *Ninth* again.

"What a bizarre sculpture. It's fab," he said excitedly. Walk back out of the building for a moment and read the sign: University of Manchester Whitworth Art Gallery. Come back in and stand behind us, contemplating the huge head in the middle of the gallery, the subject of Mark's outburst: *Sculpture* by John Davis. It was indeed fabulous, just a global head with an inane expression. Or was it? Didn't seem to exude much, yet underneath it was observing us, critically. Would look good in my flat too. We carried on idling around; neither of us was particularly struck by the Sean Mulder exhibition. Interesting shapes and forms but when the canvasses were displayed all together like this, a little samey. One of the large pictures on its own on the wall in a spacious sparse apartment; that would look flattering. We briefly skimmed the smattering from the modern collection; there were some I hadn't seen before, including a self-portrait: *Man's Head*, Lucian Freud 1963. Staring back at you rather uneasily in wild, fiery strokes of colour, our eyes locked, our minds melded. I liked this picture of this man, more than just an image. I would have this portrait to complete my collection. I looked deeper and tiptoed in.

PARIS, JEAN-LUC, UZI, SERGE

My wide eyes were just a few centimetres from his. Rather, where his eyes should have been. I pushed the painting further away to try to recapture the missing face: his expression should have been one of surprise at his new owner. Magritte's 1937 *Le principe du plaisir* mimicked Man Ray's photograph of Edward James, a fellow patron of the arts. But his head was merely a haze of light, a haloed candle burning brightly on the dark figure sat at the desk. The sombre dirty colours added to the unease, his hands tensed.

We had to get out of Paris quickly, out of France. Serge was leaning over my shoulder, his Tunisian face as disbelieving as the portrait's might have been. He remained transfixed for a moment then finally breathed out slowly. "We're going now."

"It's cool, I'm ready to roll." I placed the now frameless canvas with the other one I had acquired in London a while ago, then rolled them inside a couple of film posters and two art prints – Monet and Matisse – I found that amusing. But this meant the end of my Paris memories – let's flash back further to the... acquisition. I felt I needed to go over the details again, as they were a little muddled. Besides, a robbery always makes a good story. This was just how it happened.

In the end, Jean-Luc and I had decided to throw subtlety out of the window and go for the bold approach (some would say suicidal). That third bottle of '88 Haut-Marbuzet (rich, gamey and tobaccoey, quite superb) had made us both see reason. Also gave us a pleasant hangover, if such a thing could exist. The wine had allowed me to finally reach into Jean-Luc's soul – he was a complex man, or so I'd thought at first, but I was disappointed with what I found underneath. "So be it, young Jedi."

We were getting into the car and checking our hot weapons.

"All OK, let's hit it!" I invoked a line from a movie that he probably hadn't seen, then again, neither of us was wearing sunglasses.

The obliging car drove us down Quai des Tuileries, passing the Musée d'Orsay on the other side of the Seine, and carried on along the river. I had, in fact, changed my mind. We had spent some memorable days in the Orsay drowning in Impressionist half-light and fuzzy colour, but I'd decided it didn't have what I was looking for. Jean-Luc had seen big black-market dollar signs in his eyes; I needed something that would grasp me firmly, suit my purpose, spare me. I finally found it in the Musée Nationale d'Art Moderne at the Centre Pompidou. Visualise said building – France 2, Britain 0 – another victory for a visionary French government: modern art inside modern architecture. Designed by an Englishman (and two Italians), too progressive and iconoclastic for England at the time, with his inside-out building, internal organs, coloured pipes and tubes on the exterior. Inside the Pompidou I'd strolled with revolutionaries of the 20th Century and met René Magritte. *Le principe du plaisir* was calmly unsettling and had drawn me in – seemingly conventional, yet subtly suggestive as it invited you into the psyche of the subject of the portrait. It almost appeared to be a defaced photograph, badly developed.

Back in the car on Rue Aubry le Boucher around the corner from the Centre Pompidou. We put on our masks and tore up to the entrance, parking illegally in the gently sloping square, having taken out one of the not-as-tough-as-they-looked bollards which surround it. It was probably the last thing anybody was expecting. We stormed the gallery in a flickering slow motion montage, trapped on the security cameras; panicking visitors were smudged as they ran for cover in all directions or hit the deck. We looked menacingly chic all in black, brandishing automatic weapons. No shots were fired, apart from the initial rounds in the air just to command attention. Everybody listened then. I ran upstairs, prised the Magritte off the wall; we left. Very simple.

Jean-Luc manoeuvred along the planned get-away route; he knew Paris better than an A-Z. We blasted down Rue du Renard, pretending it was empty, a quick right, then over the bridge onto Rue de la Cité across the river. Notre Dame on my left looked down disapprovingly. Rue Saint Jacques blurred by, as did the Sorbonne on the right, majestic and still. Jean-Luc's mind-map ran all the streets together – Port Royal, Montparnasse, Départ... I had no idea how long the chase lasted. It was excitingly fast, the car handled well, as did Jean-Luc it. I don't remember what type – quick, wheels, doors – but it was a shade of red (predictably perhaps). He parked as planned about three km away in a quiet backstreet near the station, where we abandoned the guns and the gear (don't worry: untraceable, no prints, stolen car). I'd only had to waste two policemen; one car got rather close, regretted it thanks to my Uzi. It'd happened in explosive slow-motion like in a John Woo movie; I was sure I hadn't really needed to fire as many bullets into the car.

Still, would have looked very stylish on film, I thought as I recalled that art theft movie; didn't remember the name. It would have been more thrilling, more real in some ways, if it had happened like that – my imagination had taken over as I stared out of the car window; my mind flew to another universe. We didn't stay long at the gallery near Montparnasse station – arrangements had already been made, just the formality of picking up the picture. Without a frame – ironic to say the least, as it turned out to be a forgery (a very good one, mind you), as I discovered much later. Didn't really matter; it passed as genuine enough.

We sped off in Jean-Luc's Porsche, parked nearby. My Porsche now; the registration details had been changed. I rather liked Jean-Luc, but it was the last look of *The Pleasure Principle* he was to get (or anybody else – current whereabouts unknown, hence the market for top quality forgeries). He almost screamed as he unrolled the canvas and bonded with it. But silent: perhaps he saw his face appear momentarily in the blaze of white light which masked the subject's. The coiled painting fell onto the passenger seat; he was gone. I smiled without looking, although I was sad: I didn't want to peer at myself in the rear-view mirror, I wasn't sure why not.

I turned my head again to the passenger seat, still smiling. Serge smiled back. He had only arrived from London a week ago but was happy not to stay in Paris. "Berlin sounds like fun... did you give Jean-Luc my mobile number, just in case he can join us at some point?" he added.

"Yeah, he's already got your number."

"... I want you..." blurted the Inspiral Carpets out of the Blaupunkt sound system. The noisy music bounced off the motorway, as we tore past the unknowing traffic. The day after tomorrow was going to be more special for us than you, I thought. I'd never been to Berlin before, neither had Serge; another new adventure beckoned. The lines on the road ticked by, merging into one; the central reservation skimmed off my eyeballs.

MANCHESTER, BEN, DREAM

I was hypnotised by the crash barrier on the M56. Ben was driving my TVR Griffith, probably faster than was wise, and we had just passed the M63 turn-off heading back into town (it could be officially called the M60 now – they changed the name of parts of it for some reason, but it was always the 63 to me). The sounds of jamming jazz and throaty exhaust buzzed in my head and around the cockpit. So did the champagne I'd consumed in Tatton Park. I didn't return to Paris again; not in reality, anyway, but in a dream I had that night.

The central reservation flashed by again, but I stopped the car. I was on the A4 driving out of London. A girl was playing on the reservation; her mother staggered blindly through the traffic, although no car was able to touch her. A baby, the girl's sister I guessed, was playing there too; maybe it was the same person. Her toys were too close to the road, just on the edge. She reached for them, a doll with no face. I was then in Paris. It could've been anywhere, as the milieu was dark and featureless, apart from the Eiffel Tower. I followed a transparent figure into a *pissoir* on the Boulevard St Germain: it contained the faces of many others, all whispering, trapped, silenced, absorbed, trying to escape. I confronted this phantom: it was me. No, it was 'oneself', anybody, everybody, as it tried to explain. Why had I wasted my time looking for it? There was nothing to find here, nobody. Should I try somewhere else? No response.

I was glad to wake up next to Ben. Or was it Mark? It was a person, a presence, a significant confirmation of me. I couldn't then sleep so I sat up watching '*le Samourai*', because Alain Delon looked so debonair in it. I woke up again, face down on the sofa; I'd knocked over the bottle of Armagnac. Mark shook his head and laughed. Ben cleared it up, as Mark wasn't actually there; I seemed to be hallucinating. He left me to sleep, as I had indeed fallen back so. I could taste the garlic pâté in my mouth, the strong flavour returned for a moment. And cue Proust.

SYDNEY, JOHN, POOF

"Wow, there's *a lot* of garlic in this sauce," John proudly informs me. It's now a couple of years or so later, perhaps even another beyond that, and probably June as it's not that hot in Sydney. I've never been here... it's all quite unfamiliar. You'll have to rely on John to conjure up the place. I can fill in the detail on events though; it's bound to happen like this as this is where it ends. John is... yes... mysterious, dark eyes, funny. He was originally from Perth but moved here a few years ago; four I think he said. We're sitting comfortably out on the veranda at Dockside Restaurant overlooking part of the harbour. I'll pan my head around slowly to reveal the panorama to you: Walsh Bay from Pier 4. We can't see the Opera House from here, fortunately, so I can spare you the full tourist guide. But I like the Bridge; more fascinating from this angle, this close: looks like it's not sure whether it should be in New York City or Bristol.

"The locals call it the Coathanger," John says. They have a point: its 1920s metal modernism, interrupted by bizarre Egyptian pylons, hangs stylishly in Sydney's wardrobe of oddities.

John eats the Thai prawns with relish, despite, or perhaps because of, the sinus-clearing chilli kick they innocently possess. The unoaked Marsanne was a good choice, coping quite well with this excellent Aussie/Far East lunch. The stir-fried vegetables in ginger are, well, exactly that: clean, crisp, crystal flavours.

I think I'm going to spend some time in Sydney but it's a little unclear at the moment. Depends if they find me; he finds me. I can't give you many details just yet, why I left Manchester.

"Coffee?" John asks for probably the second time.

"Yeah yeah..."

He continues to reminisce while consuming more caffeine and nibbling some kiwi fruit or mango or something that looks wet and sweet... I'm drawn into his words: eloquent, witty, poetic. He is a writer after all. "*Tu les as vus!*" he says and mimics the French schoolboy pointing at his balls. I laugh; it's a good story, one of many in the time honoured style about days long ago growing up, slowly becoming aware of your sexuality (but thankfully anguish-free).

"... Jean-Christophe had obviously had enough at this stage," John continues, "I wasn't really aware that I fancied him, but it seemed I'd become obsessed with the size of his tackle, for a 14 year old, again without registering any significance. It's strange. It should've been then so clear, that I liked boys, but you still don't say: 'right, I'm gay then.' What did that mean, anyway? You can do that looking back after years of accepting and, well, growing up. That was back in Perth, when he and the school group came over to Aus, at my granddad's I think, after lunch. I'd enjoyed the trip to Marseille a few months before that – my first time in France. Kind of throws you in at the deep end: you will speak French 'cos you've no choice! Now I think about it, I did sort of flirt with a friend of his, in the most innocent way, nothing more than glances and smiling at each other..."

Jump to later. Busy yet laid-back bar in Darlo just off Oxford Street. Don't remember the name; they often all sound alike, some sort of queer pun. About 10.30 pm: I'm gazing at John while he talks and laughs with Tim, an old friend of his, former lovers. I'm amused by his looks, as it's only now it seems that I realise that I'm attracted to, and perhaps always have been, a similar type. You've guessed it – dark, mysterious, familiar – apart from the fair ones. We continue to swap 'awakening' stories, for want of anything better to gossip about: Tim's farcical encounter when he was a waiter in a stuffy hotel in England. He recounts the details, but I only pick up a brief sketch as my mind is floating: "An intriguing nervous guest on his own, staying on business... deep-set eyes, pretended not to glance, wearing a wedding ring, left a large tip even though he'd only had a coffee... his first time, shaking..." We hang on his words, laughing; he's also a good storyteller. This episode, which I'm sure I've heard before but from someone else, sets the relaxed tone for the rest of the night, for the rest of my stay in Sydney. For the rest of my life perhaps.

We've moved to a different bar on Victoria Street. I spin around on my chair to view the clientele: more pretentious than the other place but it doesn't matter; the three of us are on a roll. I'm waffling on incoherently.

"Different details, time, place, same innocence... he was right, of course, but I just denied it. To him, to myself; couldn't have been a fucking poof. You just go with the event – it happened, didn't really understand, happened again; finally something actually sexual, physical, beautiful, relieving. At last I'm gay. Oh shit, now I have to tell my friends and family: 'Yeah, and?' 'Well, it's never been proved either way!' 'We knew that years ago. How many girlfriends have you had?!' 'Shit, why didn't you tell me then!'"

Enough of the coming-out stories; it's later. We've barred out and clubbed out, and I've soaked up enough living atmosphere to fill a novel. Sydney's alright, you know. John and Tim are reclined on the sofa while I'm opening yet another bottle of red wine.

"Let's drink to us," I say. Drink this fine warm (Sydney room temperature) nectar, perfect to switch off your mind, end the day and start the next, I think.

We're now all snuggling together – it's quite a big sofa – like cats at peace, watching the telly. A film starring Richard Burton; his voice transcends the screen, us, me. I drift.

MANCHESTER, BEN, MARK, DARE

"Climb down!" Burton's voice boomed, penetrated. The man co-operated. Ben and I were avidly watching a film, yet another screening of *Where Eagles Dare*. But you can't see this film too many times if you like intelligent entertainment. That was what Mark said, anyway, as he came out of the kitchen fully armed with tortilla chips, crudités and dips. And more wine of course; we'd demolished two bottles of white – surprisingly good English from Sussex, I think: aromatic, crisp, dry, fairly serious stuff – and now had on our red wine heads. Sangiovese/Malbec from Argentina – rich, spicy, New World fruit meets European style – as I tried to read from the back label, my head tilted, the sanguine wine flowing horizontally. Superb with the houmous, disaster with the taramasalata. Back to the film, after being slightly distracted by distant sounds emanating from the Bridgewater Hall – climaxing music, applause. We watched right until the end of the credits, applauded, tongues firmly in cheeks.

How disappointed we were (shifts into movie critic mode); not with the film but that we'd been misquoting *the* line all this time. My two fellow Darites agreed – "what a superb war film," Mark indeed uttered – but the line, which Ben and I had got slightly wrong, was one of many classic cliché nasty Nazisms delivered by Nasty Nazi Derren Nesbitt, playing 'Major Bastard'. He of the whiter than blond peroxide Aryan, how German can I make my pronunciation types. "Everybody stay where you are until I know *exactly* what is going on." We'd always mistakenly (and sadly, I know) believed it to go: "Everybody stay *exactly* where etc..." You'd have to imagine the machine gun stresses on the syllables to make it sound 'German' enough. This scene came near the end of the film during the complex denouement, which Nesbit interrupted ("Is this the denouement?" I could almost hear him ask as he crashed into the room, as dark as his bitter chocolate uniform).

Dare was probably single-handedly responsible for the cliché about Germans and their obsessions with correct documentation, or at least the one which rammed it home and was remembered for it. You could tick off the papers' checking incidents with gusto; I always thought it was our exaggerated joke, but papers were asked for and found to be in order (or not) at every turn and twist of the plot. The next morning Mark announced he was going out to get the Sunday papers, answered by a simultaneous signal from Ben and I to make sure they were in order. I had a vision of him rearranging the piles of newspapers in the shop and verifying their exit visas... Mark stood up, having put his shoes on the wrong feet, and said: "I'm going to get the papers..."

BERLIN, SERGE, SUSIE, U-BAHN

"In Ordnung danke." The not blond customs official gave us back our passports. I thought it a little unfair to pick on us for a spot check; then again, it wasn't the first time I'd been singled out as a dodgy-looking character. Serge and I accelerated into Germany, top down on the car, surprisingly sunny for the time of year. I changed the CD: the Prodigy caught the sun and glinted in my eye. Music and wind fought like gladiators for supremacy; Serge and I shouted above the harmonious noise, anticipation full on. The car fast-forwarded through tinsel towns and fresh countryside, pictures on speed; we impulsively flicked through the pages of time and geography.

Eventually Berlin loomed; it threw a few images up in the air, a montage of tit-bits projected on my movie-screen mind. The new and the old: Brandenburger Tor, apartment building being erected, derelict one being demolished, the Reichstag undergoing a magnificently transparent refit, traffic, neon sleaze, people surging on the pavements, cars, industry, shopping. Exciting city.

We blasted straight down Kaiserdamm and Bismarckstrasse, then onto Strasse des 17 Juni and around the victory monument, unaware of us below. A grand procession if perhaps rather too imperialistic. But the Porsche didn't mind as it sped on through the park, destination Unter den Linden where our hotel was located, just into the 'old east'.

The cork blasted out in orgasmic haste and hit the picture on the bedroom wall; fizz water-fell onto the carpet then into our glasses. "Sorry," Serge giggled, "here's to adventure." Our glasses kissed, we drank the icy Sekt.

We'd booked in to the hotel at around 10pm after a long drive and, despite latent tiredness, we were up for partying; it made sense to have a wee preview of Berlin's finest and lowest. I was also "fucking starving", as I emphasised to my Arab-Gallic friend; first stop Italian restaurant.

"Salice Salentino, *bitte*." The waiter, probably German pretending to be Italian or maybe the other way around, obliged, nodding his approval almost unnoticed. Simple but tasty pasta for me – pecans, spinach, pesto, extra basil – chunk of bleeding meat for Serge; well, he was French, remember. We didn't hurry as we were now honorary residents in this mother of a 24-hour city. The fall-out from the waiter's zealous black pepper frenzy stung my nostrils; I almost sneezed. My nose took in, gently, the myriad aromas floating from my pasta: the spicy scented aforementioned pepper, sweet fresh and aniseedy basil and sick-stinky, but not unattractive, mature Parmesan. Serge smacked his lips in appreciation of the thick, winey sauce circling his steak and what appeared to be several different kinds of mushrooms. He missed my hand with his fork; I was too quick pinching a few chips from the plate. The Salice flowed: rustic, baked fruit and smoky figginess; I held the glass up and admired the deep red colour against the candle; the flame waved at me.

The flame from Serge's lighter glowed orange on his face and lit up the dark bar briefly around us. His exhaled smoke dispersed reluctantly but unnoticed; I caught the familiar pungent smell: Gitanes. We both observed the different oddballs who frequented this slightly sleazy cabaret club. Cancer man, also sitting at the bar, to our left by the phone where the half-oval counter joined the wall. He stared into the fruit bowl ashtray in front of him, either in disbelief at how many cigarettes he'd smoked (an American brand, I think, not seen them before) or just desolate. Hard to tell from here. He signalled for another drink: Polish vodka; I definitely recognised *that* bottle. Two bitching transvestites to the right; one sounded middle-American, one brushing ash off the other's red skirt. The topic of their derision seemed to be a couple at a table nearer the stage. I nodded agreement: bad moustache and jacket combination for him, simply awful hairstyle and brown dress combination for her. Various other misfits dotted around; then again, they probably thought the same of us. This might've occurred to Serge at the same time.

The street outside was alive with the sound of music, conversation and roasting chickens. Hot fat, beer, exhaust fumes and now rain mixed a heady cocktail of senses. We absorbed the human race out to play and crossed into Alexanderplatz, scrutinised by the monster television tower – a kind of BT tower but attractive, with a large ball attached. We'd been carried here earlier on the S-Bahn from Friedrichstrasse but decided to walk back to the hotel. So we took a short cut through some side streets.

"*Habt ihr eine Zigarette, bitte Jung's,*" a surly man called across the road. I didn't like the look of him but didn't really care.

"*Ne,*" I mumbled, as we continued, in a 'fuck off' fashion. It was poorly lit and quiet, apart from screeching cats fighting somewhere nearby; he approached nevertheless. He didn't have time to be surprised that I was now standing behind him holding the blade firmly under his throat. He had pulled the knife, predictably, after asking once again if we had a cigarette. The swiftness of my moving surpassed his comprehension and certainly his eyesight. I persuaded him to leave us alone and confiscated the weapon. Serge seemed to be initially taken aback but then casually resumed our conversation; nothing much I did surprised him anymore (not for a few weeks anyway).

Serge and I woke up virtually at the same time, entwined; stretched, surfaced. It was late morning; in fact 12.20 confirmed my watch. A leisurely lunch seemed logical; we ate lightly and drank Germanicly strong coffee sitting outside a café on Kurfurstendamm, like good little tourists. It was sunny again today, don't remember which day. Later we switched to maximum tourist mode (having warmed up conspicuously amidst gentle *Konsumerei*), ably guided by my old friend Susie who'd met us for lunch at this café. Almost always grinning, slightly mad, almost always smoking, Susie and I had shared a flat in Edinburgh several years before. Her mother was German, from Hamburg, her father was Polish; she'd studied at Herriot Watt for two years and now worked in Berlin. Unexpected character detail, it suddenly occurred to me; possible you might've thought so too.

Serge wanted a souvenir, "a piece of the Wall, if there's any left." Later; first shopping and culture. We merged with the masses on the Ku'damm, wandering and occasionally drifting into a welcoming department store or suitable clothes shop.

"Lacks a bit of glitz and style. I thought the best shops are supposed to be around here."

"Were – things are changing, moving east a bit," Susie replied. However, I bought Serge a tie with red and black horizontal zigzag pattern, good quality so it would take his weight. I bought Susie fabulous dark chocolate: bitter, powerful cocoa flavour; we scoffed it all on the U-Bahn heading back to Potsdamer Platz. Were we? What the hell happened then? Sorry, blank memory for a moment there; almost lost the entire file. I wanted to visit the Neue Nationalgalerie; could be some interesting pics to check out.

My face liquefied into Conrad Felixmuller's face on Hausmann's 1920 portrait. Black and white, if I remember correctly, oddly mathematical like a diagram. Not quite as engrossing as the strange figures in Grosz's *Stutzen der Gesellschaft*, painted in 1926. Satirical caricatures of political and military leaders: booze-flushed faces, upper class monocles, psychotic soldiers and seething corruption. No wonder old George didn't make himself too popular. However, these were not the portraits I desired; I couldn't see into the shadows.

Walk back with us to Potsdamer Platz, formally Europe's biggest building site. Frenzied activity was slowly drawing to a close in the recreation and re-launch of Germany's capital and superlative city.

MANCHESTER, DAMIEN, BOB, THE GIANT

I was watching the building work with a sense of approval and satisfaction, as the bus weaved indelicately through Hulme. The old Hulme, images associated with poverty, squalor and opportunist drug dealers, had been pulled down. New housing projects flourished on every corner, scaffolding and cranes had replaced bulldozers, family cars and Ikea blinds already moved in, shiny student palaces open for business. It seemed like every week had witnessed a piece of wasteland sprout piles of bricks, pre-packed plans and whistling workmen. Imaginative designs too; I could've lived there. But were just houses enough? These solid visions of the new Manchester coincided with the grandiose (supposedly) post-bomb refit of the City Centre. Of course, the focus of attention had been the rebuilding of M&S, the largest in Europe or the world, depending on national or local media. The site of the mammoth shop was the size of a football pitch, or maybe a golf course. Better make sure there's a new car park – people wouldn't come if they can't drive. Enough of the green – why was I on a bus, I had a car? Ah yes, remember last night? I was heading back into town after breakfast at Damien's in Chorlton (good scrambled eggs, almost as flavoursome as my special eggs with red pepper and garlic. Never used cumin before though; nice touch).

My mind cast itself back to Canal Street the night before (as I wasn't capable), the scene of a chance encounter and apparently a strange coincidence.

"I was going to ring you tomorrow," Damien said, surprised, excited and perhaps making excuses, after we bumped into each other amidst the bulging crowd outside Turners and Calle Canale. His bright smile gripped my attention for a moment; gleaming teeth the most visible feature on his enticingly dark face, his deep Indian eyes almost black. I'd met Damien a few months ago, maybe longer, at MASA, his studio in Hanover Mill near Piccadilly station. I'd been immediately hypnotised by his bizarre prints of twisted, absurd characters – expressionist with a sense of humour. We had made an agreement that I would find sponsorship for an exhibition and try to sell some of his works through my contacts in London. I'd been rather busy since then working with Ben on the opening of new restaurants here and in London; he'd been in Glasgow for a while on a teaching contract at the University.

"See you later, say in an hour or so, in the White Lodge. I'm meeting some guys there in a minute. Selling some paintings, actually. We can catch up."

Damien agreed and parted with one of his devastating smiles. The front-of-house manager greeted me with a not-so-devastating smile, as I stepped down into the White Lodge, yet another fashionable converted basement café bar. Chic (at that time), boldly primary coloured chairs scattered around metal tables, black and white photos of lonely souls framed on the walls. I particularly loved the red curtains draped all over the place, crimson camouflage for the naked red bricks.

I ordered a startlingly inexpensive white Burgundy (must have got the price wrong) from Vezelay; I knew the winemaker well. Unusually I craved Chardonnay but didn't fancy the dull Australian or Californian offerings: something a bit more subtle was required.

"Three glasses please, I'm expecting company. We may eat as well. Could you bring some nibbles in the meantime, I'm hungry... uhm, roasted almonds, olives, some of those potato things with the ferocious chilli sauce dip." The waiter smiled, noted, returned a few moments later with the wine and glasses.

"Crisp and elegant – like Chablis but better," Bob commented after tasting it. He and his associate, a very tall man indeed, had just arrived as the waiter brought the nuts and olives. I knew of Bob's associate but hadn't met him before, although it seemed so. Very pale complexion, empty eyes, a powerful presence – not just physically. Bob had started to grow a scruffy beard and his hair was now quite long, which revealed more silvery-grey-white streaks; I guess it'd been turning that way over the years but suddenly seemed more noticeable. We discussed trading my pictures – what price for those precious portraits? Enough to save my skin perhaps. We drank more wine together, switching to red, and ate more tasty *tapas*, casually munching and talking.

The hands on the huge clock had circled, as they were supposed to, to indicate an hour and ten minutes had passed, when Damien appeared, smiling for gold. Bob and the tall bloke shook his hand as they left, disappearing into the swirl of red drapes.

"So, how was Glasgow?" I asked.

"Fun, brilliant city. They paid me serious money, you know. I'll have to do more of this consultancy stuff. If I can get it!"

"There's the catch. Still, can't be that many experts on Expressionism who also paint well." He laughed modestly and talked more about Glasgow, the McFrenetic city.

"I don't know it that well – although I lived in Edinburgh, as you know, I didn't visit much. Typical Edinburgh snob!" I threw in to the word soup. Privately, I still preferred Edi; maybe not as lively but it had its own special qualities and memories. I peered into Damien's dark-cosmos eyes and drank more Chilean Pinot Noir, red velvet.

EDINBURGH, PEOPLE, PARTY, SEA

The tall glasses of Crémant de Loire slammed together in a meaningful gesture; a raucous 'Happy New Year' chorus followed, accompanied by heart-felt hugs and kisses. It was a few years ago, you don't need to know when exactly, in my flat in Edinburgh just off Bruntsfield Place. Obviously now 1st January, who was there? Yours truly, of course; Susie – flatmate; Gerald – boyfriend (hers); Gordon – boyfriend (mine); Steve, Ewan, Jane – various friends; and probably some others besides.

The action resolved to change location to all of us staggering across the Meadows in the dark. Destination, the Tron on High Street; we'd arranged to meet 100,000 people there. Picture this – infantile giggling, loud talking, tuneless singing, clouds of breath steaming then shivering in the freezing air.

No – I've decided I don't want to start there. Too gratuitous and unclear: Edi deserved more explanation and detail. Rewind another year and a few months. It was August; climb furtively through a window and walk slowly forwards inside the Edinburgh College of Art on Lauriston Place and join the audience watching a group of idiots on the stage. I was one of them. It was an interesting fortnight, our revue show on the Fringe, character building stuff. We'd been invited to do the show on the back of two plays the Edi University thesp group was performing; we'd originally run it for three nights earlier that year when we were still students there – seven of us wrote and 'starred' in the sketches. It seemed to be quite successful: in front of a student audience, performed by students with student-y (immature yet surreal) humour. We soon discovered a few changes would have to be made for the Fringe; like most of it. It was hard work trying to be funny for two weeks, especially when the material grew proportionately unfunny through familiarity (fed up with). The sketches were changed by the night; the puerile being replaced by the increasingly surreal, the content nose-dived into self-indulgent, make-it-up-as-you-go-along stream-of-consciousness. After all, how many shows could've boasted featuring the entire audience on stage? OK, so it comprised of three people that particular night. Strangely the audiences steadily swelled, as the press reviews got worse. 'Nazi swim wear' was a classic ("bad taste and just plain bad"); 'the Trial' obviously went way over their heads, an intelligent Kafka pastiche dripping with Absurdity ("cheap and unfunny philosophy student gag"). The beer-fuelled publicity stunts were correspondingly aggressive: screaming at people in the streets cunningly disguised in silly coloured, odd shoes and braces, gorilla outfit, borrowed firemen's hats. The critics' condemning words were broadcast loud and clear; odd how many more tickets you could sell by shouting "Yet another talent-less, painfully unfunny student show". What did he expect for a quid? Must have been the guy we humiliated on stage...

Edinburgh was an exciting city most of the time, in its very own understated way, even without the Festival. Then it really let its hair down and came alive, to the chagrin of the more miserable Edinburgher ("pubs and restaurants too full, traffic worse than usual" etc.) I, however, lapped it up – I mean, come on, the opportunity to see loads of comedy, films, plays, exhibitions all in one month?! I suppose all those very disposable fliers constantly thrust in your face could become a little tiresome, particularly from yet another gorilla. I fell in love with Edinburgh the first time I visited – a friend and I both had offers of places at the university and wanted to check out the atmosphere before accepting. A peculiar city to look at in some ways, up and down, built on hills and big natural bumps. And surrounded by dramatic volcanic hills too, quite close to the centre really, which wasn't difficult as it's not very big. Very Scottish architecture, all those grey stone tenement and office buildings. Let me conjure up a few twee touristy images: Thunderbird One, as we called the Walter Scott Monument; the glorious castle brooding in the rain and always on the brink of its abrupt perch; the old worn stone road down the 'Royal Mile'; the poor suburban housing estates, three junkies sharing a needle. And the smell – the sweet malty aromas, which constantly perfumed the air thanks to the huge brewery; a small town on its own charged up with a planet full of beer.

So I studied there for four years, then stayed and worked for a while in an art gallery – I don't recall for how long now; less than another four years, probably. Then I moved to London. Why? Change of job, a fugitive perhaps. This kind of decision was usually made for you – OK, it was my action that precipitated it so I had reshaped my destiny slightly. But why should work or such like have guided fate so? Few of us would allow ourselves to make decisions and actions which were outright bold, unknown and unsure of the outcome. I'd often contemplated this particular choice and how it changed my life. It could drive you mad, endlessly pondering the alternatives, the impossibility of predicting where your path might have led. What would have happened if I hadn't left Edi? Looking back, I did abandon a source of possibly unrepeatable happiness but had gained a whole extra facet; I also wouldn't have lived through all those London experiences. We would always like to think that our own actions alone shaped the future, how we were and would be judged by others. But of course other people's actions would collide with our own. Something like that happened to me. Enough philosophising, I hear you say. Let's have some of that action.

Leap forwards through the calendar's withered pages, landing on that 1st of Jan. later in the day, when I surfaced from a haze of drunken sleep, vivid dreams and unbearable warmth – a combination of Gordon's body heat and Susie having left the heating on all day. It was gentle out, already dark: I adored those Scottish winters and going to bed when light, waking up when dark. Well, we made the most of it over Christmas and Hogmanay, had to go back to work soon. There was a submerged orange glow over the pitch-black city (not as orange as Manchester's), then it disappeared. The metropolis was recovering – some snoozed, some stared blankly at the James Bond movie on the telly (we were, the universally underrated *OHMSS*), some started to party again, some hadn't stopped – the civilised Scots also declare the 2nd a holiday. However, we were content to vegetate, drinking cup after cup of lemon tea. The contrast of tannin and acidity revived my stale palate, the aromatic Indian tea washed through my head.

The bitter blasting North Sea air, crisp and tangy, rinsed through my head and lungs. We stood dangerously near the end of the pier, barely balanced on the raised, old stone part, or were trying to stand. The vicious January wind almost cut me in two and shunted the dark clouds past in fast-motion. Ugly seagulls were thrown around in erratic patterns by invisible shot-putters. The tide was out, baring the rocks in haggard toes, but the sea was running back quickly; I could hear it screaming. How could a place be so bleak and beautiful?

We'd galloped up the M90 two hours earlier in Gerald's green Lotus Carlton (flash git, although I thought they were only available in black?) until we hit the A91: "St Andrews this way" the sign had whispered. I'd smiled when the old grey (or perhaps gray) town came into view: the dominant cathedral ruins defiant in antiquity, elegant St Salvator's Chapel oozing relative youth, the half-castle melting into the sea, the tit-dome on Hamilton Hall overshadowing the 18th on the Old Course. It'd been a while since we last escaped to St Andrews, known to be good for the soul. We abandoned the pier walk and the seafront and took refuge in Pa Mellies pub, after slouching down the Scores, one of Gordon's old haunts. He was careful to avoid too many memories but couldn't stop himself.

"It's good to be back..." I listened and chased my pint of 80 Shilling with a warming Bowmore 10 Year Old, and gawked at one of the thankfully not too many golf pictures on the wall. Seve Ballesteros was caught punching the air in victory, his face contorted with excitement having sunk a monster on the 18th to take the Open. I could hear the applause.

BARCELONA, ALEX, DALÍ, TIGERS

My body lingered with Damien in the White Lodge – this time I was actually telling him one of my stories from my road movie – but my mind had returned to Barcelona, to the last episode before I departed from that Catalan catalyst.

I stood behind Alex as he recorded the enveloping view of the city from Castell de Montjuïc. In fact, I was filming him surveying the horizon on the camcorder and cut between focusing on him, thus blurring the background, and on random outstanding landmarks, which forced him to thaw into the foreground. The stately Monument a Colom guarding over the port, the Cathedral (feeling very old but un-ruined) and in the distance Gaudí's eight sun spires eclipsed by a crane, temporarily severed by a passing cable car. The sun winked off the crawling cars on the main road along the waterfront from the Colom up; the heat wobbled over the almost silent metal. Alex shielded his eyes from the summer glare with his hand and scanned his head slowly from side to side; I panned the camera, following him. The surrounding hills in a haze, white speck yachts at sea. To the left sat the maturing, brown Palau Nacional with its four corner towers and one large dome. Further left still, the spiked tyre Olympic mast thing; a telecommunications tower, I think.

"I love this city," he whispered.

"We should go away for a few days, a little seaside and sun trip," I suggested.

"Why not. Where to?" Extreme close up on his face then mouth, as the words came out.

My eyes tracked back from Alex's chops:

"Spread this on my back, would you?"

No problem young man. I took the *leche solar* and smeared it all over his dark skin; that felt real good (I doubt his constant Arabesque tan required it but that complexion demanded the attention). Another peach cruised by, kicking sand into my white wine; I forgave him as I watched his rear view blend into the others. All around golden beach at Sitgès: well, greying yellowish sand, beer bottles, sun addicts. Welcome to Barcelona's weekend escape, and most of Europe's as well by the looks and sounds of it. I'd had a narrow escape earlier when buying two bottles of Chardonnay (from Somontano I believe) in a shop – an awful chap from Leeds had started to chat me up. I appeared to have got away with being Spanish; luckily he didn't speak any. I must've been the only local who didn't speak English.

Back on the beach Alex and I were beginning to regret drinking wine in the sun – it seemed to make absolute sense a couple of hours ago. Anyway, the afternoon was disappearing and I was getting bored. We returned to the guesthouse – small, quiet, functional – and crashed out for a few sixty minutes. At that point I felt I'd truly melded with Alex; we had become one. Should I let him join me in my quest, become like me? Was his fate hovering over him at this very moment? Poor innocent, I thought, as I observed him sleeping. Good, he was dreaming. And I knew what about, as I caught a glimpse of the pictures as I drained them from his stolen brain.

Just after 10.30, my watch informed me. The airy restaurant was beginning to fill up, as fashionable Europeans came alive and out to play (remember, we were on Spanish time). And the food? Pretty good so far. Being slightly sad but an addict for the flavour combination, I had asparagus, peppers and goat's cheese to start because it was on the menu. Alex had lonely asparagus drizzled with rich, thick, yellow olive oil. My nose told me from the pungent scent that it also had... it smelled like... that herb I always forget. Alex knew, in Spanish and Portuguese only, but I didn't in Spanish, English, German or even Cantonese. No matter, it would come to me later in the most unexpected way. We quaffed the reasonable but not memorable Penedès Blanco of the house, refreshing at least. Just to take the piss, I ordered *paella* for both of us to follow. Well, I was on holiday. It was good, as Alex begrudgingly admitted, although he'd wanted something else. To get his own back he ordered a bottle of Cava to drink with it; I'd wanted something else. However, as soon as I saw the bubbles racing to jump out of the glass, I smiled; fizz was splendid for the soul. To us, Alex didn't say but implied by raising his glass. To you, dear chap, I kept to myself, grinning malevolently. Alex's charming face was trapped in each pearl of the mousse. Would the bubble burst or was he imprisoned?

"I stayed in Berlin for a few weeks last year. *Über*-city," I explained to our new German friend, who we'd met in an embarrassing bar called the Purple Parrot or similar. He was actually from Munich but was about to move to Berlin. We sat outside drinking more Cava, absorbing the warmth and the smell of the midnight population. *Sorrel*, that was it. Not his name – he was Gunther – the mystery herb from earlier. It wasn't interesting enough to tell

Alex; it interested me purely because it was typical of the way my mind seemed to work – constantly flitting around, always thoughts, flavours, things, people, places, other people's thoughts, but rarely dates and times. I tried not to think so much but "I had too much energy to switch off my mind", as words played in my head. No chance mate, I thought, as I watched Gunther chat to Alex, body language very positive. He was already mine. Predictably the three of us ended up in a stuffy, hot semi-dark club and sweated off some of the Cava, getting high on CO_2.

Alex and I slobbed in Sitgès for a couple of days, then drove up the coast to Cadaquès via Figueres in search of Dalí. And we found him. We were both silenced by the initial sight of the Museu Dalí. I was surprised that I was surprised – I hadn't been here before but assumed I knew what to expect: I'd seen pictures, heard stories from friends who'd visited, now I could buy the T-shirt. But when we arrived and entered, this place truly exuded the spirit of the man (as well as the body under foot). Not just his works but the whole ambiance, the feeling, the style. The baked-crisp baguettes fixed on statuettes, the huge eggs lining the roof about to topple and form one big surreal omelette; all this set us up on a voyage into the mind of a genius, as Dalí frequently christened himself. A tribute indeed that his gallery devoted to his memory was as bizarre and larger than life as he. I gasped when I suddenly encountered the massive canvas mounted in the makeshift hall-cum-chapel under a round glass dome. I would've had this picture, if not for its sheer size. Alex studied it intently; perhaps he sensed he would get to know it very well. The moment was almost religious. Almost.

Luckily we'd coincided our visit with a special exhibition, which featured certain pictures on loan from collections around the world. So many classics.

My head went into a spiralling spin, images flashed by in montage: Mae West's ruby lips, possessed elephants with extended legs, spindly crutches propping, dark ants swarming, melting watches, figures merging, oozing, Gala blessed me.

Alex and I were strolling aimlessly along the rocky Catalan shore. We met a man sitting at an easel painting: scary mad eyes, pointed moustache. He talked liberally about the subject in the picture – the sedate, calm, sleeping woman; the ferocious vision a second before waking. Alex jumped out of his skin as the two tigers leapt onto the beach, one of them pointing a rifle at his head. I was too busy enjoying a huge pomegranate to notice, sucking on the luscious red juice, and trying to hold the camera steady as I filmed Alex at the same time, the horror on his face as he dissolved into the sea.

I drove back to Barcelona alone – I don't remember how much longer I stayed in the city. Not too long. I decided to travel to romantic Italy – I'd drive along the coast across the south of France, taking in some of the glitz – Monte Carlo, Cannes, where I felt I'd been before in the distant past, Turin, Verona perhaps. Who would know, I could end up in Venice: vision of me standing on a small disintegrating bridge, my gaze following a slow boat down the canal. Who was that in the boat? Looked familiar. Striking red shirt.

MANCHESTER, BEN, HONG KONG, TERMINATOR

Ben and I stood and watched, hooked, as the police fished the body out of the canal, fully clothed – dirtied red shirt, black jeans – as much as I could make out from the bridge across to City café bar. The law had closed off the rest of Canal Street and Sackville Street in military style. The drone and flash of police and ambulance sirens had died down now, replaced by shouts, shocked crowds and gathering media activity. We carried on drinking red wine (Hungarian Kekfrankos/Merlot), pensive and collected yet not untouched by the mysterious drowning.

"I'm not hungry anymore," Ben uttered.

"Oh, I am," was the predictable reply. We went back inside to rejoin our guests: Charlie, museum curator from Hong Kong, and Graham, director of a gallery in Edinburgh. I used to work for Graham when I'd lived there, so didn't know him very well. Charlie was an old friend of Ben's family; in fact we had met her by chance in Hong Kong, I remembered now.

"More wine?" Unanimous nods of approval. The not-so-cute waiter was obviously psychic, as he'd already brought another bottle of Kekfrankos (the Merlot had pissed off) over to our table. The food was okay – vaguely eastern European peasant met Manchester cosmopolitan café owner and got unhappily married. We were discussing our sponsorship of a small exhibition of contemporary Hong Kong and other Chinese art. It would close in a Chinese arts' centre in London, having been displayed to critical acclaim during the Festival in Edinburgh. We'd clinched a deal to show the collection in Manchester beforehand in Ben's father's restaurants.

"Quite trendy nowadays," Ben reassured them, pointing to the handful of attractive watercolours brightening up the walls in City as evidence.

"As we've already thrashed out, we'll handle the marketing and publicity, with a little help from a friend of mine in London and your team in Edi of course," I added, gesturing to Graham.

"Includes works by Zhang Xiaogang, Sze Yuen, Wu tien Chang and Oscar Ho Hing-Kay, previously unseen in Europe," Charlie was reading out from her notes a little later, checking we had the updated information.

"I can't wait..." I continued. All seemed under control, we talked details for a while longer then adjourned to a different bar. I didn't remember which because I wasn't paying attention as we entered. My mind was darting and alert; I was sure we were being followed. *I* was being followed. A figure in the shadows; but I couldn't see anyone outside from where we took a pew in the window. My imagination again. However, I kept sensing the same feeling at night from that moment onwards. When I woke up in the morning, a touch fresher (although it felt like I was being poked in the eye), I believed someone had whispered in my ear in a dream: "I absolutely will not stop, ever, until you are..." I didn't remember the rest of the words. For some reason, my breath smelled of whisky... whiskey actually, Bushmills; it all came flooding back. I also recalled a song from the dim-and-distant playing in the bar last night: 'In between days' by the Cure. I remained lying down for a moment; my breakfast hit my head, or to be precise, Ben threw a couple of grapefruits at me.

DUBLIN, LIME, DOUGLAS, RAIN

When I returned to Dublin, stopping off en route for the USA, I couldn't for the life of me remember the name of the pub. I'd been to Ireland's number one city once before, predictably on a stag event ('weekend break taking in the history, the 'crack' and rounded off with a little relaxing golf' as far as the hotel was concerned), and we'd spent long hours in this particular pub. It had an unusual name – difficult to forget you would've thought – laid-back atmosphere, good music. It was a period house on the end of a row: two or three wonky storeys, brightly painted brick upstairs, comfortable, the odd incongruous object hanging here or there downstairs, where smoke gathered and plotted. And the Guinness was... passable. I'd arranged to meet a friend of mine there.

Flashback to previous Dublin visit: group of hungry noisy lads had taken over the restaurant in the Grafton Square Hotel (what a nightmare). The staff were professionally wearing 'serve them quickly and get them out' expressions, with a smile of course. He seems to be smiling particularly often, I thought, and at me. Assistant Manager, Douglas something from what I could read on his badge from where I sat. Looked familiar, despite his blue-green eyes. I gave him the wine list and returned beam, ordering Chilean Merlot and South African Cinsault/Pinotage for the troops. And beers. And a Coke – Coke on a stag weekend?

"Just pacing myself," was the sheepish response.

Blah... blah... several hours later, the male deer were now randomly slouched in the hotel bar, sort of in a group but looking like many cats had done much dragging. We were a few short – either crashed out upstairs or still out on the town. We'd followed the eager advice of various hotel staff and planned a route (more like a systematic campaign of attack, occupy and march on) terminating, quite literally for some, in a pincer movement on a tacky club next door. Convenient, at least, and tacky in the best possible way: picture pulsating light strips fitted into the drink-sodden carpet and curling floor, lovely glitzy Abba-reflecting mirrored balls spinning from the ceiling, enough Beck's to flood Bremen. Doug and I got chatting, he'd pretended to query something about our booking. A spark; he was on duty until 4am, we shared red and stories till dawn and beyond.

The Furry Lime, of course. How could I've forgotten that name? I was pleasantly surprised to find this pub was across the square from my hotel, a gentle float away – I'd booked into the Grafton for old times' sake. My memory had it situated a few staggered streets further away. I stepped in, apprehensive and a few minutes late; Douglas was already here, standing uneasily at the bar sipping slowly from a pint of lager. He looked quite different, his hair much shorter; I didn't recognise him at first glance. He greeted me with a beaming, reminiscent smile.

"Let's go somewhere else to meet some friends of mine. More

comfortable there, bit less red-blooded!" he cracked.

How disappointing, I thought mischievously. We spilled out into the assembling crowds, streaming from one bar to the next, and made our way down Suffolk Street, dodged the aggressive traffic on College Green then up Anglesea Street into Temple Bar, trying to head towards the river. Bad idea: the whole area was crammed full of fun seekers and somebody had forgotten to take the lid off. The noise level was fantastically overwhelming: hundreds of conversations, shrieks, shouts, laughter fought with the music pouring out of the pubs, live and juke-box, which became indistinguishable from street performers playing outside. There was no tension in the air, just lots of pissed up people getting a hit from lots of other pissed up people. I stopped for a moment, as curious as to why several unrelated characters were hanging around looking up at what appeared to be a disused building, as those people were as to why a rusty metal electric shutter was closing very slowly in a window. No light or signs of activity within. Then, when finally closed, everybody cheered and applauded. I continued to follow Doug, who'd already shrugged at my confused expression ("this *is* Dublin" were his words). We eventually made it to Parliament Street and entered into the young and beautiful crowd in The Back Room.

"This is Liam..." We shook hands, installed ourselves in one of the osmosis-inducing brown leather sofas and talked about restaurants, art, films (as you do).

"I run a vegetarian café, not far from here actually," he informed me. "I like your shirt; brilliant colour. Really vibrant red."

The next day: I was contemplating a picture. Doug and I happened to be in the Hugh Lane Municipal Gallery of Modern Art in Parnell Square. "Fantastic shade of red in the sky, warming yet sinister." I agreed with him. We were doing a casual cultural tour, not too serious though. "There's some good stuff in here," I threw in the air, "intriguing."

"Mostly 19th and 20th Century, Irish as well," he read from the brochure with a certain sense of pride, and mentioned a couple of names, such as Byrne, King, Yeats, I think. I knew a little about the Yeats clan, of course, but not much about the others, apart from their names seen in trade mags or a book somewhere. Jack B's stunning 1949 *The Gay Moon* would've been perfect: a blurry red, white and strongly blue head wearing a dark hat hogs the foreground, which echoes the white and yellow full moon; on the right hand side there's another face in profile that forms part of it. But that pic wasn't here – nothing quite as good – and I wanted something more.

"I'd like to check out the Bank of Ireland collection. Do you know where it is?"

"Baggot Street, I think, bit of a walk."

"OK, how about lunch first?" I said, and sitting watching the world go by, I thought.

Shift scenes to the "all the rage" café Potemkin: we sat and dripped in the window; Doug was smoking pungent roll-ups and reading the paper, I observed the folk outside in Dame Court, all now frenetically trying to avoid getting wet – it was pissing down black shamrocks. We drank more espressos; I needed the caffeine kick. Lunch had been simple but good, the dressing on the salads particularly memorable in a strong mustard kind of way. All nicely washed down by an eyebrow-raising Soave Classico – single estate mind you. Time drifted on, it didn't stop raining. So we accepted the inevitable and made our way to Baggot Street, strolling in the rain "to get wet on purpose" (a tune came to mind). I imagined the California sun to escape our current predicament; it wouldn't be long now.

Two drowned rats stood admiring the Bank of Ireland collection; some soaring contemporary works. Eureka.

"Doug, take a look at this one." I somehow knew this face; it looked a little like my Irish friend.

"Everything OK, sir?" the airline official asked.

"Great, especially if I can have some more red wine," I joked and pleaded at the same time. I waved goodbye in my mind to Dublin, as it disappeared from sight through the plane's porthole like on a tv screen. I sank into the seat and looked ahead; images of San Francisco blew up like fireworks. The Cantenac-Brown was sublime – rich and still deepest of reds; the flavour crashed over my tongue and gripped my cheeks.

MANCHESTER, BRUCE LEE, HARRY, BOND

I felt the shock wave from the punch breeze past my left cheek: he was very quick. However, my head had already tilted to the right to avoid it, or at least, would have avoided it, if he'd intended to actually strike me. But he didn't withdraw his arm as quickly though, giving me the chance to rotate, grab and twist it and glance him around the face with my right. We broke apart and exchanged thoughts, mental and physical free-fall in unison. Anticipation rather than aggression: what move next? Harry had been my teacher for some time now and, with a little help from Ben, I'd nearly mastered his discipline, a unique fighting art, which mixed Jeet Kune Do, Bruce Lee's street style, with more formal Chinese and Korean schools. I'd also added a little twist learnt from Gordon in Edinburgh – traditional Japanese plus a squeeze of old fashioned British hand-to-hand. And mastered was the correct word – Harry realised I was in total control. Well almost: a split second lapse of concentration didn't give me much time to dodge his high 'roundhouse' style kick. I did, just, but lost my balance and fell not so humbly to the floor.

"Keep your mind on the here, the now!" Harry rebuked and mocked at the same time, although these words sounded like I'd recalled them from a movie and probably weren't the ones he actually used.

We called it a day, showered and decided to go for a pint; we'd been working out for nearly two hours and had the devil's thirst. So we stepped out of Harry's gym and nimbly crossed Portland Street, heading for the Village. It was considerably cooler than earlier – you could rely on Manchester to be unreliable but thus more interesting and a guaranteed topic of conversation. What was predictable, perhaps, was that the evening took a distinctly strange turn. The Old Bond pub was often a source of bizarre evenings, a lively place full of real fictional characters, the likes of which could be crammed into a beefy novel. But this particular evening steadily became ominous as well as odd. On returning home, I had an even stronger feeling of events rushing to a... specific point in time, a climax perhaps, than experienced recently. I had again sensed that presence, similar to the other night, as we'd entered the pub. Difficult to clearly spot anyone in here, lots of people loitering in shadows and corners.

I could only just make out what Bob was whispering in my ear – a permutation of the volume of the music and that he seemed to be talking backwards – but I could understand him. Bob might have already been in the pub before we got there or come in afterwards. It didn't matter; he imparted some garbled information:

"I may've sold your portraits –" (the rest drowned by shouting over a microphone) "– somebody's pursuing you."

"I know," I confirmed acceptingly. Harry asked me what was wrong.

BERLIN, FUNERAL, SERGE, EXPRESSIONISM

Harry Palmer gave me his gun, smiled reassuringly and indicated that I should not make a sound. We could hear the ungainly foot-steps of our assailant, as he crunched gravel and brick dust under foot creeping around the derelict house. In fact, there was only me here dressed in a formerly white raincoat and black plastic-rimmed glasses. I didn't remember how I got here or who the other man (or maybe a weighty woman) was. I pressed myself against the wall and looked out through a hole in it. I could see the Wall, not far from the house, painted with slogans and crowned with barbed wire. Nearby stood an observation tower, tall and as alone as I in the night, armed with a searchlight. I had to get closer to the Wall; I could feel the movie was drawing to a dramatic conclusion.

I started when the chubby piece of concrete crashed to the ground in front of me. Serge laughed and came up to me, crunch-ing brick and rubble under his sizeable dusty boots.

"That's your bit, a chunk of history!" We were rummaging around in a crumbling district close to where the Wall used to be, one of the few remaining. Serge proudly carried his souvenir slab of concrete and told me an emotional account of seeing the tv pic-tures, as a few friends and he had watched on that fateful day in 1989. "A close up shot of a crowd of Berliners pushing down a small section of the Wall. An unbelievable moment, the tears and laughter and warmth, as so-called West and East met and hugged each other."

I remembered shedding a tear as well, although some might not look back so fondly now. We walked around here for a while, swapping stories and emotions, and watched how Berlin had cleared, built and grown, preparing to be the seat of government once again.

"*Putain*, not another art gallery!" Serge protested or something like that; I couldn't hear him properly across the wailing carriage on the U-Bahn. Probably even more colourful language, knowing my Gallic friend.

"Yeah, you'll like this place, *cool* pics," sarcastically, trying to downplay my authoritarian sightseeing programme.

We were now on Bussardsteig outside the Brücke-Museum. I was pleased, as we'd timed our visit with a special exhibition of Ernst-Ludwig Kirchner. His personal visions of 1910s Berlin and 1920s beyond were an eye-opener – scary and vital at once, bright colours clashed with shadows. The Expressionist style caught the dark side of his characters and cityscapes, fright of new metropolitanism yet also excitement and anticipation of the future, hopes and fears. I was reminded of Alfred Döblin's novel *Berlinalexanderplatz*, which celebrated city life, the energy of the new and the possible piled on top of one another. And also the sleaze, hardship and failure.

"Wow!" Serge uttered, "creepy." I hadn't seen these before or even heard of the artist but was immediately drawn into the faces, as Serge was. *Four Evangelists* by Karl Schmidt-Rottluff, 1912. Brass relief painted in oil – Matthew, Mark, Luke and John. Faces sucked of life, frightening and frightened yet trying to tell us something. St John was the most haunting, the dark eyes and mouth like holes in a mask, doorways to a troubled mind. Serge leaned towards it, his face seemed to pull the same expression. It was mine.

It was a very long drive to Barcelona, probably rather foolish but I had time, plenty of time. In retrospect, I should've gone through central Europe and on to northern Italy first, but that would've been far too sensible. I heard Spain calling and responded. The Flat Six purred all the way, rubber melted, many insects died. I literally sliced through Switzerland on my journey – Zurich, Geneva; tick. Appealing but too clean, too conservative; good cheese and mountains though, he says condemningly and superficially clichéd. Unfair: I remembered a hazy, warm, relaxed afternoon on a boat on the eastern side of Lac Léman near Lausanne. The water was blue/grey like the sky, undecided on rain or sun, but penetratingly comfortable; I wasn't frying but felt heated through but not perspiring but sauna-cleansed, and breathed the quasi-salty soporific air. It was one of those early occasions when it should've been obvious that I found a man attractive. Yes, we were men just, I suppose, although I've never given up the child in me. I'd been travelling with a school friend around parts of Europe – interminable train journeys, too much walking, heavy bag welded to your back by sweat and UV. He was funny and acerbically charming, handsome, dark and seemingly pure. He also only liked girls and they'd liked him. But it didn't matter; the time and place transcended such things. Memory within a memory faded.

But what happened to Serge, I hear you ask? I don't know. Maybe he stayed in Berlin, maybe he came with me. You decide, but he didn't arrive in Barcelona when I did. I was excited like an innocent as I unpacked my clothes in the hotel.

MANCHESTER, B & D, EXHIBITION, FIZZ

Ben and Damien excitedly but carefully unpacked the canvases. The Chinese pictures had arrived the day before and we had to finish hanging them in three of our restaurants before opening tonight. I chose the selective but impressive collection we would put up in the Bay of Opportunity, the newest and most stylish restaurant on Faulkner Street, where we were holding the press launch and preview the following day.

Not surprisingly, it turned into a huge piss-up. The reception was swinging, we were sure to get well-deserved publicity from it. The place was swarming with freeloading city officials, art critics and general fashionabili – all appreciated and appreciating of course. So were the dim sum – the crunchy seaweed balls were exquisite, the mini deep fried vegetable rolls epitomised very mini and deep fried, crisp and green. And the spicy prawns – big chilli, sea-fishy, *cracocant* – a dental experience. We served too much fizz – unfortunately I couldn't get enough Charlie but settled for a vintage, small grower champagne to top up, which was actually even better. Rather good for washing your hair with as well: I seemed to have poured half a bottle over a cute journalist from *City Life*, who'd come to cover the exhibition preview and to get pissed, perhaps. Ironic that *he* ended up covered, but appeared to enjoy it.

It could've been the alcohol that distorted my view or perhaps the bubbles in the fizz, like a joke mirror, but I was gripped by a sworded figure in one of the paintings and tried to sharpen my focus. She seemed to be locked in a deadly confrontation with two others, warriors meeting at sunset sort of thing. She had an almost religious aura, a priest with attitude perhaps, a sense of righteousness. Yet at the same time her expression was indifferent, uncaring, amoral. One of the warriors was tall and shadowy, wearing dark clothes and a vicious stare – presumably the bad guy. The other didn't have any discernible look, just a little scruffy and unattractive, perhaps a glint of zeal in his eyes as if after a prize. The setting was heavily stylised and ethereal, a roughly circular clearing surrounded by a mass of large stones and dotted with the odd tree. Maybe a graveyard. Swords were clasped but the figures were perfectly still, not yet engaged in combat.

DREAM, BAD, GOLD

That night I slumped into a vision in front of a movie on the tv. Acoustic guitars were strumming and plucking, then became more and more frenzied, intensified by trumpets joining at a crescendo. Hands twitched by their guns, cold eyes staring straight through one another. The sun-drenched pictures span around, cutting quickly from hands to faces, intense close-ups. The adrenalined music rebounded around my head, around their heads. The three men stood facing each other, forming a triangle, in the middle of a huge graveyard, which stretched up gently climbing hills surrounding them. The macho showdown painfully dragged on, the tension sweated from their faces. The music finally, slowly wound down until just a tune of chimes rang in my ears. Pistols were drawn quicker than a blink of the eye, yet replayed one frame at a time. Shots echoed. The dark one fell into an open grave, followed by his hat whipped by another bullet. I stepped up and peered in; it was me lying there. Yet I had a second vision, the face blurred. It was indeed the bad guy who'd been felled; I was standing there over the gaping grave, pointing a boiling gun cautiously. We'd won; I had won. I then rode off up the dried hill with my half of the loot, disappearing as a speck on the horizon. No, I did come back into view briefly – well, I couldn't leave the ugly guy hanging there. A piercingly accurate rifle shot snipped the rope. He fell. Freeze.

EDINBURGH, 80 SHILLING, DEAL, IDEA

We walked with a hellish thirst under the slightly morbid sign into the pub: The Final Drop, picturing hanging figure. The Grassmarket was busy today, some sort of hippy market. It used to be busy with curious sightseers avid for the day's hanging; Edinburgh was a much more civilised city nowadays. I said we, but in fact I'd entered the pub alone. Must've been thinking of a different occasion. I'd merely been wandering around the shops on

George and Princess Streets for a while, then crossed over past the station up to Cockburn Street. To a clothes shop, I think. I'd then decided to walk home cutting through the Grassmarket up to Tollcross. I didn't get that far: the Cale 80 wafted seductively out of the pub as I strolled past, Edi's own pint beckoned and I was thirsty.

He's so cute, I thought. Dark eyes, brown hair, fair complexion. He smiled as I took another swig of my pint (very Scottish - darker, maltier and sweeter than English bitter, but still with satisfying tang of hops) slouched in the corner. The hands on the clock moved on forty minutes, somehow actually in less time than that. I pulled my hand, clenched, out of my pocket to count the change as I stood at the bar patiently, while the woman topped up the glass, allowing the head to settle a little.

"I'll get that," the mysterious stranger insisted. He was Gordon; pleased to meet you, Gordon. We chatted in the cosiest corner.

"I work for a local wine merchant," – good start, I thought, – "down in Leith... adore red wine... live in the New Town off Dundas Street... like going to the cinema... modern art..." Somehow all too coincidental to be true.

I explained: "Really, I've just started working in the marketing department at the National Gallery of Modern Art..."

"I moved here from St Andrews in August..." He continued to tell me more about himself in much detail, curiously frank. Yet at the same time I felt he was holding back – he wanted to divulge so much perhaps, but there seemed to be something more sinister he wouldn't touch upon. I'd only just met Gordon but was getting oddly positive vibes; somehow I knew it would lead to a rewarding friendship. I suddenly believed he could teach me something, show me things I'd (only) dreamed about. He gave the impression of promising much without actually saying so.

Follow us down Cowgate, lightly sleazy in the most attractive sense, to Campbell's on the corner. A strange pub I'd always rather liked: very sparse inside, half of it appeared to be carved out of rock. Well used and engraved wooden benches and tables, bohemian but mixed crowd; students, hippies, punks, some suits. Good beer, mostly Scottish real ale, also surprising wine selection, which was ideal as both of us had pint-ed out and I craved spicy Syrah: Crozes-Hermitage please, another bottle thanks. The damp-looking streets, animated bars and atmosphere in general around here under the bridges appealed to me. Buzzing and seedy – cities ooze that style of personality and specialise in fostering areas, which combine great pubs, bars and clubs with porn dives and dodgy characters (we fitted the metropolitan profile perfectly) – all part of the experience. There was now a long, disjointed queue outside the Guilded Balloon across the road; unusual for an October gig, looked more like a heady August night.

Christ knew where we ended up (thanks to some sort of omnipotent memory loss) – before we ended up at Gordon's place, I mean – a club off Broughton Street I think. I have a very distant memory of it now but it was late, or early, when we arrived at his flat. He offered me an unusual red wine, one I hadn't savoured before. It was very dark brown in colour, old and viscous, tasted like none I had drunk.

"I don't remember," was his unconvincing reply, when I asked where he'd bought it and it was from. He kissed me smoothly on the back of my neck, and I fell into a deep coma.

All faded to dark; then a sudden blindingly bright light woke me up. The day after the next: I didn't feel well, rather drained and weak. I decided to skip work and stay in bed but still went over to Gordon's for dinner that night. I told him how I was suffering.

"I can make you feel much better, stronger, not just now but for-ever," he said, possessed. I was confused, a little scared; he opened another bottle of the special red wine.

"Drink with me, join me, join us, transcend all of this and every-one around. He does not ask much in return." I contemplated for a few moments, ticker booming and brow perspiring, then drank, sipping at first then gulped. It felt as if I'd stepped up onto a different plain – there was no going back now – I'd joined the gods (seemed like a good deal at the time). The following day the experience left me sensing fantastical bio-currents within and around me, very youthful, hyperactive and complete. In fact I was like this every day from then on.

Gordon told me many stories of the things he had done and said; how he'd surfed the waves of time and plundered history, of his collection of red wines, art and identities. The possibilities unravelled at first slowly then at light-speed in my head, terrifying and heart-pumping all at once. He revealed their limitless extent and taught me much about what I now was and could be. After I departed from Edinburgh, I hoped Gordon and I might be together again in another time, perhaps a few years on. I realised only later that I loved him, that we were destined to be united. We exchanged a few letters and calls when I moved to London, and he visited once or twice. But when I switched city backdrops with Manchester, I heard no more.

I'll wind forwards a year or so from that night of discovery, of becoming a member of the fate club. I put down the book on the floor next to my futon and breathed out slowly but noisily, an excited sigh. Could that be possible? I considered. I was emotionally and intellectually blown away by Wilde's *Picture of Dorian Gray*. But it gave me a potential idea, a way to escape perhaps without either giving back all I'd gained and learned or rendering the ultimate sacrifice. It also made me think of Gordon's cellar of souls.

The next day at work in the Gallery of Modern Art: I was staring transfixed at a 'portrait', had been for several minutes. *The Jack of Clubs* by Rozanova, one of many excellent pictures making up a major exhibition we were hosting at the time: *Russian Painting of the Avant Garde 1906-1924*. Rozanova's Jack was funny and interesting at the same time – painted 1915/16 – he had wonky eyes in an early Picasso-Cubist kind of way. A young man sporting a Dalí-esque moustache that looked broken. Cross-eyed perhaps but also piercing. And that axe, huge and grey, threatening his own life or that of the observer. Could I take this man's life and let him absorb my time? Could I store the face and mind of another man in here, so that I might live longer? I could sell it back, trade his soul for mine. It was a frightening and exhilarating thought – what size and kind of collection could I amass? How many beautiful souls could be preserved and exchanged for mine? A gallery to immortality?

MANCHESTER, ART, DAMIEN, CANAL

He was handsome but almost soulless, it seemed, from what the artist had allowed. Zhang Xiaogang's *Comrade 3* reflected the style and mood of his other Comrades and the *Big Family* series. A young man with glasses wearing the people's uniform, staring blankly yet with black penetrating eyes. Grey, black and white, sombre portraits strangely and deliberately interrupted or defaced by a splash of colour – the young man was wearing a yellow 'stain' on his cheek. I was also fascinated by Oscar Ho Hing-Kay's *Tales around Town*, a set of twenty-four sketches in charcoal on paper. An odd series of prints, which appeared as a fusion of sensationalist tabloid-style newspaper pictures and traditional Chinese ghost stories, if you could imagine such a thing, which portrayed contemporary Hong Kong news items. Damien preferred the two most facetious artists: Wu Tien Chang's *Goodbye! America*, a kitsch Statue of Liberty wearing a blindfold and sticking her tongue out; and Feng Mengbo's *Streetfighters*, painted video game graphics providing the setting for Red Army martial arts hero. He stood next to my young man in the glasses and dived into his dark eyes. Yes, you probably would fit into that frame, I thought; I could make you number four.

"Come, comrade," I said, putting my arm around his shoulders, "let's go for a drink."

We left the pictures and the restaurant, shuffled out of Chinatown, glued ourselves to the pavement, cursing the traffic on Portland Street and eventually crossed.

"I fancy Warsaw," Damien suggested.

"Lucky Warsaw." Brief pause to allow the crap joke to linger, then: "why not, haven't been there for a while." We whizzed through the sad people on Canal Street in an express motion streak, entered said bar, exited said bar. Ten minutes later, we were leaning sadly on the wall above the canal, chatting about nothing.

"Do you know him?" Damien asked, motioning his head across the street to the left.

"You noticed as well, it's not just me then. Like we're being *watched*." I couldn't resist an over dramatic line from a movie.

"Yeah," he half-laughed, "I've never seen him around here before. Can't really make out his face, he's standing in the shadow."

"Familiar but not familiar. Come on, let's walk down the road a little." We attempted to merge into the crowd, but it wasn't really a crowd, just a few bedraggled groups out for a quiet drink on this typical dull Wednesday evening. Average activity for average folk make-believing they've found some sort of gay Mecca. The figure seemed not to follow us; I couldn't see him anymore. We perched ourselves back on the wall facing the canal and peered into the murky water.

"Look at all those cans and shite floating in there," I commented.

"I can see a face, I think," Damien added leaning forwards.

"It's probably your ugly mug, mate." He appeared to be somewhat fascinated. I took a look too; all I could see were swimming ripples and frothing water, after hearing a massive splash.

AMSTERDAM, SERGE, CANALS, VINCENT

There was a shrill cry and a huge splash as the guy jumped into the Amstel. I had no idea why, but I couldn't see that well from where I stood.

I'm sorry, I've screwed up the order of things. I'd completely forgotten that Serge and I stopped off in Amsterdam for a few days on our way from Paris to Berlin. Quite unbelievable that I shouldn't remember Amsterdam, another of my favourite European cities. I'd visited once before, some years earlier, and recalled the location of the apartment letting company I'd rented from on that occasion. We managed to get a flat in the same building, very central, just off Warmoestraat: stylish and comfortable but not too fancy. It also had a kitchen – that would be a pleasant change, to cook rather than going to a restaurant (which we did do several times anyway, of course).

So, Amsterdam, fab place: the central, older part fanned outwards from the station by the port, forming a complex network of semi-circles, or semi-ovals, out of the maze of streets and canals. At least, it seemed like a maze as we first wandered around, but we later discovered it actually formed quite a neat grid. We kept coming across so many similar looking, cobbledly-paved streets and flushing waterways, we could've easily got confused and lost. But once we'd become acquainted with the main flows and location of key landmarks, it was a doddle to find our way around. And what a liberal city; my kind of town. Selected, designated coffee bars where you could buy and smoke dope, an openly controlled sex industry. Pity that other so-called progressive countries hadn't got everything out on the table and dealt with it as Amsterdamers had.

Enough politics. The flickering flame lit up Serge's North African/French features selectively; a candle-lit dinner in our apartment, how sweet. He'd made a superb starter – small (but perfectly formed, I hear you say) portion of a warm salad of spiced Puy lentils, wilted baby spinach leaves, goat's cheese in a balsamic, lemon juice and garlic dressing. Liberally sprinkled with fresh coriander. Surprisingly un-Sergian, *c'est-à-dire* meat-free, but deliciously gooey, exotic and warming on this... what time of year was it? October night (perhaps). I'd unearthed a fussily stocked wine merchant around the corner – Goulburn Valley Aussie Riesling tackled this course well (I'd been pleasantly surprised to find this particular wine), followed by more traditional fare – a single estate Chianti Riserva, Colli Senesi. The rich, raisiny and dry Sangiovese fruit complemented almost flawlessly the duck in black cherry sauce (which I'd spent far too long creating); they should've got married. But never mind the kitchen labouring, it was worth it. We slowly ate, quaffed and talked. Serge was already relaxing and looking forward to our trip to Berlin. He also hadn't been to Amsterdam before and so was eager to explore. I had to admit, we were both good mutual company, so to speak.

"I should've taken a break sooner... working too hard in that fucking hotel, too long hours." He concluded categorically and characteristically.

Walk-about time. Where did we go that night, let me think for a moment? I saw us making our way down Warmoestraat, oblivious to the matter of fact mixture of restaurants, porn shops and leather bars, into Dam square, busy with tourists trying to avoid sleazy drug-dealers and general rip-off merchants. They ignored us; I guess we blended in well. Onto Rokin, over the Singel (I only found out of late that the river wasn't all called the Amstel, just from where the Singel flowed into it heading south: what useful information) and left into Reguliersdwarsstraat, like a homing beacon. First bar – not very memorable, not even the name. Not objectionable but just as you might expect: bar in the middle, stalls around, wooden floors, comfy-ish chairs strewn around, plants, mirrors, cruising gallery-cum-upper level. I also remember the strong orange colours sticking in my vision. We both switched to beers to slow things down a little.

Second bar – I remember *that* name, sort of eastern European: Wybronov. Trendy crowd, bright white interior and a funky restaurant attached. More beer. Bar three – more memorable for Serge.

"Wow, how are you, man!" a barman exclaimed at a recognisably startled Serge, somebody who didn't usually startle at all.

"This is George," when he finally managed to introduce him to me. American, lived in Amsterdam for years, ex-lover of Serge's going back a while in Paris. We arranged to meet him later in a nearby club. Bar four – return to wine, well, fizz actually: why not, we were celebrating being here. And a little smoke just to wash it down. We had, in fact, crossed over to Kerkstraat. Things were intensifying, people, smoke, atmosphere. This place reminded me of the White Lodge in Manchester – lots of swirling velvet drapes, although purple, and odd observation-worthy clientele. The black and white checked tiled floor made me feel dizzy, a distinctly chilling pattern.

My concentration, focused on the long A to B walk I wanted to complete ASAP, was broken by a very loud screech-slam-bang-crunch.

"Fuck," Serge said what I thought but didn't express. Somebody in a brown Mercedes (deserved it for buying that colour) had chosen to play chicken with a tram – and lost. The woman had obviously jumped a red light: her car was now strangely and apologetically bent downwards on the front left hand side. The tram sat majestically still, unharmed by the trivial accident, waiting.

"That'll be expensive," I concluded. We entered the museum.

Inevitable really: we couldn't visit Amsters and not go and see Vincent. We'd eventually found Paulus Potterstraat (since when did someone called Paul Potter deserve having a street named after them?) behind the grand Rijksmuseum. The Van Gogh gallery was relaxed but full and seemed to be enjoying taking all the visitors in its stride (very Dutch). And what a collection – a rich experience of garish hues, as long as you liked Van Gogh. He was one of those painters who always surprised, or delighted and frustrated. From pictures you just didn't like and found hard to believe were by the same artist (which was possible according to certain expert opinions), to stunning masterpieces that took the words out of your mouth, bewildered by the intensity of the colours and forms, wild brush strokes and thick layers. I remembered buying a print of his *Church at Auvers*, which turned out to be so disappointing having seen the actual in the Musée d'Orsay in Paris. It was the same picture, sure, but the reproduction failed to capture that amazing bluer-than-blue deep blue sky, a colour not of this earth.

Shit, I couldn't say, and froze. Those eyes, so frightening; he was looking at me, through me, in me and at everyone else looking at him. We were lucky enough to catch a retrospective – *Zelfportretten, Parijs 1886-88*. The mad son of a bitch painted a huge range of self-portraits, mostly all with psycho-staring eyes but different coloured eyes in differing lights and shades. His fiery orange beard was, however, reasonably consistent; almost photographically faithful assuming the developer was on acid. I then caught that particular canvas, the eyes more intense and hypnotic than any of the others. So dark, deep, bottomless. It gave me goose pimples and made me shiver. Both eyes were totally black, both giant pupils. At that moment Serge moved across our sight line, temporarily breaking the spell. Vincent looked down at him and smiled, briefly.

Ten o'clock that night. We were enjoying a banquet, for want of a better word, in Destiny, a fashionably popular restaurant on Reguliersdwarstraat. The menu mixed and matched styles: Szechuan, Cantonese, Thai and Indonesian, so we did likewise and told the waiter to order us a selection of diverse dishes and flavours. We survived the onslaught that followed, truly delicious tastes of the East, and managed to walk out alive. I could smell the lingering ginger for days. The wine list was boring so I was boring and ordered safe Chablis.

Serge followed me up Kerkstraat, hanging back a little to cruise the crowd en route. We took a left and kept going until we hit the Singelgracht canal.

"Here it is," he said, "Europa." We'd agreed to meet George here, a café overlooking Leidseplein in the Europe Hotel. It turned out to be quite impressive in its Art Nouveau style, rather like the locals who frequented it.

Actually I lied, I've never been to Amsterdam before.

MANCHESTER, THAI, GEORGE, HIT

I've never been to this Thai restaurant before. In fact the menu also offered dishes influenced by Szechuan, Cantonese and Indonesian cuisine. It was 10 o'clock, I ordered another bottle of Chablis Premier Cru Vaillons. Ben and I were listening to George, a friend of his from Amsterdam, who was comparing this restaurant to his favourite there. But the food was even better here – I couldn't disagree. He also liked the Art Nouveau style of the decor: beautiful mock-brass lamps, individual coloured, patterned windowpanes, slightly cheesy wallpaper. George was American, had lived in the Netherlands for some time; this was his first visit to Manchester. And almost his last, anywhere. I'd mentioned being a bit of a Van Gogh fan and a print I had at home of some of his psychotic self-portraits. He'd seen them in Amsterdam and was particularly struck by one with frighteningly dark and bottomless eyes.

I was abruptly overcome by a powerful 'about to happen' sensation. Two men with dark, emotionless eyes entered the restaurant, coolly walked up to our table, hesitated for a second, maybe two, turned to the table in the corner next to us and obliterated the three diners sat there with gleaming hand guns. I could feel the bullets cutting through the air before finding their target. They looked as if they could've been Hong Kar-Wai's men, but I couldn't be sure. The walls were as crimson as the spilled wine on the tablecloth.

LA, CONVERTIBLE, RAMON, BEACH

The cases of red wine slid across the boot with gentle sloshing as I turned. I'd visited vineyards near Santa Cruz and Santa Barbara on the way down from San Francisco and purchased some fine Zinfandel and Pinot Noir. I'd hired a convertible, a Mustang I think, in 'Cisco and when I left I slowly wound my way down Highway One.

Even when you thought you knew what to expect, how you imagined it to be, Los Angeles was still the most frightening, exciting, sprawling, mother-fucking (to use the vernacular), huge, totally insane city you were ever likely to drive into. In reality several towns and cities all overlapping, blindly trying to find each other and brought together by thousands of cars like individual teeth on a gigantic zip. An overwhelming experience criss-crossed by freeways and wide boulevards, crammed full of vehicles streaming (or not) from one district to the next. Walk? Forget it.

It hit me when I joined Santa Monica Boulevard, coming from Santa Monica heading to West Hollywood, where the hotel was located. I'd decided to drive all the way into LA on the Pacific Coast Highway through Malibu, rather than on the freeway. But it was still manic, even for a veteran city driver like myself, but perversely exhilarating to be consumed by the metropolis. And what about those so-called 'Boulevards' – it was about ten miles from Santa Monica to West Hollywood, and this same road still continues on for at least half as much again. I became aware of a different sense of time and space – just relax (if you can) and go with the flow. Cruising through Beverly Hills and West Hollywood was eye-opening yet strangely unreal. The very apparent wealth scarcely related to other 'real' images of LA, which manifested themselves increasingly as I explored to the east and south, where physical dilapidation set in by the mile, the ordinariness of the unmythologised habitat of the most. It was odd that a city seemed to allow itself to be so consciously divided, more than any other I have experienced, and still managed to function thus. Mind you, I could've said the same about New York City, or London even.

However, I had money on this trip and so joined the fairy tale elite on the Westside. The gregarious car park attendant smiled, shiftily perhaps, as I handed him my keys, and I entered the magnificent Perth Hotel on Sunset Boulevard, plunging into Art Deco splendour. Cut straight to later, me sitting at the hotel bar around 8pm sipping a very chilled glass (the wine, that is) of Roussanne from a winery in Santa Barbara County. The dapper barman was giving me tips on where to go to eat and some good bars.

"Not too far, I want to walk from here, maybe get a cab back," I insisted.

He gave me a perplexed look and laughed. "First time in LA, huh?"

"Well, you know us Brits, like to get pissed." He gave me the names of some places on Santa Monica Boulevard less than a couple of kilometres away.

About an hour and a half later, three more glasses of white wine later (a Sauvignon, I was sure, but didn't know where from). I was invited to play pool (in Fatherhead, welcoming bar) by Ramon, a friendly Mexican-Native-American.

"I've been to London and Edinburgh but not Manchester. I hear it's lively; relaxed scene?" Ramon asked. "Yeah, it's OK." Me.

"What are you doing here – holiday?"

"Sort of. Kind of world city tour, road movie... search for metropolitan identity... new faces. Whatever." I joked. He gave me a confused smile.

"You a writer?"

"No," I laughed again. We chatted and mucked around further, played more pool. Or at least I did – winner stayed on; the locals hid their slight resentment to being beaten by an unknown new boy. The table had now become the centre of attention, I'd become quite pissed – too much wine bought for me by good losers. A friend of Ramon's arrived, a literally tall dark and handsome Tony, skin like seductive plain chocolate. They were going to eat; I joined them, now in need of solids.

Jump to camp waiter ushering us to a table in Menage à Quatre, also on Santa Monica not that far from the bar, I thought, but was scoffed at for suggesting we walked. I remembered the restaurant in a guide I'd read on the plane: 'trendy gay institution, food average', or something like that. Go with the flow, I figured. Nice colours though, the décor: a fantastic deep blue contrasted with a light leafy green and yellow ceiling, or honey perhaps. The blue reminded me of the sky in Van Gogh's *Church at Auvers*. The food was OK – unadventurous Californian – although the fish I had was pretty fresh. More wine. Good company – Tony was an up-and-coming actor (why did/do I always meet actors or restaurateurs?) currently doing some tv work. Ramon had been a little unrevealing up until now – it transpired he was a lawyer or attorney (so not an actor or restaurateur) but couldn't divulge much about his latest case (gosh, how exciting). I finished the wine, an Oregon Pinot Noir – yes, with the fish – they finished the mineral water.

"How come you Brits are such drunks?"

"It's cheaper than cocaine!" The night swirled into dancing in a not-too-far away club (by LA standards; I thought miles) into a "come back to my hotel" climax.

"Do you want to live forever?" I asked Ramon's reflection in the bedroom mirror.

I was completely awe-struck by the rambling, shimmering city laid out to the horizon and beyond. Mile after mile, block after block, grid after grid of wobbly motion, seemingly quite gentle from here. Smog and haze obscured some of the far vista, but the unending view still filled the periphery.

"One hell of a city," Ramon whispered in my ear.

"Hell being the operative word," I added. We'd driven up into the Hollywood Hills to the vantage point at Griffith Park Observatory; quite a sight.

"Beats Parliament Hill," I quietly said and explained later that morning, as Ramon looked briefly puzzled.

"Which is the best modern art gallery?" I asked him over coffee about half an hour later.

"Well, either LA County Museum or MOCA."

"MOCA?"

"Museum of Contemporary Art. It's Downtown, worth a visit."

I stood chuckling for a few moments ("I did as well, first time I saw it," Ramon commented) at the huge Swiss army knife outside the gallery.

"It's magnificent. I want one."

"Bit big for your suitcase," he retorted. A really smart building too – the galleries were designed by a Japanese architect, I was informed.

"Uta Barth... local photographer," Ramon answered my question.

"Interesting ideas," I threw in the air. Could say the same for Bruce Nauman; sense of humour as well. His 1966 photo *Self portrait as a fountain* caught his naked upper torso spitting a jet of water. I found Ramon in the bathroom drinking from the water fountain and giggled. He asked why.

Later, my hotel bathroom. I was contemplating my face critically in the mirror: well-travelled face, still appeared remarkably fresh. The razor slid slowly across and down, catching and slicing the bristles, carving a path through the foam. I was mulling over my next move, next destination: I could go to South America – maybe Santiago or Rio? (did I go there or were those someone else's memories?) My reflection kept staring back, rather intensely. The mirror seemed to slowly lose its solidity, in a Cocteau-esque way, a gentle quake of liquid silver, like mercury. My face oscillated in it. I put down the razor and touched the apparently glass surface. My fingers sunk into it; it was kind of liquid, not really like water but melted metal. I pushed them further in, then both hands. I withdrew them suddenly, slightly afraid. I took a deep breath and then excitedly climbed up on the sink and pushed my arms back through. I plunged my head through too. I could see – it was almost like being under water but different, and I could obviously breathe. I saw a bright light in the distance, then a man walked out of it towards me. Orpheus beckoned me in and so I followed. The poet told me many things and warned me. We kept walking on and on, deeper into the Underworld. We entered a dark room, although I could see well enough, a kind of gallery. There were many pictures displayed there, portraits of people; I felt I'd seen them before. As I strolled past the faces called out, whispering in my ears, quiet cries that grew louder and louder to a piercing crescendo.

I woke up, stale and unclean, early the next morning about 7am; a shout from outside. So I snoozed for another hour or two. I was really hungry, ready for a serious American breakfast. Sweet, acidic, fresh orange juice. Aromatic dark coffee, rich and strong. A pile of creamy scrambled eggs on rye toast. I fancied lounging on the beach today, to survey and join the apparently bohemian Venice crowd. The route there was easy – despite its size and the flood of traffic, LA was actually quite straightforward to drive around thanks to very long streets, which don't change name, pipe-lined neatly into the mathematical grid. So I sailed down La

Cienega Bld. for four or five miles until I hit Venice Bld., then took that for four or five miles (top down, shades on) until I hit sea. I almost got into a fight over a parking space but stood my ground and gave the elderly hippy a 'I don't give a fuck this is a hire car' look.

I merged comfortably into the crowd of locals, Westside beach bums, tourists, muscle men, rollerbladers, tramps, beautiful queens and babes, scallies and entertainers – the whole world out to play. I discovered an act, or rather he found me, I would have loved to sign up for a tacky tv talent show to scare the living daylights out of the folks back home. He was a juggler – there were many in the neighbourhood – but this show got progressively more dangerous, culminating in chain saw juggling. Over a member of the crowd. I regretted 'volunteering': "cool", as an airhead bystander observed and it probably seemed so in retrospect. He earned the $10 I gave him for not disfiguring me. I then crashed out on the beach with the not-too-many other sun seekers. Venice wafted an odd vibe, pleasingly so: I felt a million miles away from the LA metropolis. I guess that formed part of its attraction – having driven around from Malibu to Downtown, Pasadena to Long Beach and all in between, it didn't feel like one city at all. A concrete 'concept' perhaps, made up of perceptions of wildly different areas and people, all stitched together by a vast network of roads and a search for identity. Angels indeed, as the old cliché tells us. After a bite in the simple but satisfying Jim's Restaurant (he wasn't there), I strolled down the Canals and reflected on cities gone by.

VENICE, RED, GIANNI, FUTURE

I ditched the weary car on arrival in Venice, not a lot of use for it here. It had served me well on the elongated journey from

Barcelona, across the south of France and northern Italy. Roads thawed to water, boats replaced buses and I walked. I stored the car in a garage in Piazzale Roma, my loved-ones locked away inside, until I decided on the next destination and mode of transport. Venice was an extraordinarily beautiful place at that time, or in any time – a bit weird at first; then again I'd seen and experienced quite a lot of weird – like no other city I'd been to, but I quickly got used to it. The city on the sea, a disaster waiting to happen. You could get lost for weeks in the maze of back streets and alleys around the central core from Santa Croce to San Marco. And I did: for a few days, although it seemed like a few weeks. Maybe it was – I really don't remember how long I stayed in Venice but recollect exact details of other things: the food, of course, the vivid sunsets on the sea, the elusive figure dressed in red who appeared to be following me. Or did I imagine those fleeting, Roeg-esque glimpses around endless corners?

The boat sailed without complaint along the Canale Grande. I chose to go the long way round to take in the atmosphere and landmarks and got off near the Piazza San Marco, where I was greeted by a pissed up tramp prostrated on some nearby steps and masturbating inside his trousers flecked with pigeon shit. I took another boat to the Lido, one of the long banks of land that form a kind of protective barrier from the persistent sea. I threw caution onto the fire and booked into the expensive Grand Hotel des Bains in the name of art. I couldn't resist booking in as Mr T Mann; the woman behind the desk didn't bat an eyelid – I think she got the 'joke' but played along in a professional whatever-sir-wishes way.

Move on to the next evening: the somewhat pompous dining room in the hotel, in style and demeanour. It appeared to be full of rather stuffy old farts, at a glance, all trying not to bang their cutlery too hard on the plate or scrape a chair leg noisily on the over-polished floor. I deliberately let the cork pop out of a bottle of Trento sparkling wine with a satisfying, well – erm – pop I suppose, in order to turn a few heads. The guy sitting a few tables across, who seemed to be the only other young man on his own here, laughed and feigned applause with his large hands. I lifted the bottle in the air as a gesture to offer a glass. He called a grumpy waiter over, whispered in his ear and joined me. I'd seen him earlier on the beach briefly, now I thought about it, modelling a tight, stripy little number onto which his curly locks cascaded. Or that could have been somebody else. No matter: Gianni was an art historian from Rome spending a few days in Venice; part holiday, part work.

"Research on Tintoretto's paintings in San Giorgio Maggiore... told you it was obscure and boring!" In fact, I took a serene picture a few days later of the red sun setting behind the bell tower of the church on that island, underexposed to throw the gondolas and foreground into shadow with just a glistening trail of light on the water. I should have sold it to the tourist board. I don't know why I mentioned that, my mind was flitting again – difficult now to separate real memories from postcard images.

We ate the full monty for dinner – plump and fresh seafood risotto accompanied by Pinot Grigio from Friuli; melt in the mouth liver, polenta and crisp salad with a plummy Merlot from Piave; to finish a to-die-for tiramisu with Trentino Vino Santo, absurdly sweet and sensual. And supercharged espresso of course.

"I was thinking of going to the Peggy Guggenheim Collection tomorrow – do you want to come, if you're not busy? You can be my guide!" I virtually demanded cheekily.

"Of course." Gianni smiled, the set of white teeth contrasted with his dark complexion. I picked up my glass of Merlot and offered him a toast. The cooler-than-warm red wine soothed my throat and revitalised me; he drank and fell under my spell. After the meal Gianni made a suggestion.

"Let's get out of this mortuary. I know a lively bar where we can get brain-dead drinking grappa." (My translation: his words read something like "enjoy a substantial *digestif*.") Sounded like a good idea at the time; I'd obviously forgotten the last occasion I got guttered on grappa.

I ceased sleeping and could no longer picture the face of the figure I'd chased around the streets of Venice in my mind. I had run over the Rialto Bridge, but it disappeared into the crowd. Then I turned a corner to glimpse the red shirt and flowing hair blur around another corner. Then I was positioned on a smaller bridge watching a boat drift in soft focus underneath. It contained a coffin, no people and a huge wreath of red roses and white orchids. I couldn't see the name on the plaque.

It was late – nearly 11.30am – Gianni had obviously already returned to his room. He hadn't had breakfast either, so we went for an early lunch at the appropriately named Nameless Caffe in the Dorsoduro district near the Accademia. Peaceful and relaxed with a touch of Mahler's transcendent Fifth to civilise and soothe the head (although the Nazis disagreed – what kind of people could 'ban' such beauty because of a man's race?). We then strolled to the Guggenheim museum; I was unaware of the treat that awaited, along with the shocking twist in the plot. Here we floated amongst a bewildering array of imagination courtesy of some of the 20th Century's finest poets, a concluding culmination of images of confusing times re-examined: Picasso, Kandinsky, Chagall, Giacometti, Tanguay, Dalí. A collection to rival my own, almost living and breathing like my own. I lost myself in de Chirico's shadows, impenetrable corners and depth of field. I had to chuckle to myself: *Nostalgia del Poeta*; it struck me as familiar, mocking me. I thought I saw a long-haired man run into the background and disappear, unnoticed by the two figures closer to the observer, perhaps clothed in red.

Later we wandered in (or more accurately on) the liquid city, piercing the shade and randomly turning corners. We were being followed but I didn't mention this to Gianni, who seemed not to notice.

"I'll buy some wine – we can drink it back at the hotel," as he vanished into a small delicatessen. I stood by the edge of the street and peered into the far-from-crystal canal. I saw a shadow in reflection behind me and quickly spun around, but nobody was there.

"What's the matter?" Gianni inquired boyishly as he approached, a bottle of red in one hand.

"Nothing." All I saw was a blur, as the man came from nowhere brandishing an automatic. Gianni turned, confused, in slow motion and shifted his weight, briefly blocking the assailant's line of sight to me. And the path of the bullets, surely destined for me. He crashed to the ground with staged style like a demolished building (he was a tall man), losing grip on the bottle. This unexpected twist bought me a couple of seconds, time enough to move swiftly sidewards and forwards to deliver two accurate kicks. I heard the splash of the gun enter the water from the first as the second hit his chin and knocked him sideways and almost down. He ran at me, disorientated, but I swerved, took out his legs and cracked a parting blow on the back of his skull. There was no struggle as he quickly drowned. Gianni's blood ran into the red wine, liberated from the smashed bottle, and both trickled, mingled, over the paving stones into the canal, forming a red haze over the horror-struck face of the attacker below. I dissolved from the scene, the picture stuffed under my arm, feeling fresh but perhaps a tad sad.

MANCHESTER, BEN, BAR, POLICE

"Did they identify the body in the canal?" Ben asked, as we stepped over the bridge from Canal Street, pointing at the filthy water to remind me of that event a few weeks ago. I shrugged indifferently as we entered City café bar, bumping into Bob hurrying out. He didn't seem to notice who I was.

"Curious," Ben agreed.

"I assume you've seen the article in *City Life* about my father?" he said before sipping his black coffee (although stewed and weak). "Patron of Chinese art!" he giggled. I smiled and waved the waitress over to complain about the coffee, which was removed with impressive speed and without question.

"It wasn't that bad."

"Was. Anyway, not the point, your majesty."

The conversation drifted from the exhibition to the standard of coffee the Brits put up with ("stop complaining") to my travels.

"So after I left Venice, I headed up to Vienna and then Prague. Vienna was somehow disappointing, and I didn't do much or stay long in Prague. Don't know why not, it did have special appeal..." Ben laughed at my obvious plot explanation. I felt the Earth rotate as the hands on my watch advanced.

"Shit, I forgot; a couple of cops came to the restaurant last night, detectives, looking for you, asking questions," Ben continued, adopting a clichéd Plod accent: "in connection with missing persons."

"I know. They left a message on my answering machine. I'll contact them when I have to."

"What's that all about?"

"No idea," I lied. Somebody suddenly turned the music up in the bar; I froze. It was Depeche Mode's song 'Never let me down again', which reminded me sharply of a time past, symbolic of a city experienced, but also the present...

Rewind the tape.

LONDON, BOB, WILDE, BRIGHTON

Strangely I seem to have missed out London – I mean the years before that fleeting visit *en route pour Paris*, after sadly tearing myself away from Edinburgh. I'd reflected fondly on the mad capital previously, a fondness partly shattered by the reality of subsequent visits. But I'd been down just recently and had seen it in a new light, or perhaps an old one, as I'd experienced and remembered those few years earlier.

My mind picked out an episode starting on the Tube, music playing in my ears from someone's personal stereo. Why were the trains so shitty on the dreaded Northern Line? Probably the busiest line yet no investment, it seemed. Spick-and-span shiny new trains gloated on the Circle and Central with their beepy-beep closing doors, keeping up appearances for the tourists. I peered through the mass of BO-fragrant arms, stretched out for support, and steamy bodies to try to make out which stop through the dirt-encrusted window. I couldn't see but guessed it was Waterloo – it'd been half a dozen or so stops since I got on at Clapham Common. I was meeting a friend in town – Bob, old university pal (you've met him already) – for lunch, drinks and art. I lived towards the south side of Clapham Common – in fact around the corner from where Serge was later to live, by coincidence. Not too far from the centre of town, not too far to escape town, and a reasonable area. Not too dodgy, quite vibrant, growing number of worthy bars and restaurants, blah blah... I pushed my way out of the carriage after a token polite but ignored "excuse me", and said farewell to hundreds of people I'd never seen before and was unlikely to do so again. Anonymity had its attractions.

Emerging from the bowels of Charing Cross, I could immediately smell the crap in the air – good old London. I Carl-Lewis'ed across the Strand to avoid the psycho-taxis, who pretended not to see me, and made my way past splendid but subtle St. Martin's-in-the-Fields up to Kajoz bar. Bob, the old smoothie, sat in the window drinking coffee and pretended not to pay attention to the glances he was receiving. He was bloody handsome, the bastard, but we had always just been friends – a sense of mutual respect, like-mindedness and deep unphysical affection, brotherly love if you like. I was to discover that Bob was into some strange stuff – more than just gothic – and had a penchant for smoking strange stuff as well. Liberated the soul, he used to tell me... "you wouldn't believe where it led me last..." ("oh, I think I would" was a usual reply). We also had much in common.

"Tuna-mayo-salad in ciabatta, glass of *sur lie* Muscadet," I requested.

"The same; I can't be bothered to decide," Bob uttered apathetically. See, I told you so. We internalised lunch, more Muscadet, more coffee. Bob mercilessly and perhaps unfairly took the piss out of two archetypal mincing queens, who sat near us. I tried not to laugh too loudly and pretended it wasn't directed. I was unconsciously tearing up another flyer on the table into small pieces, an annoying habit I owned and inflicted on beer mats and labels on bottles of beer alike, after peeling them off. Conversation shifted from trivial to pretentious.

"I'm not so keen on Francis Bacon," Bob said categorically.

"You're just too conservative."

"Fuck off!"

"Just winding you up. I was making some notes on the Bacon's at work (I was then employed by the Tate) the other day. You have to admit, he's got an arresting style... there's one there, really scary, with a ghostly head on a black background: *Study for Portrait 2*, about 1955 I think..."

"... based on a photo of a mask of William Blake," he interrupted. I gave him a curious look. "I did study Art History as well, remember?" How could I've forgotten; he knew even more about art than I did.

"Actually, I've discovered something right up your alley," deliberate innuendo, which I ignored, "new display at the National Portrait."

"Really? Mostly crap old stuff there, no?"

"Very funny. Let's go and check it out. You'll love it."

I did: Maggi Hambling's amusing set of tributes to Oscar Wilde. I fixed particularly on *Wilde with hangover*, a magnificent blur of a face of melted colours. I could step into this one and hide behind his disguised but distinguished features under the canvas. I walked for a while with the man then walked in my mind out of the gallery, taking Oscar to a better place to start my new exhibition. You could stay a little longer and look at the other portraits. I watched you from the other side of the River – now dark, I was gazing across from the South Bank up at the illuminated 'Kafka' building, the fabulous squatting fly on top of Charing Cross station (Coopers & Lybrand's bold head office). It strangely fitted in with its neighbours, although very manifestly "I'm here and modern": Somerset House remained silent, unperturbed, it didn't deign to comment; Cleopatra carried on with her knitting. The diverse lights emanating from other buildings, the string of bridges and relentless cars, all glittered on the water, from time to time nudged by a boat or current movements. My head filled with liquid, the tide rippled over my retinas.

I could smell the crash of the unyielding waves on large pebbles before we even reached the beach. We used to visit Brighton every now and then, a good weekend escape from the big bad city. It had plenty of life, mixed bag of people and the power of the sea, enough in itself to cleanse my corrupted soul. It was too late for Bob; he'd already gone all the way down (and back). On this particular occasion we were he, me and Kevin and Rachel, fellow Londonites. We stayed at The Majestic on the seafront, indulged in a little luxury at a bargain price thanks to Rachel's work connection. We reclined on the pebbles-cum-sand in front of the Great White Bar and guzzled lager with our fish and chips. With mayo, of course. The sea air (although more sodium) and gulls reintroduced me to Monsieur Proust, as I momentarily teleported back to St Andrews – oh, I did like to be by the seaside. That night we had a few more beers before setting off to the gig. We randomly dived into one particular dingy pub to be accosted by the booming and smoky notes of 'One step beyond'; all spontaneously broke out into Madness-style dancing, didn't buy a drink and left two or three minutes later. I did wonder why as we slouched into the hall to see the Verve play – top performance from Wigan's Jim Morrison and co. Electrifying, loud and rock 'n' roll.

I couldn't say the same about the talentless busker, who was lurking in the, on the face of it, unending corridors of dirty tiles, torn posters and remote human beings within Kentish Town station. I'd had a meeting above ground in fashionable 'north Camden' – yes, I was a south London dweller who did venture beyond the Kings Cross divide. Anyway, I'd never have got them to come south of the river. Enough Londoner clichés; I remember acquiring a classic Tube weirdo somewhere between Goodge Street and Charing Cross. I obviously looked a suitable target to pester. Odd socks I could cope with, talking to yourself – all perfectly normal, but why did he offer me a cigarette from a packet full of maggots and why did he seem to enjoy eating them? I got off at Kennington, told him to follow me. He waited patiently on the platform for the next Morden train, I enjoyed watching him fry on the tracks under the wheels of that next train. What a terrible accident.

MANCHESTER, DOCTOR MABUSE, HIDE

The tram screeched to a protracted halt but it was curtains for the dog. Well it wasn't a proper dog, merely a rat with a perm. The poor woman looked devastated, the onlookers offered sympathy. Unmoved, I continued and climbed the steps into the library, then to the first floor. As I expected, footsteps followed me: probably Plod, I thought. I hadn't called them back and had managed to avoid any visits so far. But this guy had been on my tail for twenty minutes. I browsed the travel guides, although I hadn't come here for that reason, wishing simply to observe my new shadow. He'd entered the room, I was positive, but now couldn't be seen. I came back out and around to the lift, which for a change was in working order so I took it to the top floor to the language library, laboriously slowly as its strained mechanism was accustomed to dictate. No suspicious characters were waiting for me, apart from the usual suspects – a ragbag mix of students, writers, lecturers, citizens and weirdo book people from the planet Biblio. I was looking for a novel by a German author, which somebody had recommended. Predictably I'd forgotten the name but felt I'd remember when I saw it, as I'd seen a film based on it, which was quite memorable. Friederich somebody, set in Hamburg...

"Goethe or Mann?" the Doctor asked me. I was startled but not surprised; it wasn't the police.

"You," I uttered, resigned.

"Indeed. You can't escape me; it's time we discussed our little deal, remember?"

"So soon. How could I forget; I have another deal to offer, if you're interested. I need more time, more life. A collection of youth."

"A collection?"

"The finest souls frozen in oils for ever."

We were interrupted by a young woman who wanted to scream but couldn't and dropped some books on the floor. I used the distraction to exit swiftly down the corridor and stairs. The shadow upstairs faded into the air, the girl fainted. I ran out and marched to the nearest bar – not because I thought I could hide from him but to bury myself in memories, escape for just a wee while. That recent shooting in the restaurant was replaying in my head – I'd since found out that the assassinated victims, who'd tastefully redecorated the walls, were small fry in Kar-Wai's plans. He'd known we were eating there that night and had his men deliberately miss us as a warning. Should I hit back before he tried again, perhaps for real? Did I have time? Did it matter? A choice of lesser evils, so to speak: the Doctor, the cops or Hong? Who would get to me first?

The Napa Valley Chardonnay was good; glad somebody was still making it like that, fat and oaky. I climbed inside the bottle of sunshine.

MANHATTAN, ANDY, 'CISCO, ZINFANDEL

The Napa Valley sunshine was considerably warmer than the weather left behind in San Francisco. It could have been hundreds of miles away – I'd noticed the sudden rise in temperature as we headed north from the city. We were on the wine trail and my friend James had lost the toss and was driving.

But I won't start there – I wanted to talk about New York City, my first city-stop in the US (following a long boring flight from Ireland) before heading to California.

Andy gave me a tepid hug greeting me at JFK: "Buddy, how's it going?"

"I'm OK. Glad to be in NYC." We chatted excitedly on the way to his car; I told him about my recent escapades in Dublin.

"I was there just a few months ago as well," Andy added, agreeing the Irish capital was indeed a fun place to be. He was an old friend – we'd met at Edinburgh University; he'd spent a couple of years studying there before returning home to the States. He was an artist, quite successful now – he'd worked on Wall Street for a while, made a bit of dosh, then jacked it all in to pursue a talent he hadn't allowed to develop, struggled and got lucky (but deserved). "I've just moved to a new apartment in the Village."

"Very nice. You must be doing alright nowadays..."

"Not as hip as it used to be..."

We finally escaped the airport, drove out of Queens, across Brooklyn and headed for Brooklyn Bridge. As we crossed, I could hear Gershwin's *Rhapsody in Blue* in my head as Woody Allen's black and white skyscrapers of lower Manhattan filled the horizon and dwarfed us little people daring to approach. It was only at that moment I was fully aware of being in this huge and exciting city; these postcard images penetrating my eyes were so different from the outer boroughs, on the one hand more 'real' but at the same time very much less so.

"Wow," I whispered. Andy smiled, my heart thumped faster in anticipation. We drove all the way up Broadway from City Hall until we almost reached Washington Square then hung a left, crossing Sixth and Seventh Avenues, I think, and on a bit further. It had been a great taster, I felt like I was in a movie, like you've seen on tv but very much more intense. The hyperactivity, the sense of smallness below the heightless buildings in the Financial District to our left before heading north. Greenwich Village was positively serene in comparison despite its seriously busy main streets.

I looked out of the window in Andy's flat across to the River Hudson. "I could get used to this," I remarked.

"Well, don't for too long – we have plans. We're meeting some guys for a drink in thirty minutes. Then Chinatown to eat, then maybe a party in Harlem."

"Harlem? Bit of a trek."

"A bit, but hell of a birthday party, all night jazz, should be hot."

Fast forward forty minutes – the Cellar Bar just off Christopher Street.

"This is Bill, Sam, Judy..." A couple of beers were consumed.

"Who's your friend?" somebody asked Andy, "he's like a magnet."

Andy laughed as he watched me chatting and joking, surrounded by two men and one woman. "Careful guys," he whispered as his eyes locked with mine. We both smiled.

I paid the cab driver as the other three piled into the restaurant on Division Street, called something like Canton Town – I remember approving of the name. It was a bring-your-own, I'd been told, so I found a nearby offie and bought some California Fumé Blanc to supplement the reds I'd carefully stored in my luggage from Italy.

"*Ripasso*," I repeated, "from near Verona. The wine is literally 'passed over' the lees of Amarone... anyway, it's a bit dull and technical, but the wine is serious kit."

"Kit?" Sam confused.

"Never mind. Just enjoy." We toasted, drank, enjoyed.

We gave the waiter a price and told him to invent a menu: "Seafood, vegetables and duck mostly please," I added. He expressed pleasant surprise and conversed for a moment animatedly.

"You speak Chinese?!" Bill exclaimed.

"Well, Cantonese – the family of a friend of mine in Manchester is from Hong Kong, and I have several business associates..."

"There's no end to his talents," Andy cut in sarcastically, "show off!" aside to me. He was right, I guess, but I wasn't doing it on purpose. The meal was excellent: plenty of fresh ingredients and carefully spiced character.

"It's one of the best around here, we come quite often."

We stayed there for some time finishing the wine, then the others had coffee while I had tea (Chinese green of course) just to be a source of amusement. "It's refreshing!" We fell out onto the sidewalk and hailed a cab.

"Take us up the east side along the river, the view will be better for our visiting friend here," Andy added after telling her our destination in Harlem. As we proceeded northwards, familiar and not-so-familiar landmarks loomed across in midtown Manhattan: the Empire State Building stood very tall and arrogant, UN Headquarters rather clinical just to our left, the dazzling Chrysler Building beyond oozed 1930s style, the modern metal of the Citicorp Center. We moved through the Upper East Side soaking up the tidy wealth.

"What is *that*?" I exclaimed.

"The Guggenheim Museum, Frank Lloyd Wright."

"Right, of course. Still not what you imagine – magnificently out of place. I'd like to go there tomorrow; good collection of contemporary American Minimalist stuff, apparently." They laughed at my assumed pretentious tone, straight out of a review.

Later – the club in Harlem was packed, the air opaque and loud with conversation, jamming jazz and the occasional song throwing the full anguish of the soul into the cloudy atmosphere. Later still – the party continued at a friend of Sam's place off Sugar Hill. Sam was a funny bloke, a session musician (guitar) who'd been a little unlucky recently and missed out on some top gigs. But he let it wash over him.

"Hey, I didn't want to play with them anyway!" We were drinking red wine, somewhere between warm and cool, and smoking dope slouched in a corner of the lounge on the floor. I don't recall the wine – French perhaps – I was trying to read the label and dropped it, spilling loads over Sam's arm and leg. The comforting red juice trickled down his glistening black skin; I licked it off. We were one.

"Will you join me in a glass of this finest Zinfandel?" James joked, holding the bottle as if a waiter offering a rare red wine. We'd decided to book into a motel; the serious tasting tour had lapsed into a winery-crawl. We'd already eaten (so I'll spare you the menu for a change) and opted to crash out in the room and sample one of the day's purchases. I recollected the hauntingly unforgettable scene that morning as we'd driven out of San Francisco; a light mist loitered innocently around the Golden Gate Bridge as we crossed. I'd looked back at the hazy image of one beautiful city and smiled warmly. James had taken us north then east to Sonoma, stopping at a couple of wineries before heading across to Napa. The day had been civilised for us, another escape from reality. Apart from the prices poking me with a stick – so that's how Napa vintners all drove Ferraris.

Back in 'Frisco I went for a walk, completing the steep climb from James' house in Twin Peaks to have my breath taken away by the wide-angle view on all sides of the city and beyond – I could actually see into the distance this time, now the fog had cleared. Looking down reminded me of the wild experience of driving around SF off the main traversing roads – scenes from many movies became reality as we coasted up and down peaks and troughs pretending to be in a car chase. It felt good to be a temporary citizen here, the balance was right; not as frenetic as NYC but still most entertaining and charming in its very own laid-back manner. Mind you, I was yet to be cast into the LA mire which redefined frenetic. That night we stabbed it through the heart, having taken a leisurely cab down Market Street, and I saw the legendary Castro for the first time (although I had the strangest sensation I'd been here before). The reality was, well, real: nothing much here that surprised me, just a pile of folk having some fun. We bumped into some pals of James' in a wine bar, who ordered more Chardonnay – Napa I think.

MANCHESTER, NICK(ED), ESCAPE

I fell out of the bottle of sunshine and went home, confused by the physicality of my surroundings. I had an even stronger than recently sense of 'about to' whirling around my ever spinning mind. Which was probably why I was taken by surprise by the awaiting rozzers – I hadn't felt their presence due to my distracted state. While trying to snap the handcuffs binding my wrists (a little extreme, you might think, but had something to do with "resisting arrest"), I heard only selected words emanating from the officer.

"Disappearance of Mark X... Damien Y..." Nice motor though: not the familiar crap family saloon, I was escorted in a Jag, usually used on motorways I thought, unmarked. Detective Nick M something, didn't catch his name fully, carried on talking to me but I wasn't listening.

Their mistake was letting themselves think they had it sorted and that I was co-operating. I'd been taught as a kid by a magician how to escape from handcuffs, all down to subtle muscle control, the temporarily painful dislocation of a thumb and a bit of luck. As we got out at the station, poor old Nick was probably surprised to eat pavement. Shocked even to not see me melt into the night and out of his life. I'd already packed what I needed (not much, I'd concluded) yesterday, or the day before even; I seemed to have predicted some kind of outcome. I was at the airport before they could say the word and was showing my false passport in an extremely relaxed way, the subtle disguise matched the picture well enough.

Manchester evaporated behind us in a puff as the aircraft contemplated the long flight ahead. I sipped red wine – Burgundy for sure – and chatted peacefully to my neighbour, reclining as images of past and future were typed through my head as if read from a hefty novel.

"Yes I have," I answered his question ("have you been to Hong Kong before?")

"Business and pleasure." I had to collect some freight I'd sent there a few weeks ago, before flying on to Australia. Quite often I wouldn't encourage fellow passengers to be so talkative on a long distance flight, but this time I didn't mind. With the inevitable conflict or showdown or whatever awaiting me at some point somewhere, I felt I needed to indulge a little in confirmation of my own existence (I think the passenger's name was Jean-Paul).

Part II

A Rare Vintage

EDINBURGH, THIS TIME (ALMOST), RECRUIT

I met this really interesting bloke in the pub today; he must be pretty special as I even opened a bottle of the incomparable '87, barely tasted by the precious fortunate few. Knows his wine though, he appreciated it; into art and films too. It's true I'm known as Gordon, but only in this time. I didn't assume that identity until quite recently actually... it's a long story.

EDINBURGH, REPUBLIC?, CROMWELL, THOMAS

I was struck by lightening in 1649, on the 30th January to be precise, and haven't been the same since. I remember the date very clearly as it was the day we executed the king. Back then I was called Roxburgh, soon to be Colonel Roxburgh, George; my real name in fact.

The 30s had been frustratingly mad and confusing, Edinburgh was drowning in a thick broth of muttered rumour, sensational gossip and tit-bits of news, when any actually arrived from London. It seemed unbelievable that Parliament had been dissolved for so long – how could they have allowed the king to carry on like that? By 1640 it all came to a head; we, like many others, were totally fed up with Charles Stewart (or Stuart as preferred by the English). The po-faced Presbyterians were behind us – but at a safe distance – thanks to his now impossible attempts, as they argued, to turn the religious clock back; but such issues didn't interest me. So, many of my eager colleagues in the Scottish army joined in marching into England to attract attention to our little protest. And it seemed to work; it was reported a few weeks later that even Cromwell had demonstrated sympathy to the cause. But this cosy comradeship didn't last too long; he grew increasingly weary of the Presbyterians (who could blame him) and their demands to remodel the church only from their point of view. I decided I couldn't be associated with this any longer and made my move. So I left Edinburgh for a few years; first stop was London to entwine myself in the real action. I offered my services as a respected soldier and certainly no fan of the king, whose contempt for Parliament and any such organisation had now piled up to a precarious stack of pure treason, as far as I and others were concerned. I was commissioned as a colonel in the New Model Army and was fizzing with excited apprehension, as the campaign against clustering royal supporters ignited to a blaze.

It was an omnipotent day, the sunshine and blood curdled, heavily enhancing the supernatural aura that hovered over the battlefield. My strongest memory of the war returns to me often – the 'righteous' (it seemed at the time) victory against Charles at Marston Moor on that infinite June day of 1644. So many men – I don't now remember numbers of living and dead – locked horns, so intense was the din of weapons, shouts, screams and horses. Yet the power of the battle left me behind, quite distant from my comrades in arms even though I was swimming alongside them in a choppy ocean of bodies, hate and fear. This was a crucial day for our parliamentarian forces; in the aftermath we guessed we'd cut wide open a royalist vein that would bleed dry. And my men certainly knew how to celebrate; the camp was alive with song, beer and wine (but few women apart from the odd local or officer's wife), even the wounded were intoxicated on victory.

"Where are you from lieutenant, I haven't seen you before?" I asked the handsome fading-blond officer, his dark brown eyes glowed orange on and off, as the fire hopped from foot to foot.

"Essex, sir, a small town by the sea," he informed me whilst tightening the bandage holding his damaged arm; another strapped it to his shoulder. Otherwise his upper torso was uncovered. "It's not serious, sir," he added assuming perhaps I was scrutinising his injury.

"Good. We need you all fighting fit." I averted my lecherous gaze and responded, suitably colonel-like. "There'll be more days like today; not too many, I hope."

"My parents own a down-to-earth inn..." he continued to tell me about his home and family.

"What's the name of it?" I interrupted.

"The King's Alms. Honestly!"

"Ironic to say the least."

"It's quite busy with travellers passing through, and the locals like the food and ale. That's what I do normally – I brew the beer." He noticed my glance at the bottle of red wine he was drinking from. "I like wine too!" he laughed.

"So do I." We shared and savoured; I found it a little harsh but it fitted the occasion well enough. Nothing to compare with those splendid bottles I was to seize from the Earl of Manchester, his entire cellar in fact. We removed him from power under the terms of the Self-Denying Ordinance, a pompously titled but simply interpreted law, which I and others often (mis)used: "... unsympathetic to the cause, obstructive...", the words on his arrest warrant ran through my mind. I confiscated his wine and horses.

Thomas, the talkative lieutenant, bolstered the narrative further: "I joined the army because..." he seemed to pause to think for a moment (motivation was perhaps always elusive; I found that too), "quite frankly, I really do believe the king has just gone too far. He can't rule without Parliament, although I trust some of the men there even less. Now we have the opportunity to make him understand that for good. The opportunity to..." He caught himself, suddenly wary of his words and my company and realising the drink had loosened his lips: obviously that pause had been more deliberate than I thought. But he was reassured he had nothing to fear by my heated approving smile and nod. I was to enhance the strength of our forces by encouraging people like this, intelligent young men with deep-seated morale and committed discipline who *believed*. Fortunately, Cromwell and others backed me up when the nobles and so-called professional soldiers objected. Thomas served under me at Naseby, where I promoted him to captain, and later in Ireland in '47. There he stood by my side as we tried to stop the brutal carnage that was unleashed. Ideals dissolved on that campaign, actions slipped out of my grasp.

REVOLT, FAIRFAX, THE KING IS DEAD

I instinctively grabbed Thomas' arm, just in time; he turned to stone realising his mistake, then quickly stepped backwards out of sight of the token yet alert guards. I thought he, of all people, would be more careful. As it happened, the element of surprise was thrown back in our faces like a thoroughly rotten egg: this mission to seize the king was a non-event. He'd already fled with a handful (more like a thumb and forefinger) of loyal troops; obviously our plot was considerably less secret than I was led to believe. "News travels fast when you don't want it to," I spat out, furious at first but then amused by the debacle. "Let's ride back to Fairfax. He should know straight away there's a traitor amongst us."

Sir Thomas Fairfax was mightily pissed off and, uncharacteristically, he let it be known. He allowed himself a spontaneous outburst, then relaxed, his face automatically reassuming its serious and 'down to business' expression. I'd been acquainted with

Fairfax for a few years; he proved to be a bold and intelligent military commander throughout the war, pretty fair and down-to-earth for a noble. "This is not good," he understated, "Charles will already be heading north to rally any sympathetic Scots he can find. With this damn revolt in the army, he could make a timely counter strike."

"I wouldn't like to see any of my countrymen helping out that bastard," I snapped, widely overstepping the mark. Fairfax threw a bitter stare at me that went straight through my eyes and bounced off the side of the marquee, then continued.

"You know some of these men, don't you, these so-called Levellers?"

"Yes. They have... justifiable grievances," I suggested as tactfully as possible.

"Go and talk to them, they trust you. We have to gain control of the situation; we may need them again." I'd already left.

The New Model Army had been forced to disband after the final, or so we thought, defeat of the royalists but were owed back-pay, promised but not forthcoming. The more radical men used this discontent to stir up calls for political and social reform, underlined by the latent threat posed by such a number of triumphant but hungry troops. I had to admit, I had great sympathy for their ideas, more than I would admit to Fairfax and other senior officers or members of the House; they were landed and wealthy men after all. We seemed then to be on an extraordinary historical doorstep (I guess that's easier to say as I look back on these distant times) – the possibilities and opportunities to make sweeping changes were inviting us in. But even Cromwell was revealing a disappointing streak; then again, he was a politician as well as a soldier.

Anyway, the Commons were surprisingly obliging in voting through full payment of arrears to my men, after a show of muscle. We still decided to take a gamble and push our case a little harder, and I proudly led one of the regiments, now a mixed bag of infantry and horse, on that fateful march on the capital to call for a newly elected House. Londoners lined the streets and cheered us along; I could taste the optimism and hope in the air.

Things, as they had a habit of doing, started to go horribly wrong after that celebrated day. Cromwell was thickset, stubborn and convinced about what to do (as were many of the ruling class), despite the lengthy discussions my fellow Agitators and I had with him.

"To stabilise the country and public order, we have to restore the monarchy and introduce a new constitution, which includes it and the Lords"; his pompous words are embedded in my mind with a chisel and summed up the position of the gentry and himself 'very nicely thank you'. We argued in vain, the proposals too radical, it was obvious. I suppose he was just a country boy at heart, didn't seem to have the appetite for a bold new future. The king, the arrogant snake, rejected Parliament's proposition outright, wanting to completely undo what had been tightly tied up and go back to the way it was. On the other hand, this played into ours: too late *sire*, your fate was wax-sealed. Couldn't you see that sword dangling over your head, clean and crisply sharp? I licked my lips in anticipation.

Predictably Charles charged back to Scotland, looking for support and crying like a spoilt regal baby. I shadowed him, accompanied by a small but fierce team of steadfast men – no warriors; I've forgotten; we had a couple of fighting women in our midst – with like-minded drive. We were determined to find out more about and scupper his plans and rendezvoused in Newcastle with some old friends of mine from Edinburgh, no fans of the Stewarts and also wanting to make the most of the potential, which served itself up on a rotund plate for dinner that night.

"Hamilton, that bastard!" I half-shouted and half-laughed.

"Indeed, he's already assembled several battalions in the Borders," replied Hamish, more worried than I.

"He couldn't command a couple of well trained dogs let alone a few desperate royalists," I mocked haughtily but with some justification. Fortunately, I was proved to be a good judge of Hamilton – his troops were soon driven back after invading England, where they'd combined forces with the last fleeing henchmen of Charles the Finished.

It was now late 1648 – I confidently, but also strangely nervous, pushed open the heavy oak door to Cromwell's private chambers. We were all greeted with hearty handshakes (my group comprised six); I braced myself for the serious task ahead of us, this kind of negotiating and dealing was unfamiliar to me – to convince Oliver that the king had to be executed.

"I too can no longer tolerate the man and agree he does have to pay for his treachery against Parliament and the country. But regicide? Are you fully aware of what we are contemplating here, Roxburgh?"

"Yes, sir. Extreme perhaps, but there is no other way; you know what he's like! He can't be allowed to raise another army or just step back onto the throne as if nothing has happened. We have to remind the country this man is evil (I knew that word would stir something inside him) and there is no going back."

"Parliament will decide," he replied, now resigned to the outcome.

FOREVER, IRELAND, HAMISH, PROTECTOR

So what happened to me on that day in January '49? Hard to describe exactly. I try now to piece together the elusive details, and have on many occasions since, but the lightening itself remained the most powerful image; a fast and furious blow that burned into my mind. I was struck, that can'ne be denied, in the midst of a rainstorm so intense, so wet, I'd never seen the like before or since. I thought I was going to be nailed to the ground and my skull shattered by those polished drops of stone. And then... supercharged light bored through my left temple, electrified my brain. I'd got horrendously steaming the night before; we all did in celebration of a new dawn, as Charles was sweating his last hours away. Somebody, who appeared to be one of my soldiers, a sergeant I think, came over with a bottle of the most ecstatic wine I'd ever tasted. He didn't look familiar at the time – I believe I knew all of my team so I should've been suspicious – but was hypnotised by the occasion, the soothing liquid and his enveloping charms. He told me stories about an acquaintance; "the Doctor" was how he referred to him, and offered me the wide world. Then he left me, and I slept for a solid twelve hours but felt sick when I finally woke up; my legs and arms had changed places, my tongue was glued to my stomach. But after that sadistic storm, I collapsed, dead to the world for a further twelve hours. Then... I opened my eyes like the first time I ever did, a warm, fresh light filled my view and I sunk into profound relaxation, which has stayed with me since. I saw pictures of people, unfamiliar objects, exciting things I didn't understand for very many years.

In a dream I also had a vision of four costume-clad, flag-carrying figures thrust shoulder to shoulder, representing the separate nations ruled by independent democratic parliaments, yet all part of a commonwealth republic. A lively coloured, idealised painting ostentatiously displayed in a gigantic public gallery somewhere. Unfortunately, the new regime shared no such vision; England was king, Wales essentially no longer existed, Scotland melted into the whole and Ireland was beaten into a cowering colony. By March '49, I had to leave the army, as I refused to go to the Emerald Isle as a whip-wielding oppressor. However, I did go on my own steam, joined by Thomas, now similarly disenchanted, and Hamish, who couldn't return to Edinburgh as he had a price on his head for some irrelevant misdemeanour (the Puritans had no sense of humour). So we set sail once more to stir up trouble, a common cause, call it what you like.

Owen O'Neill was an odd bloke; I knew we couldn't really trust him, but he was probably the most suitable ally at that time. Our *confrérie* didn't survive the clash of personalities and ideals, despite mutual ground against Cromwell's bullies. Our numbers were also swelled by a boatload of escaping Levellers, looking for new converts and the downtrodden to take up arms together (if not, legs would do). Back in London, history was becoming depressingly linear. There were no social reforms, no redistribution of the vote; Cromwell and his gang only wanted to look after their own and make no further waves (or so it seemed to me – some dismissed my opinions as too idealistic, too 'opinionated' perhaps).

Thomas woke me up early, about a quarter after 6, and apologised but had news worth the initial shock. He looked even more handsome today than he had last night, as I sniffed the revitalising aroma wafting from his hair and body.

"Not good, sir," offering an expression that would have suggested it was his fault.

"Please drop the sir, Thomas, we're not in the army anymore. Now we're friends, comrades in thought, in cause, and in death," I cut in, somewhat dramatic but reassuring.

"Sorry, I keep forgetting." Such a naive face in a lived-in body.

"Ludlow and Lilburne have been arrested. They're still alive but others have been executed." I had no immediate response but sat and considered for a few moments. Ludlow and Lilburne were the most influential and visible of the radical leaders and had been fighting to keep the fire fuelled and burning hot.

"We have to return. They need our help."

"I was hoping you were going to say that," Thomas almost sang,

113

"... but we'll have to tread very carefully; you're well known in London and Edinburgh."

"I know, but we can probably be more useful over there."

"This all sounds suspiciously like Cromwell is using the army to force his will, to impose a dictatorship?"

"It's already established: 'in the name of order and the threat of foreign invasion' of course, those old chestnuts. If we can get Ludlow and Lilburne released, maybe there's a glimmer of hope. It'll be dangerous – you and Hamish don't have to tread down my unstable path," I added tokenly and received the desired and expected response.

"Danger is our motivation, sir, if you are in it," Thomas the fateful.

"Ach, they'll be looking for me too, remember!" Hamish the down player.

So my two trusty protégés returned with me to Edinburgh – it was good to be back home, even if we did have to remain under-cover for the time being. Luckily, the moon moved in an unprecedented way and did strange things to the tide. Ludlow and Lilburne were emancipated from jail; not only that, but they quickly regained favour and power. It was reassuring to see that London was still essentially radical – Parliament had obviously realised it could only squeeze so much – and that our small efforts from afar behind the scenes had helped in some way. Ludlow replied to my letter and supported wholeheartedly our plans in Scottish affairs. He even offered money – better still – I didn't ask where it was raised.

And then, unbelievably, the royalists poked their ugly heads over the wall once more. Within two days, Edinburgh was virtually overwhelmed and an army heading south to meet Cromwell's flying devils skirting up the coast. They collided at Dunbar: Cromwell's superior force buried them finally and totally then and there. He arrived in Edinburgh in September 1650, the lesser of two evils it seemed, so I reluctantly persuaded my ally, the Governor of the Castle, to surrender. I thought the old stone street up the hill would be worn flat that day, so many heavy feet did clump and stomp and shuffle past.

In the next few years the anticlimax was tangible, what could have been deflated to nothing. We and many others pushed Cromwell to influence fundamental changes – proper union of Scotland and England, law reform etc – he reacted by moving further towards the traditionalists, still favouring a treaty with Charles' son. I saw no other route apart from declaring a full republic and burning the Stewart's crown forever.

Disaster followed disaster throughout '53, Cromwell dismissed Parliament twice and then iced the cake – he was declared Lord Protector just before Christmas of that miserable year.

"Sounds just like king to me." I'll never forget Hamish's words, joking and bitter at the same time. Our hopes seemed to be finally squished under the sole of his substantial boot. Some of my Leveller friends even turned to the royalists rather than the new regime. But not me; I spent the following two years half-hiding, half on the run, involving myself in any republican conspiracies I heard about. By '56 military rule was firmly imprinted on the nation; there's not much more to tell; these were difficult times.

And that fluid, death-scented night where we nearly perished, the luckiest of many lucky escapes I encountered during those dark days. Although, looking back now and understanding what I'd become, perishing was not on the cards. Nor Thomas and Hamish, for we were one. It was only then, seven years after that strange and unnatural occurrence, I realised I was invulnerable, that time had stood still. I suppose it should've been obvious; I hadn't changed one tiny bit physically, and mentally was also super-agile. And Thomas and Hamish had become so much part of my life, of me, that we hardly needed to express our thoughts in words. We drew on each other's strength, conviction and love.

That night in February '56, I'd already sensed the presence of the killers; their violent intent hung in the atmosphere weightier than their bad breath. Thomas dropped the bottle of wine as Hamish came crashing through the door.

"Broghill's men, just up the road. They're searching every building. Seems, at least, they don't know exactly where we are," he stuttered, disorientated. The glass and red liquid mingled by his feet. We were able to leave immediately; we were always prepared for such things, never allowing ourselves the luxury of settling in any one place. The horses were as hyper as we were, eluding Broghill's thugs the common goal. And we believed we had: suddenly, an ambush on the tight lane the other side of the village, a sly lane which didn't reveal itself easily to strangers to the area. Thomas was quick to react, very quick, his sword quietly removing the life from the first of the soldiers to appear out of the not-too-dark evening (for us at least, our eyesight was heightened and finely tuned). Hamish drew his pistol, unaware he'd already received a hit from a hidden musketeer. His shot rebounded off the treacherous trees alerting the rest of the bloodhounds to the scuffle. My pistol sprayed hot shot into the face of another attacker (I was beginning to get turned on by these aggressive men). I felt the burning pain of his sword in my leg; he'd managed to follow through before collapsing under my horse's feet. It was warm and numbing at first, but then I didn't feel any further discomfort. We galloped away up the lane, then cut into the bottomless woods – they wouldn't find us here. About two hours later we could risk stopping and let the horses rest. We took in events as they replayed in our heads, all communicating confused yet unified thoughts and words.

"My leg!" I exclaimed, "it's barely scratched." Hamish prodded his chest once more, trying to locate the evaporated shot holes. We felt blessed but magnificent.

We departed from Scotland again (I wasn't to return for more than thirty years) and re-embarked for Ireland – there was work to be done there, stirring up the Catholics or whoever was interested against Henry Cromwell's occupying army.

RESTORATION, AMSTERDAM, REVOLUTION

His father finally died in September '58, the tough old bastard, and the Protectorate slowly trickled down the drain after that. Despite the efforts of my unofficial regiment, now numbering some 180 disillusioned republicans and the last disparate groups of Levellers and Agitators from London, Charles II was crowned in 1660 and turned the whole country on its head, as if nothing had happened. Depressing days. A core group of our men and women, about half of them, voted with their feet with us and sailed to the Dutch Republic. We settled in Amsterdam, a growing city port, which was flowering into an exciting and bullish trade and cultural centre, enriched by the nationalities and ideas that passed through. Some of the band remained here, married, had children, died; some drifted back in dribs and drabs to England to grow old and fade away. Hamish and Thomas eventually went their separate ways; Hamish may've ventured to the Americas, or so I was told a few years later. Thomas fell in love in Amsterdam and lived with his partner, a talented painter. They enjoyed the freedom of that progressive city to the full, a freedom not tolerated anywhere else in Europe. Thomas recounted many stories of wild parties and debauched scenes painted in blood on the fair and fresh skin of fellow revellers. They subsidised this life style by selling a few pictures, supplemented by myself from fortunes previously stolen from those who hadn't deserved or needed them. His lover, too full of life and good times, died ten years later from cancer, or so Thomas was able to guess a diagnosis a few hundred years later. He was very sad at first but I talked him through it.

"I'm afraid you'll have to grow accustomed to this. Your beauty will never fade, many more will melt away in your arms."

"Difficult to get used to." At first monosyllabically subdued, then his eyes lit up as he pondered on my words: "Unless the devil finds me first!"

"Don't worry about him! We have each other; you'll... *create* others like us too. Look forward to times ahead, shaping events, the thrill of passing through human history but always transcending it!" I was on a frenzied roll; he smiled a smile so warm, so meaningful, the likes of which I didn't see again for three centuries.

I met some interesting people here too, an inspiringly diverse crowd that you were unlikely to find in such concentration even in London. It appeared we weren't the only 'undesirables' who'd settled here, also rejected by Europe, ever in turmoil and transition. I used to enjoy meeting and chatting with Spinoza, an extremist philosopher (and only in his 30s I'd guess), who'd been expelled by the Jewish community. It was positively enlightening to discuss politics and the world with one so frank and unafraid of his views on democracy and other 'unacceptable' ideas. Pity such a man had no influence in the England we'd deserted.

I stayed in the Republic until 1688 then rushed back there with these thoughts in mind to join in the "Glorious Revolution", as my countrymen coined the phrase. Political and religious dissatisfaction had brewed and fermented right over the edge – James II was deposed, Parliament seized control and invited William (III) to sit on top of the new constitution. This seemed an acceptable compromise, I suppose, as good as we were going to get at the time. He was also a known quantity from my point of view, having shared his country for the previous thirty years, even though he was an Orange prince and James' cousin. For this reason, Thomas remained in the United Provinces; I received a few letters from him, then we lost contact. I did see him again though – after a chance meeting in Berlin in 1922. I celebrated the turn of a new century in my very own Edinburgh and was there seven years later to finally experience the union of Scotland and England. Then? Destination France, in search of wine and trouble.

PARIS, CLARET, ROBESPIERRE, JEAN-BAPTISTE

I tasted my first bottle of the Mouton '87 in early 1793: still young, dark and unrevealing. So was Robespierre at that time, although in his mid 30s, but wore it well considering the pressures of the job and how hard he was working to keep the momentum going. We were soon to fall out severely after he set up the 'revolutionary dictatorship' (as historians later came to describe it; I called it a pain in the arse of the nation) in the autumn of that robust year. I'd liberated ten cases as payment from the Marquis Léoville de Beaufort and forgave him his crimes against the people. I'd also got involved in confiscating and redistributing vineyards in Burgundy. I made sure a long-standing colleague of mine, Edouard Cassenous, received holdings in a village close to Beaune to divide amongst his substantial family, as a reward for his services to the Revolution. In fact, one *domaine* there remains in the hands of a descendant – he's changed the style of the wine a little but it's still one of the best Pinot Noirs I've ever drunk. And believe me, I've polished off some bottles over the years.

I still have three bottles now of the towering 1787 – no, two actually – of course, I opened a second the day after I met that mysterious yet naive young man two hundred years from the very first apprehensive bottle. The drink the night before, so heady and strangely intoxicating, put him in my grasp; the next fused him to me forever. I didn't give Robespierre the pleasure of a further sampling; I ensured the life-blood was removed from him by another's hand, not offered for eternity. A disappointment *malheureusement*, but also with deepest regret. Anyway, this drifted through my consciousness over two centuries ago, so let's return to that point in the story.

I don't remember exactly when I assumed French nationality but I was known as Jean-Baptiste Lefèvre. Certainly thirty or forty years before; I think it was the name of an old acquaintance of Voltaire, who disappeared in suspicious circumstances without trace. Or was it one of his characters? It'd been a trying year, to say the least. Paris was intense, very intense; the air was as concentrated as the Mouton, the streets were redder still.

LONG TROUSERS, TERREUR, MARAT

I'd written an article in the paper in June '92, a discourse which stoked the fires of hell; its language matched the bloodiness of that carnal summer. I'd decided to stick my neck out (but not far enough to catch a blade) and launch a bitter but justified attack on the war against Austria. "As if we didn't have enough problems, *citoyens*." The article attracted the radical attention of the so-called *Sans-Culottes* leaders, branded thus by unimaginative bourgeois bores as nothing more than uneducated lower class men; and later Robespierre, who seemed to be manoeuvring behind them, although I thought they had little in common. Things, as they had a habit of doing, led to other things that led to my collaboration in an uprising to remove the king from the equation for good. Just the plotting, mind you; I'd had enough of the physicality of rebellions by then. And they wanted to use my contacts to cement useful support. Let's say unofficial backing from sections of the revolutionary government, who saw, as I did, the absolute necessity in nailing down the slippery Louis XVI. And so the *Sans-Culottes* thugs seized the palace at Tuileries and the king but were compelled also to massacre the guards, which didn't help to cast their actions into a favourable light. More massacres followed in September, more French blood tarnished the *Tricolore*. I was surprised it still had any white and blue left on it.

I succeeded in denying my involvement in this violence and wrote a piece condemning it. Ironically, I turned the story around to stir up support against Louis by effectively blaming him, and urged members in the new Convention to vote him guilty, stop beating about the bush and declare a Republic. Finally a majority count sealed his fate. I was hyperactively pacing back and forth in my apartment all afternoon, waiting for the news from, in the end, a rather apathetic messenger.

The crowds gathered, excited but also scared, on that day in January the following year – I really can't remember which; it seemed like Thursday. What was it with January and regicide, anyway? The execution cut the day in half, ominously dividing the past and the future as well as physically Louis' head from his neck. What a good excuse for celebration.

"*Santé*," I said to Robespierre lifting the glass. He gently clinked his against mine, the Mouton '87 sat like a particularly dark night shaded by deep velvet curtains. We drank.

In retrospect, I should've perhaps stood by Robespierre. At heart, I now realise he had a peculiar vision, perversely logical, cold and ruthless (but he personally wasn't once you grew to know him, in spite of his reputation) to achieve that elusive goal whatever the cost. Then again, I kept forgetting he was a trained lawyer. But at the time the price seemed too high, even for me.

"Ha, you've turned a bit soft, that's all!" Marat would taunt me a couple of months later, "Like him. He's just not bold enough; what we need is something extreme to get to grips once and for all."

Some of Robespierre's posturing was a front, I sensed, to hide insecurities. However, I, like many, undervalued his self belief but can't help thinking now that he spread it too thinly on the surface to submerge a lack of ability to see clearly ahead. Easier said than done; I wasn't the one in up to my boots at the *épée*-sharp end. And I was fortunate enough to live through what followed without his mortal fears. I was even prepared to give him the benefit of the doubt... but the Committee of Public Safety; that was impossible to justify and marked the beginning of my slow and subtle retreat from Robespierre's entourage.

"There's too much power centred in Paris," I took another deliberate sip of the claret, paused and enjoyed the moment, then continued: "the provinces won't take much more of this." Robespierre stared at me in disbelief, twitching his hands and neck once again; he looked puzzled. It'd obviously passed him by; he'd been too embroiled in what was going on in the city to have spared a thought for the rest of the country. He seemed to have conveniently forgotten his words of a year ago (I hadn't), one of the reasons he gave for resigning as Public Prosecutor for Paris.

"I wish to serve justice throughout the nation, not just in Paris," more or less word for word, as I'd written a piece about it back then. He'd quickly learned to get back into bed with the people in the capital, as I'd done. Politics appeared to be appealing to me again.

"Well, you did ask me to be honest," I continued, keeping these thoughts to myself.

"*Tant pis, citoyen*," he commented rather disdainfully, biting his nails, and added, indifferent: "this wine is making me feel a bit peckish. Let's go out and eat." I was a little taken aback but not for long; I knew what he was like, why he was unpopular. His curious and complex face seemed very calm, some would say dour. I suppose he was handsome in an odd way – that noble nose, neither large nor small, a flat sleigh-slope; penetrating, deep-set saucer eyes and forehead sanded by time and events. But not ground down enough to conceal his pitted complexion, viciously carved out forever by smallpox.

So we ventured out to our local restaurant, Le Couchon d'Or just around the corner not far from les Halles. It was too dangerous to walk any further afield, although I really wanted to stroll for a while to clear my head. But it was now Brumaire Year II (November '93) – a lot of dodgy desperate people lurking around and opportunistic opponents looking for an excuse for an execution. I had the same dish that night as I'd eaten the last time we came here back in January. My memories seemed to have fused; it was eerie that those two nights were strikingly similar. Even the rabbit tasted exactly the same; same sauce, same texture, superbly succulent each time. Was this an omen or was I overreacting? Anyway, we were lucky to get rabbit at all amidst the food shortages and crazy prices endemic in Paris. We didn't inquire where they obtained it.

"Just consider it a special privilege, in return for your kind favours," Michel the proprietor answered our unasked but obviously hinted at question. I threw a brief glare at Robespierre, serious face as always, then smirked; I also didn't ask and didn't want to know what favours Michel meant. I was surprised Robespierre ate any of it, let alone *all* of it with such gusto. Perhaps I'd exorcised some of the puritan in him, perhaps the political atmosphere had instilled a new hunger, a lust for flesh.

So we rolled into 1794 and crisis followed in our shadows, ready to pounce and stick a knife through my ribs; or rather Robespierre's. Too many bad things had been carried out in the name of necessity – opposition in Paris was effectively silenced and the army had sorted out any unco-operative elements in the country. It all seemed very familiar, I could hear the rebounding sound of history repeating itself. Nevertheless, he'd neatly boxed himself into an impossible situation.

"What was it all for?" I asked Philippe over lunch a few weeks later. He was an old comrade, who'd left Paris to get away from the smell of blood and hypocrisy and exchanged it for the sweet odours of tranquillity and anonymity in the countryside. Until now, that was, until his apparent rural idyll was rudely interrupted by city politics and death. The murder of his sister by a soldier had carried him back to Paris with revenge in his heart and renewed revolutionary zeal. I was fond of Philippe and admired his active mind, but he appeared drained and to have lost that committed passion.

"I don't think I know now. I don't think I know anything any more." He was also prone to over-dramatise, a pessimist when he wanted to be. But the truth could hurt. The violence hit a frenzied peak by the summer, the guillotine seemed to be working night and day.

I remember visiting the hall of the Convention one day amidst all this wall-to-wall terror; I needed to escape for the afternoon and, for a change, the hall was strangely inviting, empty and quiet. David had finished *The Assassination of Marat* about six months before, and the painting had been proudly exhibited here since. Marat, the Editor of *L'Ami du Peuple*, an influential publication keenly read by myself for one, was murdered on 13th July 1793 (a date I easily recall) by royalist scum. David's popular and populist picture possessed a powerful beauty reflecting the mood of the period, or at least the image painted by government propaganda. His romantic patriotism nevertheless provided a useful myth to focus attention on anti-revolutionary upstarts. A gentle light illuminated Marat; his head was wilted and arm and pen dropped to the floor. His face was communicating both nobility and outrage; a final and fulfilled peace as he relaxed, marinating in a bathtub of his own sacrificed scarlet life-juice. Although somewhat flattering and stylised, in an odd way it did resemble him. With a tiny tear tingling my cheek, I stepped up to his limp body and touched his vulnerable shoulder. We had a brief moment together before somebody came down the hall and shattered it.

I'd met Marat only in March '93, unfortunately too late to save his soul, and we hit it off remarkably quickly. An impressive and vocal writer and agitator, he knew what he wanted and how to go about it. In some ways similar to Robespierre, in others they were most unalike, not least of all their appearance. Marat was a bit of a scoundrel and seemed to deliberately cultivate the scruffy man-of-the-people look. Robespierre, although from or perhaps because of a poor upbringing, preferred rather outdated even aristocratic clothing, what with that stupid wig and precious buckled shoes. They shared similar principals; Marat was even known to sometimes praise him! I must say, I was rather attracted to Marat, despite an unkind skin disease that was slowly eating away his fragile and, underneath, still youthful face, for a man of 50. I felt sorry for him, having done so much to keep the revolution going and fight against the resurgent royalists. Yet he seemed so mortal, almost helpless, sitting across from one so unravaged by the past. He exuded an intriguing mixture of masculinity and tenderness, violent bloody-mindedness and genuine understanding of others. He'd come over to my apartment one ordinary early July evening, ordinary apart from the fact that he'd been followed. He must've been distracted, as it wasn't in his nature to be caught out so easily – Marat seemed to have an extra sense, always aware of others around him, behind him. But on this evening he succumbed willingly and was seduced by my charm and a couple of bottles of Burgundy. Would I let him join me on that higher level or leave him to try to escape his own fate?

"It's the only way. I agree he's given great inspiration in the past but now Robespierre is right; Danton must go. Sacrifice to the cause, if you like."

"But... some say the same about you, you know. And he is popular." I stuttered without making it sound like a threat (which it wasn't). His facial expression responded without words; he knew what I meant and wasn't bothered. But he was right: I had no defence, nothing I would say could make any difference. I was also a little surprised by the affectionate intonation he placed on Robespierre's name. The way he softened the consonants and drooled the R's at the end, yet spat out *Danton*. Perhaps I was being naïve to think he'd still hold a grudge against Robespierre for not supporting him, when the *Girondins* in the Assembly had impeached him a couple of months ago (although he was acquitted). On the other hand, the mutual dislike and mistrust of Danton had obviously soared to a high; they just wanted him out. Then again, I didn't know why Marat had showed any respect towards him in the past (assuming he had – I hadn't known him that long). Politically, they were poles apart, although I suppose they were both men of passion, unlike Robespierre, which was probably why I'd gravitated into his circle. I suddenly sensed Marat was aware I was reflecting intensely, almost as if he felt left out of my thought processes. I replaced my expression and feebly rethread the conversation.

"Erm... I certainly don't want to go down with him, if it's inevitable."

"It is, and you're wise to think about this unemotionally."

"But I believed. What happened, Jean-Paul?"

"History happened, human beings made it happen. And along the way our former friend Danton was lining his pockets." I gave him a sympathetic glance, then one of unashamed lust, I have to admit. It went right over his head. I knew then that he was already lost. Strangely, he understood that too but his interpretation had differed from mine; he'd predicted his own downfall.

"And it'd be better for you not to get closely involved with me. I'm not popular in the Convention; certain people will try to remove me from the arena."

"OK, but bugger them. What about the people on the street? They like you, they trust you. Try to use that more."

"I have; you've read my articles. Unfortunately the *putains Girondins* still seem to do whatever they want, despite what I rant on about!" I offered an understanding nod and switched my words back to his kind warning.

"Besides, you don't need to worry about me – I'll survive. I always do."

Marat laughed and snorted, mocking: "I've heard that said before!"

"No one can harm me, believe me." He was confused, suddenly aware he wasn't understanding me, as he'd believed he was on the same wavelength.

"Never mind," I pitched in firmly to save him going over the futile possibilities.

And that was the last I saw of him; he parted my company and disappeared into that heavy night. And soon after the clutches and blade of an assassin: Charlotte Corday, a *putaine Girondiste*.

I was shaken right to my bones by the murder, but not as much as Robespierre, who thought himself a more likely target and possibly the next. This tragedy more than justified the powerful editorial I'd written merely a few days before, urging the Convention to move against Danton. Just as I did against Robespierre a year later: he was arrested and executed on 9 Thermidor Year II (the month of heat, late July of 1794 under the *Ancien Régime*). Foolish, really stupid, but then I did realise it was bound to be bad judgement on my part in luxurious retrospect. The next five years saw some sense of law and order restored, yes (although too slowly for many former *Jacobin* comrades who were systematically butchered, particularly in Marseille and other southern cities), but the revolutionary breath had dissipated into the stale Paris air.

NAPOLEON, VICTOR, DEPRESSED

By the end of the century I'd had enough of France. Why? I'll skim over a few distant memories for you, try to put things in a chronological perspective without tainting events too much with the kind of judgmental hindsight that only I enjoyed. After the Constitution of Year III was established (1795), Bonaparte, the sly bastard, rose and rose. The 'People's' armies were carrying out popular – it has to be said to be believed – imperialist (call it what you will) campaigns outside of France. He was also clever enough not to be seen to be connected with the widening cracks in and, let's face it, downright balls-ups of the Directory (the subsequent republican régime). But the official propaganda cloaking the foreign wars back-fired in 1799, when the 'glory' sold to us temporarily evaporated. Defeats in Germany and Italy wouldn't be easily covered up; I could almost smell the masculine adrenaline and sweat emanating from the Russian and Austrian soldiers, who'd now advanced closer to our borders. Napoleon hurried back to France and proved useful as a timely figurehead for his cunning brother, plotting in the wings like a manic actor in that year's hit tragedy. Anyway, it all culminated in the overthrow of the Directory in Brumaire Year Eight (towards the end of '99) and his declaration as First Consul of the Republic. *Merde*! I was furious, almost as furious as the *Députés* thrown out of the Council of 500, some of whom I met the following day.

"Can you believe it, expelled by troops!"

"That scum Murat pompously waltzed in and had the nerve to take over the floor..."

"Yeah; then he shouted to the soldiers behind him: 'Clear this fucking crowd out of here!' I mean, *crowd*, as if we weren't supposed to be there."

I smirked (in fact nearly smiled but they wouldn't have seen the funny side of it) and shook my head in empathy but wasn't surprised. Unfortunately, most of the country didn't appear to be as angry as us. Call it resignation, call it apathy; at least Paris was, for once, as silent as a significantly quiet graveyard.

I fled to Italy, as I'd written one too many articles criticising France's favourite and most glorious general. I settled in Naples where, in comfort and relative peace far enough away from Bonaparte's satellite states to the north (it seemed), I was working on my first novel. It was here I heard the news – this was four or five years later, by the way.

"What is it?" I quizzed my intensely faced companion Paolo, who approached me on the veranda with slow, ominous steps and stared down at his ponderous feet.

"A bulletin from Rome..." he stuttered, shocked and perhaps a little frightened. "Napoleon... has been crowned Emperor."

"Well, *quelle surprise*. But it may not make any difference to us down here." I added as convincingly as I could manage.

Bonaparte continued the vendetta against me, or so it appeared from where I was standing. But in reality he'd never heard of me, of course; I just happened to keep being in the wrong place at the wrong time. You've guessed it: the French armies then took hold of the whole of Italy with an embracing and crushing hug. The south was annexed and the Kingdom of Naples, as it was renamed, became another tamed vassal of the Empire.

In about 1810 (sorry if I've lurched forwards somewhat, but you wouldn't want to know all the gory details of the debauchery in which I indulged in Italy) I ended up in Russia, more by luck than by design, after a whore of a long, sprawling and rather random journey. It also cost me a lot of money; too much in fact, and I arrived in Moscow as one well travelled but flat broke man. I decided I had to marry money to survive and buried myself into the Russian aristocracy, much to my distaste. I pretended to be an ousted *aristo*, down on his luck. It worked – Countess Sasha

Kutunov took me into her home, her arms and her conjugal bed. I played along, well I believed, and enjoyed spending her money; a temporary loss of principles, you understand, but I'd been acquainted with too many corrupting influences, and certainly felt no guilt considering the circumstances. Anyway, there was a further incentive to prolong this unnatural situation. Madame had a cute younger brother, who most definitely preferred the company of gentlemen. So we entered into a passionate affair – his name was Victor, about 28, gorgeous green eyes, bigger and greener than his sister's most prized emeralds. It transpired she was perfectly aware of what was going on but just turned a blind eye. Underneath all that charm, perfume and sumptuous clothing, Sasha was applaud-worthily devious and cleverly manipulated people without them having an idea of what she was up to, before being sucked into her tight-knit world.

But I had to leave Victor, poor chap; he was devastated. I was wrenched out of my new pampered lifestyle and thrown back into reality in September 1812, when Bonaparte's forces finally occupied Moscow. I couldn't believe it; anybody would've thought it'd become personal, although deep down I hadn't underestimated his craze for power and imperial drive. Where next? Nowhere in particular, I just bummed around Russia, keeping a low profile, week by week being pushed further and further east like a hapless player in some giant board game, over which I had no control. I learned after the event that I needn't have been so hasty in deserting my Moscow playground and vibrant Victor. The French Imperial army soon retreated, thwarted by Russian obstinacy, lack of food and eventually the bitter winter. Thankfully, Napoleon was finally defeated and kicked out; I'd considered going back to France but a bombshell dropped on the threshold of my decision process. In 1815 Louis XVIII was restored to the throne. I was so depressed, I emigrated to America (via Japan!): a fresh start, I thought, new places, new faces, new blood and no kings, more or less.

AMERICA(S), WINERY, INDIANS

I got a real high from injecting a grade 'A' virgin shot of purest, unadulterated history into my veins. The downer was, I'm afraid, that the remains of the 19th Century is a bit of a confused haze! I don't really understand why – much of the detail of events from, say, a hundred and fifty years before are stuck like sharpened pins in my mind-library. Perhaps the air was richer here than in Europe; perhaps I entered a totally inexperienced consciousness; perhaps my body was reacting to lack of nourishing red after the interminable, cold and hazardous trawl across Alaska and Canada. A few days into the journey my thoughts and perceptions of my surroundings became indistinguishable from the harsh physical geography. I felt myself being folded into the innocent crisp snow like an egg in a wispy meringue, put my head down, dug in my heels and let my mind go, dematerialising into the rapid and frosty molecules of wind. I woke up on the east coast months or probably years later, although it only felt like minutes. Where was I? Boston, I was informed in disbelief in a friendly eatery. Something/body then grabbed my hand and stole my memory and led me further down the coast, let go and vanished. New York was where I was meant to be and I was glad to settle here for a few years.

The city was just beginning to blossom from its roots as a busy trading port and boasted a fulsome population of nearly 100,000 at that time. It was to double in just ten years as floods of German and Irish immigrants arrived and set up home in Manhattan's Lower East Side. I became acquainted with two or three struggling but determined families living in the slums, which bloated out and up around Chatham Square. In this area, and in fact in much of Manhattan, the streets were still narrow and haphazard, most unlike the newer, straight and wide boulevards such as Broadway, with its neat lines of trees. Here the unpaved walkways separated the rotting dwellings; dodgy wooden layers built on top of old Dutch houses and crammed full of new arrivals. I heard many stories of fires, disease and death, and indeed saw the evidence with my own eyes, as I didn't live too far away. Eventually the rats, filth and roaming pigs were ousted by reforming humanitarians and the brick sidewalks with tidy curbstones. It was calming to make new friends, but I also bumped into old enemies, or rather their ancestors. I wasn't the only one to find dismay.

"So I went along yesterday with John Hughes and his delegation, and he told him, the mayor, face to face, 'If you can't guarantee the safety of honest American citizens or protect their churches and homes, then we will be forced to station hundreds – maybe I could even muster more than a thousand – armed guards around our buildings.' That soon quietened down the Puritan bastards!" Eamon told me passionately, one of many who'd fled Ireland to escape this kind of persecution. I was fascinated to meet this Hughes character and did shortly after these events. He was an impressive figure and confident speaker, a priest who'd arrived about the same time as me, and became an unintentional political leader.

In contrast, I used to stroll down Wall Street when I needed to visit certain merchants, or to chat and drink coffee at the Tontine Coffee House, *the* place to be seen apparently! It was an unassuming, mostly wooden (the norm) affair nestling on the corner next to a couple of grander, tall-windowed brick and stone edifices. Not far from it stood City Hall with its subtly proportioned, rounded tower on top of two storeys supported by eye-pleasing columns and arches. I would enjoy absorbing some of the growing wealth being created in this centre of fashion and finance. On an uninspiring and average Wednesday afternoon in 1819 or 1820, one such conversation gave me the desire to tap into some of this prosperity and an idea of how. I was sitting with Samuel Waldman, a moderately successful businessman, who liked to reminisce on his pioneering days, and I took pleasure in listening. He'd been born into a tobacco farming family down south but later shrewdly switched to cotton, and moved north to export and import.

"This city's changed so much. I mean, it's a city now but it does-n't seem so long ago when it was just a bunch of towns with a port. But so much about Manhattan Island and across the river still gives you a distinct feeling of New Amsterdam, even a hun-dred and fifty years on!" He paused to take a satisfying drag or two on the impressive cigar perched on his lips, then explained, "You should read William Byrd's accounts of his visit to New York in 1685. Evocative writer; it's absorbing stuff – ask at City Hall."

"I will; sounds interesting."

"He talks at length about the white washed brick houses with high gabled roofs; very north European. And so was Brooklyn over on Long Island; that was a lovely Dutch farm village once." How transient a romantic idyll can be.

"But true character can't be erased so easily," I added and point-ed here and there. "Take all these stylish buildings. They're here to stay."

Samuel smiled. "Wise words from a youngster."

"Well, I've a good feel for places and time."

"You were in France recently, no?"

"Yes."

"It's just that... sorry to keep harping on about the past."

"Please carry on."

"I suddenly remembered... had a flashback to just before the turn of the century. That tune, it came into my head. The *Marseillaise*. I remember refugee revolutionaries singing it in these very streets."

"*Jacobins*?"

"Yes; you remember too?"

"I was... involved."

"Really... how?"

133

"I'm older than I look!" We laughed.

"So, what are your plans here?" he asked, switching his mind back to the present.

"Not sure exactly. Thought I might look into importing goods from Europe."

"Like?"

"Spirits – brandy, whisky – wine maybe."

"Why not. Have you tried any of the wines made up-state?"

"No; didn't know you produced wine over here. I mean, in this neck of the woods."

"Yes, but it's disgusting! From wild American vines; the flavours are very strange, nothing like European wines."

"Really? Interesting."

So I set up my own business and got so thoroughly stuck in to it that I abstained from the company of others and pleasures of the flesh for a while. Except what I had to, of course: that which propelled me. I decided to contact my friend Edouard in Burgundy, to try to ship over some of his fine reds. The news eventually returned that he was dead, but his son Bernard had taken over and was keen to do some trade abroad. In the meantime, I'd written to a few properties in Bordeaux and had received a couple of favourable responses. Minor setbacks ensued – largely out of my control – although in reality a serious drain on finances, but I'd become rather laid-back and relaxed about such things since arriving in New York. The problem was finding reliable and honest transportation but it was quickly overcome, when I discovered and went into partnership with a reputable little company who paid well for the best captains and crews. It was a bonus that it was run by Jan, similarly easy-going and so dashing with those polar bear eyes and thin, sharp face. He was married, but that was just a front to evoke an air of respectability and avoid scandal and didn't stop him being a free spirit, sexually speaking. He and his wife also liked to have a good time and make the most of the city.

"Come on, you've been working too hard. And I've already bought three tickets."

"OK, what's on there?"

"The new play by Moncrieff – that English writer – *Monsieur Tonson*. I've heard decent reports." And so we descended on the Park Theatre and eagerly took our seats right at the front below the stage. It was the first time I'd been here; it was an astonishing building, with more than four tiers and an ornate dome of a ceiling. The first of several, for I'd discovered another source of pleasure.

Meanwhile, the business grew from humble beginnings, as did the number of satisfied discerning customers. Plus, on a personal level, I was able to top up with the kind of red I'd become accustomed to back in France. A fresh and exciting cellar devoid of the past and contractual obligations. For the moment, at least.

However, America was absolutely dripping with promise, so I decided to move on and left the business in Jan's small but capable hands. I sensed I'd miss New York, but would return briefly nearly a hundred years later (conveniently dissecting stints in Mexico) and catch the concert of a lifetime. I slowly trekked across to California – I know, I know, not very logical or well planned my west-east-west manoeuvring madness – taking with me some vine cuttings I'd shipped from France. I figured the climate would suit much better than on the east coast; suit the vines and me, in fact. I'd temporarily lost touch with the startling geography of this continent: wow, America was one huge piece of land, although when I reached the west, of course, I was sharing Mexican soil. And friendly warm-hearted earth it was too.

I accidentally rejoined the USA in 1848 without moving even one centimetre, when California reluctantly became part of it after the war with Mexico. But I was happy to go with the flow at this stage, as national borders had become as fluid in my consciousness as most were physically, as history took its toll and human beings stomped back and forth in the name of territory. Unlike my contemporaries, who had to either stay and accept their new flag or head off south. Towards the end of that eventful year I heard news of a revolution in France, which finally got rid of the wretched monarchy. Nice timing: I had a little celebration of my own, the bicentenary of the stopping of my corporal clock, my 200th birthday if you like. Plus several years – I didn't now recall how old I was when I was struck by that bolt of metaphorical or metaphysical lightning. Around a third of a century perhaps.

I was relishing every minute of every year that I lived in San Francisco. Soon after, California became a further Star to supplement the Stripes, a wave of incoming adventurers flooded our small city. In particular, the so-called '49 Gold Rush caused hoards of thirsty pioneers to flock here. The population of San Francisco seemed to explode overnight to over 50,000, embracing many fresh-faced Chinese immigrants. I used to get my laundry done by an efficient and amiable couple in what became a kind of buzzing Chinese quarter on Sacramento Street. One distinctly memorable evening in 1850, on my way out to the lively characterful bars in The Barbary Coast – the city's red light district further up Grant Avenue – I was drawn down this street by pandemonium and smoke. A few buildings, including my friends' home and business, were swarmed with hot flames and poisonous fumes. Luckily they were standing out in Sacramento Street, terrified and weeping in disbelief as their livelihood disappeared before their eyes. At least they survived; we witnessed charcoaled adults and children as they jumped to the steaming ground. Later I found out that this fire had been started deliberately; it wasn't the first or the last of the attacks on hard working Chinese residents. Fortunately, my neighbourhood was a little more peaceful; out of my window I could survey the view over the Plaza, the neat square newly planted with trees and shrubs and paths marked across. In the background, a rounded hill spotted with houses; the Bella Union, smart two storey structure fitted with sizeable shuttered windows, dominating the square; along with a taller stone-looking edifice next to Eldorado, a hotel and saloon.

I stumbled into a Romanian count – seriously – named Zarnesti who'd also travelled west with imported European vinestocks. We formed an amicable partnership and founded a winery in Sonoma Valley just north of 'Frisco in the early 1850s. We carefully selected and placed the best vines from our joint rootstock; the Count was knowledgeable about soil types and climatic influences in relation to the aspect of the land. Ideal – I was glad one of us knew what he was talking about. I worked hard there and derived substantial pleasure from toiling the land; obviously, I was turning into one of California's great romantics.

"You know, I'm really enjoying this new venture, quite a departure for me," I plucked out of my thoughts and threw onto the dinner table one evening. Or rather the solid wood table that lounged outside on the porch in the sunshine for much of the time. We'd gently consumed a savoury meal of fresh vegetables, heavily spiced beans, cured Spanish sausage, pungently mature cheese and sweetly ripe fruit. The Count poured us both a second glass of some ferocious central European *eau de vie*. I forget now what it was made from; he did tell me once. Distillate of Satan perhaps.

"Departure?" He looked up and screwed his face up in misunderstanding.

"Yes, a change from what I've done before. I haven't really told you much about my background."

"This is the new frontier; no-one has a past here."

"Except the ones who were here already!"

"Fair enough. But what counts is what you're doing now, what you want to make of this vineyard."

"Good wine of course. But it's more than that. I... I'm experiencing a magnificent sense of tranquillity, of peace within myself."

"Presumably you weren't before."

"Not really. In New York, yes. I guess I'd got too heavily involved in politics in Europe. Too stressed."

"I know what you mean. It's amazing what a simple undiscovered satisfaction can do for the mind and soul."

A few years on we were rewarded for our efforts by beating Major Ballejas at the State Fair, in 1858 I think it was. Our French Colombard white and Ruby Cabernet red impressed the pants off the judges. The Major was previously the Mexican governor of California, who I'd bumped into in the late 40s. He was also a sore loser; I learned not to cross him again. I made matters worse (and blew my cover) by seducing his sensuous son Juan and allowing him to roam for eternity. It was a clear, tepid night; Juan and I were cavorting in front of a serene San Francisco backdrop as if in a painting, when his father and a couple of malevolent swordsmen materialised out of the purpley blue half-dark. A fight followed; a bright steel skirmish of metal, sparks and blood, as whipping blades sliced through the very molecules of air and flesh. The assailants unleashed a dazzling display of anger and strength. Of course, I could've conquered all of them but decided just to withdraw from the scene and disappear with the Count, who had itchy feet anyway, and embarked on a trip to chart Central America. But I travelled with him only for a few days; we separated in southern California – apparently he was never heard from again. He knew more about me than he let on, as I found out from a conversation we had on one of those final days.

"Of course, I know who you are, what you are." I tried to give off vibes of cluelessness. "In Romania we are... enlightened about... the supernatural. Don't worry, I'm neither afraid of you nor jealous of your gift."

"Interesting word – gift. Sometimes I'm not so sure. Sometimes."

"I pity you as well." I hadn't encountered such understanding anywhere else or at any other time, although I must've sensed something about him, as I never once desired to take him.

After this I found myself roaming further south from town to town and over vast waves of dry, peaceful desert. Here I was penetrated by a profound sense of comforting isolation, and from time to time came across people other than Mexicans, who were very different from any I'd met before. This was Navajo territory, once considered one of the most ferocious Native American tribes in the eyes of settlers, but I discovered an intelligent and spiritual culture and at heart simple, rational desires. They didn't appear to sense any threat from me (as indeed there was none), as I was never harmed and, on the contrary, often welcomed into their 'villages', even though we spoke no common language. However, I did seem able to communicate my thoughts and interpret theirs. The Navajo had given up the predatory and wandering lifestyle I was told about and had adopted some of the customs of the Spanish colonials and Pueblo Indians. They'd embraced and showed a natural aptitude for and pleasure in farming, sheep herding and making pottery. How quaintly bourgeois! As a people, they only numbered some 12,000 or so, thanks in no small part to the persecuting campaigns waged against them by the American occupiers of New Mexico in the 50s and the resident Mexicans before that. The Apache had to be handled with greater caution as they had no love of white men and were quick to strike. I'd never seen such skilful horsemanship – I could've used them back in England! They moved around a lot so they could avoid being easily tracked down.

Anyway, I lived for a while with the great chiefs Manuelito and Barboncito and their families and followers at Canyon de Chelly, the Navajo's bottomless, rocky and impenetrable stronghold on the modern Arizona/New Mexico border. In fact, I settled with Barboncito's complex and alluring son, known as Little Barboncito or so I translated/guessed; such a handsome charmer and bit of a wild boy. I found it bizarre and irritating that my fellow Europeans had rejected and hunted down these fascinating people because they were "uncivilised". Not only were our cohabitation and lusty sexual shenanigans tolerated but positively encouraged! The chief only seemed to care that LB (as I nicknamed him) was happy, and for some reason rather liked me: it struck me he sensed something spiritual or wise about me. The four of us, including his quiet but strong-willed wife, would sit together and smoke and try to tell stories, usually mostly by drawing in the fertile earth or on kind of canvases fashioned from hides and the few words of their expressive tongue I'd acquired. I believed I felt fully accepted into the tribe, known as Dark Mountain by the way, after taking part in a whirlwind attack on Fort Defiance alongside LB and his father and their ally Manuelito. This was in April 1860, and I wouldn't have wanted to be in the US army on that frightening day in that isolated spot, however many guns they could call upon. In a tornado of painted flesh and bone-splitting screams we overran the fort and seized as many animals as we could manage, then melted back into the mountains faster than we'd descended. It was a straightforward tit-for-tat mission to replace our herds lost following a raid by soldiers, who'd recently wiped out Navajo cattle. Fair enough, I thought. As time went by the Dark Mountain split away from Manuelito, who never seemed to tire of war, but Barboncito grew weary of fighting and increasingly favoured peace with the new bosses. But they were betrayed and forced to resettle to the east on mediocre land, although eventually were allowed to return to their homeland in vastly reduced numbers. With sublime sadness I parted from them, but the bonus was LB decided to accompany me full of the excitement of adventure. It was also a sound moment to get the hell out of there and avoid the escalating war between Union and Confederate troops, butchering each other over possession of New Mexico in 1861/62.

So from around that date we found ourselves mostly in central and southern America. The Latin infusion did me good and I didn't hold back, I have to admit. Nor did LB – did I mention that he'd become more than just a travelling and bed companion? He was now a history addict and drifter of centuries, proudly plugged into my guiltless psyche and soul. Crazy genes were absorbed, but it all helped to keep us occupied and to refresh our mind and body. As did the discovery of some super red wines in Argentina sometime in the late 1880s, especially those made by a certain pretty black-eyed wine producer. He had European roots – his family had travelled from Italy forty years earlier but he was born here – his name was Ennio Bianchi, or something like that. Unfortunately for me he was married to Eva, but fortunately for him, perhaps, because she ran the place as he wasn't too bright. I slowly drained his cellar but had to make a speedy departure before his family could lynch me (Eva was wise and devout). The last memory that sticks was getting hooked on gambling in casinos in Chile, then finding myself on board a slow boat to hell. The would-be-assassin sea and storms hiding in the wings around Cape Horn pounded me like a heavy-weight boxer, until I descended into hibernation-like sleep. I missed my port by a long, long way and woke up, once again, on the east coast of the USA.

Inevitably, I suppose, I was drawn back to Mexico: the 20th Century had already opened the door to possibilities wide open and welcomed me in, and Mr & Mrs Conflict and their whole diverse family of bellicose and colourful human beings. I seemed to have acquired a skilful knack of sniffing out political turmoil (we're talking about one uniquely developed sense of smell here, after all). Reluctantly at first, then full-on passionately, I donned my red cap and helped out the Partisans with their little revolutions from 1910/11 onwards. Why not? I had more experience of uprisings than most and was in the mood for some action.

I returned to Europe after the First World War, to Germany. Why there? To be honest, I let chance decide by closing my eyes, taking a deep breath and pointing at a map: the Weimar Republic, freshly established and declared, had chosen me, a man of many stories and still keen to tell/learn more.

BERLIN, BLUE RIDERS, DESSAU, BAUHAUS

First, I needed a new identity – my previous incarnation was wearing a little thin and suspicions would surely be aroused, particularly with a name like that. Not that they would've known what to be suspicious of, but these were strange times we were living in. The Great War certainly wasn't that – the populations of Europe and beyond had a whole new outlook on the world now; humanity had had a good look at itself in the undeceiving mirror and didn't like what it saw. However, Berlin was determined to put all that behind it and reinvent itself; and, wow, what a new start with two bangs and a half. I became known as Peter Rötingen, architect, and soon a friend of Walter Gropius, having been introduced to him at a meeting of new designers, sculptors and artists, all brought alive by the liberal aromas of a very *nouvelle cuisine*. The radical spirit in the air brought with it reborn perspectives on a new era. I learned a great deal from Gropius, whose designs for modern living influenced generations to follow. I quickly hoovered up a lifetime's experience of design and engineering from whatever sources (and whoever) crossed my dangerous path, and added them to my increasingly bulging personal portfolio. I also acquired a greater passion for art and form in general, but in particular the 1920s Berlin visual art scene.

I think it was Kandinsky who was to blame! We first met in May 1922, about six months after he'd returned to Germany from Russia (or rather, what was it now named, the Soviet Federal Republic?), at an exhibition at the Galerie Goldschmidt-Wallerstein. He looked quite Russian but could pass as German, if anybody ever resembled his or her nationality. He was wearing serious glasses and a curl of hair on top of an exposed forehead; in his mid 50s I guessed. Gropius had the air of a banker but with subversive eyes and a dark moustache; fashionable at the time but didn't look very attractive. He'd recently offered Kandinsky a position to teach at the Bauhaus in Weimar.

"This is Peter Rötingen, a recent and most enthusiastic recruit to our movement," Walter introduced me.

"Wassily," he modestly stated and shook my hand, as if I wouldn't have known who he was.

"I'm honoured... I'm a big fan," I stuttered out like a pathetic schoolboy meeting a Hollywood star.

"So, what interests you in particular?"

"Everything really – it's pretty exciting in Germany at the moment! But painting above all, I suppose."

I'd already made friends with some of the burgeoning population of Russian emigrés in Berlin and would go regularly to Café Leon in Nollendorfplatz with Vladimir Nabokov, a young aspiring writer. Here, other writers and publishers would gather for meetings and general chit-chat. I first went there in 1921, I think, and not long after this, poor Vladimir, himself only in his early 20s, lost his father to a Tsarist assassin. He'd established a publishing house and a controversial newspaper, but caught the bullet intended for his guest speaker at a meeting he arranged at the Philharmonie.

But it wasn't until 1926 when I joined Kandinsky's painting class in Dessau, where the Bauhaus relocated itself after the Nazis had taken power in Weimar. I'd wanted to earlier but couldn't be bothered to travel all the way to Weimar or go and live there. Bit small and boring, I thought. Dessau proved to be a regular civilised escape when Berlin, much as I loved it, became too intense. I was often invited over to the Kandinskys' home to have tea in their garden, where I also met Paul Klee, and we would discuss contemporary issues far removed from the bad old real world. The two families actually shared a specially built Bauhaus 'double-house' designed by Gropius, who also had a studio in Berlin where he did much of his work. So it was in Berlin that we often got together, and sometimes with such architectural luminaries as Ludwig Miës van der Rohe and Eric Mendelsohn, who were to be responsible for several of the excitingly modern glass and steel office buildings which grew up from Berlin's lush ground. And from here an opportunity was born that would help me shape the future of the new districts now amalgamated into the swollen Greater Berlin.

"Peter, I'd like you to get involved in this project," Walter asked matter-of-factly as he presented the plans to me. "Our team has taken on a, well, truly inspirational challenge to design a housing development in Charlottenburg."

"Fantastic, it's just what I was hoping for," I responded, ecstatic. To put into practice everything I've been taught, I thought.

"Indeed; at last the world is taking notice and prepared to bury the past," he added somewhat philosophically but with a zealous glint in his eye. I flicked through the documents quickly but sufficiently to take in the crux of their contents.

"These look great; I like the idea of gardens and parks too."

"Yes, having somewhere to live is all very well but I want to build a community in these estates as well."

"And a mixture of houses and flats?"

"To give a balanced feel on the eye and in the mind. Style is one thing, but these will be for living in at the end of the day. And the flats won't be too high either..."

"Well, there's plenty of space. This isn't New York City!"

Gropius retired from the Bauhaus in 1928, and I later heard the whole movement changed scenery yet again, setting up in beloved Berlin from 1931 to 1933. In that terrifying year, Hitler finally abolished it for good; Kandinsky fled to Paris.

THOMAS, GANGSTERS, DECADENCE

I have to single out an earlier chance meeting back in June 1922, now that it presents itself in my head, as by coincidence it was around the time Kandinsky had arrived at the Bauhaus in Weimar. I was bored on that unfamiliar Friday evening but couldn't be bothered to go out with the usual crowd to the usual places. So I just went out alone, started wandering the streets of Kreuzberg, decided half-heartedly to go for a beer then perhaps to a cabaret show. I wasn't watching where I was going and tripped over a man sitting on the pavement, propped up against the wall. I'd stumbled on his only leg and kicked over his cap half-full of coins, which rested nearby.

"Sorry, guv," he muttered.

"No, it was my fault."

"Spare some money for a wounded serviceman ignored by his country?"

"Of course." My heart sank and I scooped up the spilled coins and added a pocketful more, then gave him my flask containing the remnants of a fine brandy. "Keep it." By coincidence, I'd just walked past Der Rosaflamingo on Zossnerstrasse, where I could combine my aforementioned desires, probably more. It wasn't too busy inside; a few random couples, threes and fours occupied a few random tables. The show wasn't due to begin until at least midnight, so I sat at the bar and ordered a Pils. I surveyed the three others, who'd similarly decided to stay as close as possible to the source of drinks. Two together: a man in his 20s, smart dark suit with wide chalk pin-stripes, crisp white shirt, very bright blue tie, plain features but not unattractive; a smoking older woman who was talking much more than him, slim, dark dress, small hat. I smiled to myself, as I was impressed by the quality of *his* outfit and make-up, but should have expected a guy in drag in here. Both were drinking champagne and intermittently took turns in snorting cocaine (I assumed) off the bar. The other man was... Thomas! I couldn't believe it; I had to sit and stare for a full minute before I was sure, even though I knew it was him the moment I clocked him. He hadn't noticed me as he was looking down at the bar, maybe reading something. Yes, a letter. I quietly rose, picked up my beer and edged around the bar, despite the fact that it was square, and approached my long lost comrade.

"Hello, stranger," I whispered and put the glass down beside him. At first his eyes rolled across to the beer, then slowly scanned up my arm, then jolted up to my face. He smiled a Thomas smile in disbelief.

"My god, Colonel!"

"Peter nowadays, just Peter. How the hell are you, er, Thomas?"

"Yes, I've stuck with Thomas, just changed the surname every fifty years or so." I melted into his gaze; I'd really missed him. He sensed this and carried on smirking in the cutest way.

"I don't know what to say, where to begin," I said clumsily.

"Perhaps: where the fuck have you been, what have you been up to?!" he joked and added, "How long have you lived in Berlin, assuming this isn't just a visit?"

"No, only about a year. And you?"

"Twelve years. I managed to avoid the War, somehow." His 'somehow' sounded a little hollow, as if there was a longer story behind the word. Maybe a story I would find out more about, but for the moment I decided to let it lie.

"Know the feeling; I've seen a few since England, Ireland and Scotland."

"Tell me about it. I was even teaching military history for a while, in Athens, before I came here."

"And partners?"

"They've come and gone, quite literally. I've been single since I came here, didn't want to lose anybody else. That's why I left Greece."

"So how have you... replenished yourself?"

"I've got by. I've consumed as I needed to." He paused and looked a touch sad, so I took up the thread of the conversation.

"Right, let's have some more drinks." The bartender must have overheard me as he was already on the way towards us. He carried out Thomas' instructions to the letter – a very good, very dry vodka Martini apparently – and carefully poured me a generously large brandy. He took the opportunity to make idle conversation while he served us.

"So, I guess you've heard about Rathenau; shocking, huh?" He fixed on the topical death of the foreign minister out of the blue.

"Yeah, well, hardly a day seems to pass without an assassination nowadays!" I threw in flippantly but accurately.

"I went on the protest march," Thomas came out with, to my surprise.

"Really, he wasn't exactly a national hero and defender of freedom! A heartless tycoon, from what I heard."

"Perhaps, but one of the few left who are vaguely sympathetic," he defended his actions, "and we can't just let the military upstarts get away with killing whoever they want." Fine words, but ones whose weight soon seemed to diminish, as I took a closer look at what Thomas was wearing. I'd already noticed the striking silk sash he had across his slim torso, but it was only now that I spotted his unusual ring. Quite out of the ordinary, it resembled the ones I'd seen before worn decoratively by, shall we say, members of a rather exclusive club.

"Does that mean what I think it does?" I said pointing to his hand resting on the bar.

"What do you *think* it signifies?" he replied almost aggressively.

"A, what do you call them, sporting club? Which *Ringverein*?"

"The *Nordpiraten*. Does that bother you?"

"Well, you have quite a reputation. But I've long since given up making judgements about what people do for a living, what motivates them." I paused, more dismayed than I pretended to sound.

"I can't deny I'm pretty close to Gustav... Coke Gustav, as he's known; but if it helps, I try not to get directly involved in drug deals." He offered some degree of apology.

"You don't have to justify yourself to me." Reticent pout in return. I continued:

"From what I hear, you must've done some time behind bars then, to be *eligible*?"

"Yes, five years." He wasn't going to elaborate so I didn't push the point. "So, what do you do for kicks nowadays?" He changed the subject, but with tongue in cheek, to gloss over the purposeful switch in tone.

"I have an extensive, er, cellar." Thomas didn't at first follow my words but then threw a glance at me, so warm that he stepped into my soul just for a few seconds. "Red wine – some of the best from across time, nourishing life force slumbering in bottle. Do you want to come back for a drink?" It would have sounded corny if I'd said it to anyone else.

Thomas grinned: "Of course."

It'd been such a long time since we'd lain in each other's arms, and the mutual comforting touch offered a refreshing top-up of unadulterated love to our well-travelled flesh. We drank a bottle of beautiful Rheingau Riesling, all petrolly elegance, one of a few Thomas had 'bought' a few years before: 1899 vintage. I was later to acquire six cases directly from the Schloß, an impressive and stately estate perched on steep slopes above the town of Johannesburg. (That was sometime in the late 1920s as I left Germany; the economy was collapsing and Weimar spirit fading away.) After that ageing exquisiteness, I treated Thomas to a mature, sanguine Italian monster and told stories of the men I'd already shared some of this wine with in the previous century. He drank with me, fascinated.

MOSCOW, JAPAN, SOUTH AMERICA

"The winter in Russia that year was a killer; the cold ate right through me and filled my soul with liquid silver ice..."

"Don't tell me your frozen phantoms could get any chillier!" Thomas interrupted – ever so funny.

"1812," I continued. "So a couple of months earlier, for some reason, the city was just abandoned and Bonaparte's men started to appear in the streets from about mid September, I think, looking like death warmed up. Amongst this chaos fires were being started, deliberately I assumed to stop them getting supplies and shelter. I had to get out quickly; my face didn't match the locals, my alias, as a refugee aristocrat, wouldn't exactly have *endeared* me. And Victor's quarters were just too damn close to the flames for comfort – he was the roof over my head by the way!"

Thomas smiled and slurped red deliriously, strangely similar to the way Victor used to gulp down wine.

"Then I was overcome by some kind of weird driving force that wouldn't let go of my limbs. I just kept travelling east, on and on; the sheer width of Russia continually egged on my curiosity to try to map it all."

"Intense! The closest I've got was when I made a voyage through the Baltic States on the way to Finland, and then back across Poland heading south. So how far did you get?"

"All the way! I ended up in Vladivostok eventually – the rest, well it seems nothing more than a list of place names now. Kirov, Omsk, Irkutsk in southern Siberia, then I cut through northeast China to reach the coast faster. The easy bit was finding a ship to take me across to Japan – I landed in Sapporo."

"Japan, must've been interesting?"

"Yeah, it was... more Italian red?" I noticed Thomas' glass was empty, as was the bottle that stood guiltily in front of us on the table. "Are you hungry? This wine's crying out for cheese, at least for the cheese I have." Thomas nodded; I laid out a selection of fermented dairy and freshly broken dark German bread.

"This red's excellent; what's it made from?" Thomas.

"Mostly the Sangiovese grape, appropriately perhaps!" I then paused and thought for a moment; it made me jump on a few decades. "Aye, I also came across this grape in Argentina, in the 1880s..."

"Argentina – no! Hamish was living there around then; still does I think. Buenos Aires the last I heard."

"Shit, unbelievable! But we weren't there for long, mostly over in the west side of the country – Mendoza."

"We?"

"Me and my Native American friend, Little Barboncito. He made the journey with me all the way from Mexico. We passed through and stopped for short breaks in a whole host of places; a few weeks in San José in Costa Rica, then edged the Caribbean coast and took a train to Panama; the city, that is. Next stop Bogotá before the long haul through vast uncharted Brazil, staying in Río de Janeiro for a couple of months. Then we cruised the coast down to Montevideo, across the *Río de la Plata* and on to Buenos Aires. We'd intended to settle there as it looked very up-and-coming and full of promise, but the stink of lousy sanitation and too many Brits forced us to head west! Finally ending up in Mendoza, as I said."

"What was happening there?"

"Well, at that time it was a poor area rather cut off from the east. Had more in common with Chile."

"So you sat around in the sun all day drinking nice red?"

"Cheeky bastard! No, digging for silver too; people were just beginning to mine it. Anyway, we amassed quite a stash but blew a big chunk of it in Santiago. The rest helped finance campaigns in Mexico." I could see I'd lost Thomas and so embellished: "You know, the Revolution!"

"Again – hadn't you had enough of them by then?"

"Well, I thought so too, but a brief jaunt back to New York City prior to that wetted my appetite. Somehow I got the taste once more for rebellion."

"Bit of a long way round, no? I mean, my geography's not as well honed as yours but..."

"Yeah, I just sort of ended up there. It's a long story; odd really, can't explain. I left – LB remained in Santiago..." I sailed off on a memory for a waterfall of seconds and touched my chest. "He gave me his mother's pendant," affectionately pulling it out of my shirt, "it's supposed to hold the spirits of the gods and the dead."

"Wow! Magnificent stone. Valuable I'd say." Thomas was wide-eyed and mesmerised.

"Only to me... anyway, where was I? Yeah, um, I left on a ship from Valparaíso, and from what I can remember, sunk into deepest delirium."

I shrugged as Thomas looked puzzled, then he added: "What drugs did you discover in South America? I've heard good reports!"

I laughed and went on: "Anyway, Mexico. Still interested?"

"Of course. I did teach history for a while."

"Well, I discovered it wasn't that simple. I allied with Zapata, one of several squabbling factions, as you're probably aware. And there wasn't just one revolution, more a procession of failed governments followed by yet another overthrow..."

"Sounds familiar," Thomas cut in appreciating where I was coming from.

"So our army battled on – I think I was on the most just side, difficult to tell anymore – and marched on Mexico City at the same time as Villa's division in... 1914. It was a brilliant feeling: the streets were crowded with tired horses led by even more tired soldiers, their expressions hidden under big sun hats. People were hanging out of cramped windows, cheering us on, giving us a welcome boost as we trampled on down that warm, dusty road.

Predictably after that the different leaders couldn't agree amongst themselves, which pissed off me and many others. So our combined armies carried on the struggle until we were virtually crushed the following year, but I managed to fight on with Zapata until he was murdered three years ago, in 1919."

ROARING BERLIN, MONEY, BROWN SHIRTS

From time to time (OK, most of the time actually), Thomas and I would party it up with the high life set in the west end, fleetingly oblivious to the financial traumas engulfing the city and the country. By mid 1923, the government was printing so much money it would have put any honest fiscal forger out of business. It all spiralled out of control after they'd started to devalue the mark about a year before, and panic gripped everybody's wallets, savings and just about anything, really. But we 'survived'. I'd allowed myself to be drawn into Thomas' gang's shifty underworld – only enough to keep my head above the garbage pile, mind you – and by the end of the year the crisis was temporarily over as a transparent stability was restored. Within a couple of years, I'd joined the lucky loaded few after borrowing some money (as everybody seemed to be doing in Berlin) and made a killing on Wall Street through some wildly improbable speculation.

Move on about a year to sometime in 1926. Thomas, with full-moon excitable child eyes, gawked up at the cinema and muttered once more the headlining film title.

"*Faust. F-a-u-s-t*; who's the director again?"

"Murnau," Vladimir thankfully obliged, as I'd already told him twice in Café Leon where we'd partaken in a movie-aperitif earlier.

"Amazing theatre; looks like a cathedral," Thomas continued as we approached the front doors of the grandiose UFA Palast am Zoo.

"You've not been past here since it opened?" I asked.

"No. I mean, I probably have but didn't pay any attention. I've rarely been to the cinema; don't know why."

"Well, you're honoured to be in the company of a film star tonight, eh Vladimir?" I joked.

"Hardly," he paused to chuckle then cough. "Not exactly stardom, some walk-on extra in a second rate movie."

"When?" Thomas jealously probed.

"Last year, at UFA's studios just out of town. When you need the money..."

We slowly waltzed down the aisle to soak up some of the plush splendour before taking our seats not far from the orchestra. With beating hearts, stimulated by anticipation of the event and a couple of strong cocktails in the bar, the curtain rose simultaneously as the full-scale orchestra warmed up the score with slow, low notes, and the pictures rolled.

The eating was good too. A number of great restaurants opened in Berlin in those frivolous, hedonist, swinging (well not all of them) and gastronomic Twenties. The greatest of which, in size at least, was Kempinski's Haus Vaterland in Leipzigerstrasse, allegedly boasting three thousand covers all housed in a swanky, austere and curved-modern building. We went there on and off, usually opting for the Hungarian village inn or the Wild West bar, as you do. In fact, it was in the latter that I first met Christopher Isherwood sometime in '29. I was gladly stimulated by this young – he was about 25 then – writer's enthusiasm and thirst for ideas. We bumped into each other again before I left Berlin – just after Christmas that year, as Germany was once more guillotined to its knees by domestic and international financial crisis – at an outrageously magnificent fancy dress ball at the dance hall In den Zelten, where Isherwood had a room. He was decorated from head to toe in a purple silk ball gown, powdered wig (I hadn't seen anyone wearing one of those for a while) and skyscraper heels, which was a pity as it made him much less attractive, I thought. I was a bit boring and declined attending in drag, opting for a simple but scary white mask and black cape combo. It was a lively do, to say the least; debauchery of the highest order.

Unfortunately I had to part company from Thomas, forever. It was hard – such an extraordinary chance reunion and fun few years were surely never to be repeated – but I could never approve of the new set of intimates he became associated with. After all he'd learned, all we'd fought for and against together in the distant past, he became slowly sucked into the sordid world of new German politics. The Fascists seduced his seemingly incorruptible soul step by step, as he climbed up the ranks of power; I think the rot set in around the turn of '27-'28. We'd started to protest outside their headquarters at 44 Lützowstrasse since Goebbels launched the Nazi paper *Der Angriff* in the summer of 1927. He used this to stoke up even more trouble between Left and Right, actively encouraging battles in the streets. Thomas and I were unwittingly drawn into one such conflict – call it being in the wrong place at a particularly incendiary moment – as all available objects (and those brought along by some) were seized and turned into bloody weapons. There was so much noise that we had to rely on our other senses to pick off the Brown Shirts one by one. It wasn't too difficult, as their army comprised mostly untrained and disorganised thugs at this stage (Röhm wasn't back on the scene till 1930). I took special offence to one very arrogant, objectionable individual and derived real pleasure in ripping his head off. Such bloodlust had escaped my mind and limbs for almost ten years, as I'd tried to focus on peaceful, constructive activities in line with the spirit of Weimar. But this bastard, not one of his scummy band, wasn't going to join *my* élite.

"Looks like you singled out the wrong chap there," Thomas informed me the day after next, handing over a copy of *Der Angriff*.

"As you well know, their headlines never correspond to what actually happens," I replied indifferently.

"Yes, I was there too, remember." It turned out that I'd killed one of Goebbels' favourites, who he was grooming as a fellow candidate for the Reichstag elections due the following year. The paper made a right tasty meal out of this sacrifice to law and order and emphasised, in the most flowery and poetic language, the dangers represented by the Communists. I was no member of the Party but, increasingly, was glad to help out when it came to a spot of Swastika bashing. Despite taking ten seats in those elections in May '28, it appeared most Berliners continued to share the same point of view, which was one of hostility to the Nazis. For the moment anyway.

But Thomas kept secret the acquaintance he made on that afternoon of crazy brutal action. In the midst of the scuffle he fell in love with a beautiful blond Brown Shirt; he was just about to clock him one but froze when he gazed into his Mediterranean eyes. Thomas and I'd lost each other in the final stages of the skirmish, when the police had finally arrived. I didn't know at the time he ran off with this cute 'soldier' and went straight back to his place for masses of sweaty passion. I suspected something had changed about him and we saw less and less of each other from then on. Over a year later, one day early in 1929, I visited him in hospital after I found out he'd been caught in a shoot-out in a bar with some of his dodgy *Ringverein* chums.

"No, I'm fine of course. I only came to keep up the front and Rutger over there company," he explained pointing across the ward. "And to stay out of court too. I persuaded the doctor to *exaggerate* my injuries. Make up, I mean."

"So what was it all about?"

"A gang of members had gone to Dixi – in Breslauerstrasse – to avenge a stabbing. It all got out of hand very quickly and we got a call for help, but us turning up too transformed it into a bloodbath. It was fucking chaos... you should've seen Muscles Adolf, he was possessed... he only got ten months, not bad huh? Obviously the bribes were good value. As I said, I didn't go to court but was acquitted anyway." I listened closely; I was torn between finding the whole episode amusing and despairing about where Thomas was heading. My anxiety was confirmed and heightened when in walked another visitor, the aforementioned pretty Nazi dressed in his not so pretty uniform. I said nothing for a moment, partly taken aback and partly waiting to see what Thomas would say. He looked as surprised as me, not, I think, because he wasn't expecting him or didn't want to see him, but couldn't believe his timing. I was left in no doubt that this was a meeting Thomas had been trying to avoid for as long as possible.

"Oh, erm, this is Ernie..." he pathetically attempted to introduce us but was unable to divert from my face on fire. I said nothing, spat on the floor and marched out. And that was the last I saw of him; the rest of his 'progress' was discovered from hearsay.

I'm afraid I'd now lost the appetite for opposition – a terrible thing to admit I know – and I returned to Britain for the first time in more than two hundred and fifty years. I can tell you, I was feeling seriously old.

EDINBURGH, WEDDING, START AGAIN

I remained in London during the 1930s, which was gradually forging some beginnings of prosperity as the population dragged themselves out of the Depression, and industrious in attempts to reposition itself as a modernised capital city. I rapidly moved to Edinburgh in the early 40s – I'd had enough of wars – and settled with ease, although it was as if I'd never been there. The city was virtually unrecognisable to me, apart from the always-recognisable old town nurturing its history-washed sentiment and buildings, which would never leave and were happy to see a familiar face from a bloody yet gilt-edged era. Edinburgh, like all people magnets, had gently oozed its boundaries outwards to accommodate them. I established my own humble wine shop and restaurant on Rose Street. This was a fun distraction and did quite well despite circumstances; I gained quite a reputation for my unusual, even avant-garde style of cuisine (very multinational, as you can imagine, quite *outré* for traditional Edinburgher tastes) and exceptional wine list. Strange how I hadn't done this before – now I look back, it seems as if it'd always been my destiny. Of course, I had some experience of trading in wine (and stealing it) – remember how those eye-opening barrels I imported into the States had made me a few dollars – and making it in California, but not catering. I later returned to work for the same wine merchant in Edinburgh, or rather the company, which had developed from it and moved to larger premises in Leith.

I married for cover: a feisty young lady called Emma, very ahead of her time in outlook, which obviously appealed to me. She was a stimulating companion and didn't appear to be aware of my alter ego or activities in the underworld. Sadly, she died very suddenly, run down by a bus on the Lothian Road, but this did at least provide me with the opportunity to create a fictitious son, born in 1951 as his mother passed softly away in Casualty. It was easier to falsify records then, and this tragic twist-ette of events allowed me to assume his identity at the necessary time.

I want to run forwards a little, only a few years, to the point where I became Gordon. In the late 70s, a slowly nurturing desire to commit myself to education came to a head. I decided to go to university, kind of; to teach and work on the research for a PhD at the same time. Although I'd passed plenty of time studying here and there, I didn't actually have a qualification on paper. I'm not sure why this need possessed me so vividly all of a sudden, particularly as I'd learnt and experienced much more than a few years at a simple university could ever hope to 'teach' me. I guess I was hankering after some romantic notion of reliving a 'lost' youth (so to speak), to indulge and surround myself in a cosseted and safe world of modern education. And in addition to pass on some of what I'd absorbed, and to have some fun too. Besides there was always something else to discover, as I felt the hours, days and minutes had overtaken me somewhat in this briefest of centuries. I thought I could do with adding a few new skills to my universe whilst I was at it, such as using computers or business management or something practical like that. And so I became my son, after a fashion, dressing to the nines in the whole identity and soul of Gordon the Tutor, who'd been born of Emma's unfulfilled wishes and my even more fertile imagination.

SEA, TOWN, DANNY

I suppose Edinburgh University would have been the logical choice but I decided on St Andrews: the pull of the North Sea was stronger than mere logic. Conveniently, I was then offered an academic post in the French Department and the possibility of a doctorate. Besides, I could always escape back to Edinburgh whenever I felt like it; St Andrews was only about fifty miles away. Mind you, if I'd stayed in Edinburgh, I might've met Eliot sooner than I did instead of four years later. But you'd think yourself into the ground if you kept reasoning like that, always in retrospect; my head probably couldn't handle much more twisted logic than had already been fed around it.

The town possessed a grey freshness that penetrated to the core. The succulent sea was calmness itself, even when (frequently) rough, with a looming sky towering over it. The sky was definitely bigger up here, an overwhelming cosmos, often clear, often bleak, but always large. I remember total bodily osmosis with the air, which had a primordial coldness stripping you bare yet warming your bones. The place held an eternal fascination and always will; from time to time I encouraged Eliot to accompany me here on weekend escapes from Edinburgh in the proceeding years. The light could also be hypnotic: in the winter it never really seemed to get light, just black to grey to black. But in the summer, I'd forgotten what the reverse effect could be like, a sight I'd not taken in for a long while. Even at night it could glow purple and you could see the houses on Venus. The wind was pure and purifying; I'm sure it contained more oxygen than elsewhere. I remember one very weather-intense day; the wind was so strong it could've pushed everything off the edge of the world, all possible winter weather flew past my eyes and ears within a few minutes. I was almost blown to a complete standstill; I just didn't seem to have the strength to drive onwards, although this was obviously not so. But there was something more to this elemental force, something deeper and more beautiful; it told me not to fight against it, to succumb – I could never win.

Danny, the first light-emitting being I laid eyes on, was one of the most refreshing I met there, and in some ways had similarities to Edi-man. One of my students, he sometimes emitted feelings of being overwhelmed by so many unseen faces and the grand task ahead, so I took him under my wing. He seemed a shy bloke at first, from a once posh family languishing in the rural suburbs of north London. He and his brothers had thrown their father out because of his abusive behaviour and a string of affairs. Unfortunately, he took all the money with him and couldn't be tracked down to drag into court. So they closed together and looked after their own; Danny managed to get enough of a grant to get to uni. He was short but lean and quite strong for his size, sported bomber brown hair, kind of cute looking with unusual features; something rodent-like that I found appealing. But underpinned by Côte d'Azur eyes, which burned like a Roman candle 24 hours a day. He became my protégé; I wouldn't allow any harm to come to him and, ridiculous I know, I felt him too fragile to protect himself from a superior physical being. One afternoon in the pub we were enjoying a couple of games of pool, as was the fashion, accompanied by almost flat beer. Two pissed-up rugby thugs – the university team had won the league the previous day and these two hadn't stopped celebrating since – were hanging about waiting to play, as the other table was busted (probably thanks to a pissed up rugby thug). One of them, who really did look like a giant chimp, decided to vent his frustration on Danny and pushed him onto the pool table; fortunately all he could manage at that particular moment. Nevertheless, I didn't underestimate his potential for violence and attributed that half-hearted attack to loss of balance, rather than being totally incapable.

"Pick on someone your own size," were the words that involuntarily came out of my mouth. What a crap cliché; I winced, but it sufficed.

"Oh yeah... grunt... grunt... mumble..." loud response followed by grabbing of the cue and swinging it at my face repartee. He couldn't have even seen me duck out of the way and stand straight back up, as he now squinted at the cue in disbelief at its apparent temporary fluidity. He then tried again; I caught it in the palm of my left hand, clenched and snapped it. My right hand then grabbed him under the chin, squeezed and lifted his bulk of a body off the ground. Not far, just a few centimetres, then swung him into the wall like a sack of second class Marfona potatoes.

"Why don't you both go home and sleep it off?" I politely suggested, sound advice I thought. Sorted, they obliged.

Danny wasn't often picked on – I assumed in this instance the guy cowardly went for size – as he projected an innocence that wasn't really there. I detected a disturbed psyche too, which manifested itself every now and then whenever he would get almost unconsciously drunk. No cause for alarm, you might think, but he would rant on incoherently, threatening to kill himself, and that "nobody understands". Although I would never take lightly someone's deep-down desolate cries, I didn't really believe Danny would follow through with his potentially suicidal but ultimately attention-seeking threats. He told me about his late night or early morning walks down to the ruined castle where he used to sit and stare out to sea and contemplate.

"We all do things like that," I replied affectionately, "the air's powerful here, helps clear your head." But I miscalculated, misread his mind on this occasion (I should've taken that as a sign of his compatibility). One night I suddenly heard his screams in my angry dream, a call for help drowned by colossal waves and cold salty water. I flew into his arms by tracking the signal of his mental energy and outpouring, and rescued him from the harsh sea and malicious rocks just beyond the castle. He soon came to and tried to tell me something; I pulled him closer.

"No hospital or doctor; please take me home," he implored.

"Of course." I had no intention of rushing to A&E; I'd quickly realised he required no medical assistance.

"We should talk more often; you can't go on like that," I stated softly in the morning.

"I know," he admitted, embarrassed but grateful for the sympathy and understanding. You're welcome, I kept to myself; it was time to gently invite him fully into my circle.

ORPHÉE

The first time I entered the underworld in the Gordon era, I was alone. I remember that exceptionally blustery day as if printed on my frontal lobes, as it was then I realised that the same man/woman (this person gave off no discernible gender) was on the bridge last time I went home by this route, and the time before that. And he/she was there again, watching me. Well, not really watching me but just there, staring. I could never remember his/her face once I was in the distance, as if he/she had no features at all, just a blank face. I'm not really sure if his/her presence made me uneasy, but it did give me a sense of foreboding, a hefty 'about to' sensation, but what?

I walked home the same way the following day, and the day after, and for the rest of the week. He/she was not there. I forgot about the incident eventually, or so it seemed, but still passed under that bridge once a week just to check. He/she suddenly reappeared seven months later in the mirror in my bathroom as I was shaving. His/her 'reflection' (for want of a better word – I don't think there is one to describe what I actually saw) was positioned to my right and slightly behind me. I looked around but he/she was no longer there. I turned back; it was gone. The same thing happened in a clothes shop where I was trying on a leather jacket and checking out how it looked in a long mirror. He/she was there, nodding as if they approved. Later I walked past the university chapel on North Street and turned off towards the library, strolling nonchalantly alongside the large brooding windows. The figure was shadowing me, but wasn't really there whenever I turned my head to observe.

I thought I was hallucinating: I was being haunted, but nobody else could see him/her; my friends thought I was mad. But I gradually realised or sensed who it was; inevitable perhaps after all this time. Surprising he/she hadn't come sooner. Then he/she disappeared again but only for about a week. It was an arctic-cold November evening, the other residents of the house were out, and I filled the bath with steaming water, causing a scented fog in the bathroom, wet and encompassing, clouding all the mirrors. I sunk into the tub and floated on the warmth. I was surrounded by an aura of total relaxation and meditation. The steam swirled slowly, the mirrors dripped and became opaque. I entered my mind as my body cleansed and became aware of the steam around the large wall mirror turning inside out, being sucked in and then totally dissipated. A path was clearing; the mirror was arid dry. I felt myself rise from the bath and move over it; my reflection began to shimmer, the surface was liquid. I could see the man/woman in the mirror, beyond the mirror beckoning me, calling me in. I confidently put my fingers against it, they flowed through; and so I stepped in, into the dark light, naked.

DANIEL, TRISTRAM, HARRY AND LIZA

And love? I swam around the pumping life force that glowed within a few hearts. Well, you've met Danny already – that elusive feeling of child-like innocence gradually evaporated, or, at least, the appearance of it gave way to a latent minor evil. I don't mean out and out bad, or that he was already signed to a long-term contract like myself. But he was darkly mischievous; at first I just thought it was his grim sense of humour, which appealed to me I have to admit. Some girls fell for his complex charms too, and he provided visceral pleasures, or so he claimed. But nuance and whim were seeping through the amplifying cracks, as he also seemed to be intrigued by men and wanted to know much more about me, amongst others. And I discovered he was willing to go all the way down.

"Where were you last night?" he asked one morning, having turned up at my house unexpectedly. "*All* night. I knocked at 12 and 8 – sorry, but I couldn't sleep."

"Really?" I didn't believe him. "That's a bit sad, traipsing all the way here twice. Anyway, never mind, nowhere in particular. Just out."

"Out where?"

"A few pubs, to eat, then a late party."

"Thanks for inviting me."

"Another time maybe."

"Next time I hope." There was something in his tone when he said that, something accusing and suspicious but also hinting at revelling in confirmation of those suspicions.

"You really want to know?"

"Really."

"Not now, I'm tired," I pretended. "Come round later, I'll crack a bottle of something *extraordinary*. Then we can hit the town; I'll show you the sights from a whole new perspective, if you can handle it!" He didn't know what to say; he looked ecstatic and deeply anguished all at once.

Harry was a nice guy, to use that overworked and ultimately inexpressive word. He was a fiery and heady mix of Irish and Spanish; his father was from Derry and mother from Seville. He'd been a student here a few years before but decided to stay in St Andrews and opened a bar-restaurant with his girlfriend Liza. His appearance was very medium in most aspects: average height, not slim but not overweight; neither fair nor dark, handsome nor unattractive. Our relationship was different – he was straight for a start – and unravelled comfortably in a platonic realm. We became close friends and hung out a lot, mostly just sitting around drinking and bitching about people, the world, music, films, whatever. Liza was usually there to mould a loquacious threesome; she blended easily into most surroundings and conversations. That's not to say that I didn't like her or that she wasn't interesting – far from it, she was very independent and displayed a wicked sense of humour and observation – but just secreted effortless sociability. They were the first couple I brought over to the other side, willingly of course; we all knew they were destined to be at each other's side. They still are, or were when I last saw them, unfortunately the only occasion when we were reunited.

As regards Tristram, desire would've been the right word but he didn't seem to want to play. I adopted him and his entire gang of pals as academic sons and daughters, one big happy dysfunctional family. I'd come across some odd traditions and rituals in my time, but this university won the trophy; it had a curious one all of its own. To help introduce new students to the awesome world of learning, other folks and self-development, third and fourth year undergrads would adopt families. Even though I was 'staff', as a post-grad I could get involved in this strange but entertaining scenario. It was all very cosy and resulted in a whole network of friends spread throughout the campus and town. It also involved carved-in-stone, unstoppable initiation ceremonies, the zenith of which were the Raisin Weekend festivities. Dad took the siblings out and got them all hammered and humiliated. He was also responsible for providing a Raisin receipt in return for dried fruit or preferably a bottle of wine for services rendered (the origins and meaning of all this were shrouded in the pagan mists of time and bastardised by historical Chinese whispers). In the beginning, whenever that was, the receipt had been a simple scroll in Latin. The legacy was any old object found or stolen, daubed in dodgy, half-baked Latin (or bits of French or Italian to fill in any blanks): large rocks, non-functioning tvs, Nelson-sized papier-mâché phalluses, scrapped cars, road signs etc. These were proudly exhibited, carried and pushed around the streets on the Monday following the weekend, the lucky participants (cross-)dressed up or down by mum, who also laid on tea and sandwiches the night before. Anyway, Tristram was game-on for all this silliness but oblivious to my affections. Pity, he was quite sweet really, despite a ridiculous *de rigueur* haircut involving long floppy fringe, which woefully covered one of his two pretty green eyes. He had a noble nose – he didn't like it, believing it to be too bulbous – which set the tone for the rest of his face. But I have to own up to losing my patience and temper and tossed him into the cavernous pit of the universe.

DANNY, ESSAY, BANALISM, JOKE

The little known revolutionary movement of 'Banalism' (*Banalisme*) was started accidentally in Paris in 1932 by Jean Arnaud and the great Spanish abstract painter Juan Carlos. I was lucky enough to interview Jean in 1986 a year before he died; I remember that warm July day when I drove up to his very ordinary house near Versailles. He greeted me like an old friend; now an elderly man of 81, he reminded me of Samuel Beckett, who I met a few years before that under similar circumstances. He looked haggard and tired, yet still had a youthful and slightly frightening glaze in his suede-brown eyes. I asked him about the group and how it came into being:

"There was much going on at that time," he explained, "a lot of revolutionary and pretentious artistic activity. I bumped into Juan Carlos in a bar in St Germain in the autumn of 1931; he'd been in Paris for about two years and was searching for new inspiration. I'd had enough of the fight between traditionalism and modernism and had begun to write fresh inspired works, which were basically…" he paused to think. "Well, rather plain."

He offered me a glass of under-chilled 1985 Sancerre, but it didn't take us long to get stuck into this, conversing more freely as time went by.

"It was only when we met Philippe Loiret," he continued, "and Peter Dietrich-Fetzer in March '32 that things seemed to come together. Their writings and paintings helped to focus our disjointed thoughts; from the middle of that year we all had a clear image of what became known as *banalisme*. It was Juan who coined this expression after Philippe penned possibly his finest piece ever:

The leaves are falling,

The grass is there,

I look around me

And see various things..."

It loses something in translation and certainly didn't fully convey Arnaud's emotional state, which was mesmerising. Apparently he hadn't read this poem out loud for quite a while.

"... erm, you see the implications were shattering at the time," he stuttered, then gathered himself and his memories. "He'd managed to create such depth of feeling with such ordinary non-expressionism."

Arnaud then started to produce an important series of Banal paintings, including *Scenes of a wall* (1932), *Fully clothed bathers* (1932) and *la France inchangée* (1933).

"It's perhaps ironic that all three of these pictures now hang in the Museum of Modern Art in New York," I ventured.

"No, not really," he replied.

The group was supplemented by the Polish writer Mischka Nicolaski, renowned for his political apathy, another Parisian Laurent Perrière, and the English sculptor James Edwardson. This formed more or less the core of the movement for over three years, although Edwardson parted company from the rest for holding at least four opinions at once. *Le Manifeste Banaliste* had been published in October 1932 with the startlingly bold headlines *Aucun Avis!* (No Opinion!) It was a tame anti-political treatise, which took the bourgeoisie by storm and the talking point of many afternoon teas. The main points were:

Man's fundamental will to apathy

The power of opinionlessness

The un-inspiration of nature on our inevitably limited vision

The death of politics

The beauty of the mundane

The plain-ness of existence (this clause was later removed as it was deemed too philosophical).

The manifesto contained deep pieces made up by all the artists off the top of their heads, including 'Blank Space' by Nicolaski, a poem so banal that the editor forgot to print it. The literary world's reaction was remarkable – an overwhelming sense of the ordinary pervaded the reviews and supplements.

The first exhibition took place in Paris in early 1933. Arnaud and Carlos had produced by this stage ten paintings each, every one a work worth considering for at least a minute. Carlos' *Empty Street* and *Workman doing his job* exemplify the neo-didacticism, which led onto his disinterest in film. Edwardson's magnificent sculpture *Satan* was far too expressive for most of the group and became the centre of an argument, which resulted in him leaving them. Arnaud told me of how he was arrested in 1934 during an ugly demonstration, where the Banalists clashed with Fascists in Munich (or rather they happened to be in the same place at the same time). His placard daubed with no slogan allegedly smashed a shop window, but Arnaud claimed the Nazis started all the trouble, and frankly I believe him. He never struck me as a violent man. However, the public and other artistic movements grew tired of the constant demonstrations that appeared to achieve nothing. By 1935 the group was already showing signs of creaking, and the artistic output of some of the members was becoming alarmingly communicative and sensitive.

In late '35, Carlos deserted Arnaud and ran off with the Catalan filmmaker Binos Manuel to concentrate on a new genre. Ironically, his first short, shot in a small seaside town in Scotland, portrayed many of the events from the period 1933-35, with a classic rendition of Loiret's 'Time surrounds me' poem. The ending boasts stylish flourishes from the director, as the French actor Pascal Vialard stares meaninglessly at his stopped watch and the lulling tide wets his feet on the empty beach. The re-enacting of riot scenes in the town's streets is graphically violent, as the police gratuitously beat up the band when picketing the local *charcuterie*.

Dietrich-Fetzer's paintings are of particular interest, and I have the personal pleasure of owning his 1932 masterpiece *Conflict over in Nature*. He was the most prolific of the Banalist painters, having created 42 canvases, the last in 1957 when he tragically passed away of boredom. His most well known were *Painting* (1934), *Another painting* (1941) and *Selfish Portrait* (1955), all spanning his whole unremarkable career. The use of texture is particularly appealing to add rich tone to his obsessive sweeps of brown and black colour. His paintings are also some of the most sought-after of his contemporaries.

Perrière was the only true novelist of the period but only produced two complete works before he committed suicide in 1937. I have a collection of his early short stories, which already showed a soul tortured by the mundanity of art. His first novel *Voyage* (Journey) was published in 1934, but it wasn't until his second *Un Jour* (One Day) appeared in 1936 that he received the critical savaging he deserved. His third, untitled, was only half-finished when he died, a timely exit in some ways, as the movement was pretty much expiring with him...

As I said before, that Danny had a commendably strange sense of humour. But it was back in Edinburgh where I met the most truly desirable *citoyen*. Yes, I sensed he was eminently suitable to indulge with the Mouton '87, slumbering in overcast magnificence and as old as time but faring better, denied to all but the very select. He also bolstered and helped prolong the new lust for life I'd picked up as a 'teacher', when I'd immersed myself in books and pursuits of the mind (OK, and some of the body) for far too long.

Part III

To the End of Time?

EDINBURGH, THIS TIME (MORE OR LESS), ELIOT, RACH

Gordon was sitting, without motive and unarmed, in the Final Drop enjoying a quenching bevvie, when that noticeable stranger walked into his universe. He watched him closely for a few moments; he did rather resemble Thomas in many ways. The object of attention became aware his presence was being recorded, so the observer transmitted one of his irresistible smiles. About half an hour later he went back to the bar to get another pint – Gordon followed.

"I'll get that," he said forthrightly, "I'm Gordon, by the way."

"Thanks, pleased to meet you; Eliot," he offered his hand and added, "I always accept drinks from strangers!" They sat in the corner and swapped introductory stories. Some time elapsed.

"I work at the Gallery of Modern Art, started there recently actually, in marketing," Eliot explained.

"Sounds interesting; I'm quite into modern art," Gordon said, keen to impress.

"Pop in some time, just ask for me."

"I might."

"What do you do?"

"In the wine trade, for a merchant down in Leith."

"Nice one – I'm a big wine fan." His eyes lit up, shining and naive. He continued: "Lived in Edinburgh long?"

"Not very long," Gordon lied, face surprisingly straight; then again, he must've become pretty good at telling lies by now. "Moved here a few months ago after finishing at St Andrews," he plumped up the fabrication, then added a 100% spoonful of truth; "I'm staying in a flat in the New Town, off Dundas Street."

"I was at uni here, decided to stay. I love Edi," Eliot elaborated affectionately, "I'm sharing a flat in Bruntsfield."

Gordon found Eliot very easy to talk to and was probably a little too forward that night in terms of what he told him about himself. But enough to get him curious, hooked even. The two companionable men moved on to Campbell's and on to the red wine; good choice, Gordon thought. "Do you fancy going to a club later?" he asked.

"Club, er, where?"

"The Red Bar, off Broughton Street," without sounding too familiar with the geography of Edinburgh.

"Oh, right. Heard of it; never been there though. Don't know why not."

"Too intense an atmosphere perhaps!"

"Ha! Yeah, let's go for it."

They did. Then back to Gordon's place – having opted for the nearest – much later. Then the 1787, the old smoothie. Eliot crossed the threshold into another dimension; he didn't regret it, and signed on the dotted in purest red. Gordon really enjoyed having a new soul mate and relished telling Eliot about many of those previous adventures; he always seemed to be interested. He was particularly jealous when Gordon mentioned the artists he'd known; one night as he revealed his collection of red wines, that cellar of souls so to speak:

"You met David?" Eliot strained out.

"Yes, he was a friend of Marat and president of the *Jacobins*; well, for a few weeks."

"*Jacobin*?"

"Our party, the revolutionary party. Do you like his stuff?"

"Yeah some of it… in a certain way."

"Meaning?"

"Well, you know, it's a bit dramatic and posed; stylised propaganda."

"On the right side though, on our side," Gordon countered, all high and mighty.

"Catches the mood of the times, no doubt?"

"Aye. I remember when Jacques-Louis was arrested after Robespierre, in Thermidor... I mean August, erm, 1794, and held in a studio. It belonged to one of his pupils, an *acquaintance* of mine..." He laughed at the way he'd unconsciously stressed the word but didn't divulge his thoughts on this person, "... Anyway, I took him some painting materials, to apologise for going against Robespierre and to explain why. He seemed to understand."

"How long was he locked up for?"

"To the end of the year. He was finally pardoned the following October, I think."

"What was he like?"

"A big bloke actually, quite fit and active. Hell of a fencer too. He had lovely bright eyes." Gordon paused for a second or four as he briefly jumped time barriers. "He painted an extraordinary self-portrait after he was imprisoned in this studio; most unlike any of his 'grand classical myth' stuff," gesturing suitably flamboyantly, "very simple and honest. Shows the essence of the man, still shaken by Marat's death, as I was."

"Yeah, I know which one you mean. It's in the Louvre, I think. Lots of browns, quite romantic in fact."

Eliot joined Gordon in relishing the moment; the hazy French red rendered the night as fluid as the memories and quietly closed it down.

"And lovers?" Eliot asked the following morning or perhaps the one after.

"Lots. But most were just for the pleasure of the moment or whenever necessary for... rejuvenation... or short-term company, whichever. There was one who will always be part of me, the first I suppose in some ways, but I had to separate myself from his charms sixty or so years ago... Thomas..." Gordon paused, "... he looked, erm, still looks probably, a bit like you in fact." He carried on describing Thomas, what they did, the chance meeting again, his downfall.

Eliot also had a great love for music; very varied in his taste, some would say bizarre; Gordon thought eclectic like himself. But it was Gordon who heightened his appreciation of 'classical' music, to use the misleading generic term loosely, and he seemed to be especially fond of the piano.

One distinctive lazy Sunday afternoon, they went for a walk (how amorous) and found themselves drawn into the Jug & Joanna (how predictable). A cosy, magazine-advert scene awaited them: medium-roaring fire, couple ensconced in melted settee, a forest of Sunday papers strewn around read and unread. A few other miscellaneous punters helped to populate this barn of a bar, two or three of them eating the pasta of the day, no doubt. Gordon and Eliot bought drinks (as you do), a glass of white and a creamy cocktail; Gordon idled over to the piano and sat.

"And?" Eliot said sarcastically and approached. He attacked the keys; Eliot was instantaneously mesmerised by his companion's playing. But he was performing Rachmaninov's *Second*; who wouldn't have been wooed by such a beautiful and compelling piece? He ebbed and flowed for a few minutes on a musical ocean, then stopped as quickly as he'd started.

"That's amazing. I've heard some Rach, of course, but that bit just on the piano, incredible." Eliot blurted out excitedly, visibly shaken; perhaps even a tear-ette. "Then again, I s'pose you learnt it first-hand and have had plenty of practice!" he joked.

"Not quite, but something like that. I'll never forget the concert in 1909 in New York City where Rachmaninov actually played himself, the newly written *Third Piano Concerto*. The audience was awe-struck, I cried... so complicated yet spontaneous, deeply soul-touching. And to see those amazing hands in action; his long fingers were streaming so gracefully and nimbly." Gordon waved and wiggled his hands passionately then went on: "He wasn't that well known in the States then; the Première of his *First* had been a disaster, he was completely traumatised and didn't compose anything for a few years until this, the *Second Piano Concerto*." Gordon repeated the climax, high on Russian emotion.

FRIDAY NIGHT, HUNTING, SIMON

"Come on, stop faffing about. What *are* you doing in there?" Gordon quizzed Eliot, who'd been in the bathroom for over ten minutes. Gordon had already put on his clean but not shiny favourite black shoes and tapped impatiently on the hall floor. They co-operated and signalled their approval of the piece of music that was playing them out, the climax of the *1812*, which was obviously too loud but conjured up a memory or two.

"What?" shouted from the bathroom.

"What are you doing?" Gordon repeated in competition with Russian canons.

"Coming already, just putting on a tad of scent."

"I can smell it from here – sure you've used enough?!"

"Up yours!"

Our two night-on-the-towners eventually left the flat and noisily descended the cascade of soiled stone steps. Echoes of footsteps and words bounced around and up and down, then fled. They entered the uneasy evening and turned onto Bruntsfield Place.

"Christ, it's not raining. Unbelievable."

"Boring but true."

"Shall we walk or grab a cab?"

"Walk, I think. I fancy inhaling some Friday before we get poisoned in some smoky bar."

"Which particular smoky bar did you have in mind?"

"Oh, don't care really. We could stop for one at the Student Union on the way. I've still got my old card," Eliot continued.

"Guaranteed smoke there. Yeah, why not."

It was obvious that both of them wanted to indulge a little in some studenty atmosphere, for old times' sake; youthful if not fresh. The crossing beeped its message so the guys traversed the road, checking out the grey faces of tired/excited motorists – depending on whether they were heading up or down the hill – as they gently crawled by. The Meadows (Bruntsfield Links to be precise) seem quieter and softer than the last time I walked this way, Gordon thought, then again that was Hogmanay. Doubt if I was paying much attention then.

"Neither was I," Eliot said. Gordon smiled, not surprised at his growing abilities, but pleased.

"Good, you're learning."

"Top teacher."

"Thanks," Gordon uttered modestly and strolled on further, then increased the pace, then dashed across Melville Drive, as he couldn't be bothered to wait for this crossing to change to green. Eliot had to freeze and let two cars drive past, then followed.

"Still much more to learn. Bit slow there – you would've made it. Go with your feelings; you'll soon sense the full energy of that surge, to use your vital inner power. Those cars would've made no difference. No importance to you." Eliot was a bit confused but listened intently; Gordon hadn't been wrong so far about his heightened facilities. He felt as high as snowy mountain air. They merged into the beginnings of the university as grass transformed into path to buildings and streets; they then came to Teviot Place and charmed their way into the prison-like mini-castle that housed the SU.

"G&T I think, for a change."

"Nice one, me too." To bar girl:

"Two large G&Ts, please." Duly placed on the bar with all the delicacy of a clumsy giraffe (she was quite tall). No ice. Nor lemon. E tutted, spotted a lonesome ice bucket and pushed the queue sideways slightly to reach it.

"Careful, mate," annoyed student (or so he seemed) proclaimed, having lost a third of a mouthful of flat lager.

"Sorry, but no one's gonna hear in here if I ask nicely," Eliot answered, facetious and a little bit threatening.

"He's not worth wasting your effort," Gordon whispered in his ear pre-empting.

"No lemon though," Eliot replied now indifferent to the disgruntled one, who stood his ground like a territory-protecting gorilla and continued to block part of the bar, which pissed everybody else off as well.

"We're talking about wasted lager here!" Half-seriously. Eliot laughed, Gordon watched.

"It's not funny." Student put the drinks back on the bar, presumably to free his hands. Indeed, he made a move for Eliot's throat, who in a blink snatched the approaching arm and squeezed hard, while taking a sip of his now cooler G&T. Gordon wasn't in the mood for aggravation so just focused his thoughts on the stroppy bloke.

"Just go and sit down and carry on having fun," Gordon's words blasted through his skull, although he sounded extremely calm to the surrounding masses. The guy stood, fazed for a moment; Eliot had let go in surprise, so he picked up the neglected drinks and waitered them to his friends in the corner. They were looking over at Gordon and Eliot, concerned but not indicating any malice, as if this was usual. Our two protagonists glared back at the now two lads and one girl. Mr Angry appeared to have forgotten the incident already and was chatting to the young lady. The other guy continued to stare back, grinning. Gordon and Eliot exchanged knowing brain waves without looking at one another, then both slowly proceeded through the semi-crowd and heavy smoke towards him. He had long-across eyebrows, wore a red, blue and green checked shirt and two African style wooden bead neck chords, which enticed the viewer down through the open buttons to the smooth chest below. He was one to two days unshaven, which suited him and made him look a bit older than he probably was.

"I'm Simon," he eagerly shook hands.

"Gordon, Eliot."

"This is Murray and Jenny."

"Sorry about your drink," Eliot offered, conciliatory.

"Nee bother," Murray replied.

"He's very attached to his lager," Jenny quipped to lighten the situation. All smiled. Simon subtly manoeuvred himself in between Gordon and Eliot, or so he thought, as Jenny deliberately restarted a conversation with Murray so the threesome could engage.

"So guys, what are you studying here then?" Simon attempted to ignite a dialogue, but with that line it resembled a feebly struck match.

"Nothing now," Eliot quickly saved him an embarrassing pause, "I mean, I was at uni here. I'm working now. Gordon was at St Andrews," he added to remain convincing.

"Oh right. Never been there. Pretty apparently?" Simon nervously.

"Quiet compared to here, but nice place yeah; peaceful but plenty going on," Gordon.

"I haven't been out of Edinburgh much – just to Glasgow to see a band and up the west coast. I'm not from here, you probably guessed. Born and bred in Cardiff," Simon.

"Oh, Welsh blood. Passionate!" Eliot.

They all laughed, Gordon more so; then he added: "Anyway, home is where you are now; where the heart is, as they say."

Half an hour or so passed, they seemed to connect.

"I need a piss," Simon proclaimed and departed.

"Seems willing enough. Bit naïve but not a closet case at least," Gordon analysed.

"No, just inexperienced," Eliot said deviously, and considered following him into the loo, but Simon returned strangely quickly and offered to buy more drinks.

"How about somewhere else?" Gordon.

"Where?"

"We were thinking of heading towards the New Town. Broughton Street perhaps."

"Yeah, come along if you want."

"Why not," Simon, now relaxed in their company.

Outside: black drizzle, light wind spraying it back and forth.

"This is your fault, you know," Gordon joked to Eliot, "now it's raining because you willed it by being dull and talking about the weather earlier."

"Fuck off!" Eliot snapped. Simon related to their sense of humour but was struggling to keep up at their walking pace.

"Come on, hurry up," Eliot nagged him unfairly and stroked Greyfriars Bobby *en passant*, who looked wet but content. They chased the buses over George IV Bridge, and Simon glanced back for a moment: the Royal Museum sturdy to the right, Cowgate oppressed underneath, then Parliament House ahead to the right. They turned onto High Street towards it then left down some hellish steps all the way to the bottom on Cockburn Street, across Market Street and over the not-too-busy bridge, keeping the submerged station to their right. Princess Street sparkled like a black ice rink, shadows of pedestrians, glared up by orange lights, danced by. The threesome skated into South St Andrews Street and then over the Square up to York Place. A blunt right was succeeded by a final cut through York Lane into Broughton Street.

"I wouldn't mind a quick snack, bit peckish..." Eliot.

"As usual," Gordon. "What about Café au Lait, we can get a drink there too?"

"Sorted," Eliot. They entered the café: pretty busy but luckily a couple were just leaving their table, Gordon barged through to occupy it. The other two followed in his wake.

"What's the soup?" Eliot asked the waitress.

"Black bean and chorizo. Comes with bread too."

"I'll have that, sounds fab," he machine-gunned in response.

"What do you want to drink?" Simon timidly suggested feeling neglected.

"Oh, wine I think. Not bad selection here. That OK?" Gordon.

"Er, yeah, why not. Don't usually drink wine, but..." Simon.

"Well, you should, don't know what you're missing," Eliot emphatically, and somewhat tongue-in-cheek.

"Red OK?" Gordon.

"Should go with the soup, and I fancy red." Eliot.

"Any more food?" Waitress.

"No, I'm not hungry. Simon?" Gordon.

"No, I'm all right." Simon.

"Just the soup then, and a bottle of that French Grenache please." Eliot.

"Fine."

Move on another forty minutes, all consumed.

"That was superb, really rich and smoky," Eliot enthused.

"Eliot is our resident restaurant critic, by the way." Gordon sarcastic.

"It's interesting though. I've never met people who're so into food and drink." Simon.

"Pity; these are natural pleasures after all."

The conversation had begun to fire up – the topic changed from gastronomic hedonism to education to students to art, for no apparent reason. Perhaps because of the large poster next to them on the wall, advertising a forthcoming exhibition at the Scottish

Modern Art Gallery. Eliot had already noticed it but at first didn't offer further information, even though he was involved in the publicity. Simon prompted him by also spotting it.

They carried thoughts of pictures, photos and sculptures across the road to Bar Nowhere. The atmosphere was so hip they almost tripped over it; heads turned as they approached the bar.

"More red?" Gordon pitched into the noisy air.

"Not sure, I'll probably throw up," Simon joked. Gordon and Eliot ignored him, bought more wine and proceeded to throw it down his neck.

Later Simon bonded further with them at Gordon's flat; big mistake for going there perhaps, but he didn't know that. He was intrigued by Gordon's collection of CDs, tapes and vinyl; a hotchpotch of musical taste including some recent purchases influenced by Eliot (Techno, Indie etc.).

"Some great LPs here from the 70s and 80s," Simon excitedly. "Classic Zeppelin, early Siouxsie…"

"Gordon's a bit of a collector." Eliot.

"Not so keen on the classical stuff." Simon.

"Huh, heathen," Gordon sighed deliberately, "the youth of today." Eliot chuckled, so did Simon, but understood the gag in a slightly different way. His dark brown hair with wispy fringe looked blacker in the low-lighting permeated room. It was short but not shaved-short and matched his small orang-utang nose. His greeny brown eyes (more turquoise-hazel than Lincoln-chocolate) darted around, checking out the features and fixtures in the apartment; he was slumped on the floor, leaning against the wall by the hi-fi system, next to tidy-ish stacks of CDs.

"It's more comfy on here," Eliot said as he stroked the sofa seductively. Simon, shy at first, then beamed and sat beside him. Gordon observed from across the living room as he sipped red from a huge, lovingly rounded bowl of a glass. Its aroma was magnificent and lifted him away just for a moment – Paris and

Revolution cruised noisily through his head. He watched Eliot tentatively kiss Simon, who seemed to have forgotten Gordon was there.

"After you," Gordon transmitted to Eliot. "Good to see you're learning to appreciate young full-bodied reds," he kept to himself. Nobody heard the muted cries of pleasure and pain; nobody saw the filtered red empty down the plughole, dripping away into the sewer.

PARIS AU PRINTEMPS

"It's just a bit corny; I mean, come on, there're loads of other things to check out," Eliot whinged, but frankly.

"No, really, I promise it's fab at night. The view from right at the top is superb." Gordon subtly chipped away at his will power.

"So you said." The conversation was briefly interrupted by the delicious waft of saliva-sizzling *merguez* proffered by the grinning middle-aged proprietor, brought straight from the grill-chef's inferno. The gastronomic scene located itself inside a humble but recommended Tunisian kosher restaurant on the main road through Belleville, one of Paris' more pulsating, diverse and multicultural districts. Gordon and Eliot had already tucked in to mostly unidentified but tasty *hors d'oeuvres* bites, followed by a mountain of succulent vegetable couscous and a *tagine* dish, whose resonant lemon-spices-almond-olive sauce was performing a lip-smackingly thorough job of making even chicken have some flavour.

"Ah ha," Eliot drooled and impatiently attacked one of the redhot sausages, then quickly spat out this morsel on his plate. "Shit, they're boiling!" Gordon just laughed; no comment was needed.

Earlier that day they'd walked down to the Eiffel Tower, reluctantly and unplanned originally for fear of being swamped by other tourists. It'd loomed closer still as they were crossing the grand imperial Pont Alexandre III pitched against a schizophrenic sky. Over one side of the river, charcoal and threatening, the other showing off chunks of a grey-tinged but nonetheless blue backdrop. A bright white cloud, touched by an intermittent sun, stacked up in juxtaposition to the rainy dark blanket trying to eat up the horizon and all in its path: the glass-domed Grand Palais just on the north bank and the Arc de Triomphe way beyond, essentially invisible but tangible all the same. The dazzling rays breaking through flamed up the impeccably golden Pegasus-invoking mythical statues, which stood guard above each end of the bridge; ethereal torches putting to shame the pollution-tainted columns that supported them. The woman sitting at the base of one of these, perhaps *la France soi-même,* briefly covered her eyes with a hand, glad for a glimpse of warming sunshine.

"I have to admit I'd forgotten how spectacular it is," Eliot owned up as they approached and then placed themselves underneath the Tower, gazing up and from side to side at the strutting iron structure. "It still looks, well, sort of modern even after all this time."

"Imagine what people thought of it a hundred years ago then!" Gordon.

"Yeah, radical."

Let's move on a few hours to that night: the sated duo had Métro'ed and RER'ed their way from Belleville back to *la Tour*, and now we've spotted them huddling within a long uneven queue between lifts waiting to ascend to the next level.

"Maybe this wasn't such a good idea," Gordon regretted and sighed.

"It's OK," Eliot more tolerant, "anyway, you promised a great view," he re-emphasised, but light-heartedly. Ten minutes later *voilà*, the much-hyped perspective out across the whole city, obligingly lit up like a forest of yet-to-be-felled but nevertheless daintily sparkling Christmas trees.

"Wow," Eliot, suitably wowed.

"What's that big building down there?" His dreamy contemplation was broken by a (dare I say it without making an inane racist cliché) loud American tourist with colonialist assumption that English would be understood and answered.

"Le Trocadero," Gordon butted in, stunned but in his best French accent.

"What's Trocadero?" came the drawn-out response.

"Tro-ca-de-ro," Eliot joined in deliberately unhelpful and as vociferously. They both smiled at him then turned their backs, but in their minds imagined picking up said person, pulling off the safety fencing and chucking him to a violent but scenic death; all witnessed by a shocked but forgiving Sacré Coeur, bathing in a splendid and flattering light up on its distant Montmartre pedestal.

Still panting – although lightly compared to a hapless mutt – from extreme step climbing, Eliot found himself tastefully framed in a holiday snap looking down from the tree-lined fence at the base of Sacré Coeur. Peering under the accommodating branches of one of these trees, which improvised the top and one side of our canvas, the erect Eiffel Tower was again being greedy by hogging the limelight over myriad rooftops. But hey, what a landmark. Eliot's gentle tracking shot then panned thoughtfully to the right and slowly zoomed in on the Arc de Triomphe, breathing life into it and blessing it with that tangible feel once more. They stepped across the airwaves and time itself.

Wertingen, Guntzbourg, Prentzlow, Lubeck, Raab, Mohilew. The names of the battle dead are strewn across the front of the frantic smoky scene; musket, pistol and sword are drawn and create a deliberate focus on the central figure; the *tricolore*-waving woman whose breasts are shamefully exposed due to her torn dress, *la France violée*; citizens unite and cry out around her amidst a revolutionary bloodbath.

"Shit," Eliot exclaims as a rusty but sharp-enough bayonet kisses his left cheek. He rapidly wakes up and relieves his attacker of said weapon and, without thinking, plunges it in his stomach, dispatching him to the corpse-piled ground. Gordon just about sees what happened through the smoke and chaos, then unleashes a volley himself in reaction to an approaching malevolent liberty-taker. They both glance over to the immortal flag bearer; la France, *la Liberté*.

Gordon and Eliot evaporated from the street battle – Delacroix's masterly propaganda portrayal of the 28th July 1830, *La Liberté guidant le peuple*, which they perused the day before in the Louvre – and faded back to the names carved respectfully on the inner edges of the Arc. Eliot touched his cheek and wiped off a morsel of dried blood.

"Awesome," was all he could manage. They loitered underneath the Arc for a little longer to enjoy the bravura sweeps modelled by long wide avenues: down the wet but glistening black Champs Elysées to the tall needle of the obelisk thrust into the middle of Place de la Concorde; in the opposite direction beyond Av. Charles de Gaulle and the looping Seine, the eyebrow-raising modernity of the buildings at la Défense demanded attention. Holding the picture together beautifully was the just visible but applaud-worthy square hollow torso of la Grande Arche.

STUDENT, HALL, BICYCLE

"What the fuck is that?!" Gordon abused the building they were passing in the car as they disembarked town, heading for the Forth Road Bridge.

"Andrew Bernard Hall, a university hall of residence. I lived there for a while."

"Who designed it?"

"I don't know."

"Well, he or she should certainly have been shot." Gordon downloaded his critic's speech: "Interesting 1970s practicality combined with a love of white-washed concrete, prison-block symmetry, low-cost business sense and an unusual lack of vision or of any kind of artistic aestheticism."

Eliot chuckled and played along: "Perhaps Andrew Bernard designed it and had the breath-taking wisdom to name it after himself."

"Or perhaps our AB was a famous academic who had the fortunate pleasure of teaching at this fine establishment and discovered anti-matter; in his honour they named a student hall of residence after him."

"Poor man."

"It might've been a compliment if it'd been a magnificent, grandiose Victorian edifice or a cutting-edge statement of modern architecture."

"But it's not; it's Andrew Bernard Hall!" Eliot interfaced.

"Anyway, let's not bother getting to the bottom of that mystery. It's just that it really hits you in the eye, a total monstrosity."

"Ach, you're just a bit of a design snob."

"With good reason."

"I agree it's pretty ugly but it found a place in my heart. It was my home for two of those fun four years."

"Two years!"

"Yep: room number 26 in the second block on the right there, also named after yet another fascinating explorer or politician whose history was a mystery too. My own square box with fitted wardrobe subtly hidden by nice wooden sliding – well, most of the time – door, plastic sink, tiny bed and engraved work desk; by knife rather than sculptor's chisel! It's a big hall; it was quite a shock being thrown into a whole new world full of so many naive faces."

"Including yours no doubt!"

"Ha, yeah I s'pose. But I made loads of friends, a bunch of really sound people. Some of them will remain close and dear friends until the day I die."

"The day they die."

That evening, or the following day perhaps, our heroes were *en route* to no particular destination, gossiping as usual and not paying enough attention to the world around them. Well, Eliot wasn't. Gordon stepped aside quicker than him so Eliot nearly got whacked by a marginally psychotic bike rider, who happened to resemble a student.

"Bastard!" Eliot said quite angrily but knew he should have anticipated the hazard more effectively, since there were many cyclists enthusiastically pedalling back and forth. Especially in the cycle lane, where the two plonkers had been walking.

"Come off it; it's got to be better than more cars on the road," Gordon defended the now disappeared wheeled-one.

Eliot looked puzzled for a couple of seconds, as he'd not heard Gordon express such right-on opinions before; then added: "I know, I know. Even I had a bike once."

"When in Rome...?"

"Well, it soon became apparent that beloved Andrew Bernard Hall, glorious as it was, was a sodding long trek to lectures into town. I resisted the temptation to buy a car – that would've gobbled up my grant forever."

"How wise," Gordon sarcastic, but at the same time his tone egged Eliot on.

"Most of my fellow students weren't famous for their walking prowess, let alone the desire to place one foot in front of the other in order to cover distances." He demonstrated in the exaggerated style of a 'silent' movie, "unless there might be some sort of worthwhile goal at the destination, eg a drink. Hence the ocean of bikes which flood every corner, road and pavement of our cosmopolitan town." Gordon pointed to such a pack of neglected and injured machines lovingly tied up outside a university building, then stepped into Eliot's story by putting on the narrator's glasses.

"Certainly a useful way of getting around; more efficient than walking without expending much more energy, I would've thought. Almost a form of non-deliberate exercise, if I was being cynical."

Eliot nodded and continued: "Student bikes have other uses too, you know."

"Such as?"

"They make an ideal trampoline for drunken locals – or other students, come to think of it – on a Friday night when you fall out of the pub and let out some aggression. It all added to the rich and entertaining experience of trying to ride the bike the next day, sporting a couple of croissant-shaped wheels, minus obligatory stolen lights, kicked in spokes, bent handlebars and vomit on the saddle. Another top ten favourite was to create a modern 3D montage combining lamp post and hanging bicycle motif."

"I find the symbolism inspiring," Gordon retorted as, without moving any closer, he levitated the saddest looking and only unchained specimen off the ground and gently hooked it onto a nearby lamp post. Eliot pissed himself laughing; then they withdraw from the scene more speedily than that cycle was probably capable of. The chaps found themselves, fifteen minutes later, ensconced in a Spanish restaurant gulping a rich and satisfying Ribera del Duero red. Gordon encouraged his mate to pick up the thread of his bike story.

"So, after a whole term of walking down those predictable stretches of road, I decided it was time to join the bike owners' club and become a 'non-pedestrian'." Eliot made quote marks in the air with his fingers. "I use this terminology loosely as what I actually bought could only be loosely termed as a bike. But for £15 I couldn't complain. It was one of those 'adventure family fold away into your boot and take it on holiday' bikes with ridiculous-ly small wheels. In fact, it was a 'girls' bike' as I was frequently reminded by Peter..."

"How sexist language can be," Gordon interrupted, then "Peter?" Intoning upwards.

"A, erm, sophisticated drunkard, friend and general mayhem-seeker/creator." He paused to finish off the mushrooms. "These are delicious."

"Were!"

"It was also one of those bikes, where the saddle and handlebars were in constant disagreement about being level. And the chain kept coming off. And the gears were knackered. And the brakes were a little slow. Anyway, it survived the first year and proved invaluable when it came to the frequent rides returning home 'the back way' after consumption of too much alcohol. This also avoid-ed the police as lights and other roadworthy, 'legal' requirements were very much optional extras, I'm afraid, and usually stolen if you did buy any. However, this was to lead to an encounter with the law and the beginning of the end for my faithful bike. One Friday night coming out of the student union on my trusty steed – and really quite sober, which pointed out a moral to the story, as if I'd been drunk I would've returned the back way, and the fol-lowing events would never have happened – I encountered McPlod, the local constabulary.

"'You're walking home tonight, pal. No lights,' he rightfully reminded me, pointing at the relevant bits just in case I hadn't noticed." Eliot had attempted his best Scots accent; Gordon screwed up his face. "'I wouldn't dream of it,' I reassured him, and subsequently dismounted, then started to stroll with the offending item. Of course, this didn't last long and when I felt I was out of sight, I remounted and cycled off. But not far – McPlod was cer-tainly on the ball and drew up alongside, telling me to pull over; in case I out-ran them no doubt. After the 'right to remain silent' treatment, they took all my details with a view to doing me!"

Gordon chuckled like a child and rolled his hands in a 'please carry on' gesture.

"I played along quietly – not the first time I'd come up against an officer – but performed, for their benefit, a suitable range of faces and voices expressing 'this could mean thirty years hard labour'. Then I walked back."

"What a good boy!" More dishes arrived so they made some space and ordered another red.

"Obviously McPlod had a bit of a session that..." Eliot stopped briefly to choose the right word, "... unprepared night, as when the official documents came, I wasn't the only one queuing up to sign for a recorded delivery that fateful Saturday morning at reception. The statement was a masterpiece of legal jargon and ran something like: 'under the hours of darkness, the accused was caught in possession of a two wheeled cycle machine which was not bearing a forward facing lamp, namely white, or a rear facing lamp, namely red...'"

"Good to see, in some ways, things have changed little. I've known some lawyers in my time; doesn't surprise me."

"I had to fill in a return coupon to the local magistrate indicating whether I pleaded guilty or not! Alternative strategies were pleading insanity or claiming the officer was lying and the testimony was false. Both seemed likely to piss off the court, so I put my 'it's a fair cop guv' hat on," Eliot demonstrated with imaginary head wear, "and paid the fine like a good little law-abiding boy. Mind you, they were lenient and only sentenced me to £15 instead of the customary £20, on grounds of poverty and a promise to buy some lights."

"Did you?"

"Yeah, actually."

"Ha! That's funny – you're good at stories, you know."

"Thanks. Mind you, this is my version or memory of the story.

Somebody else witnessed the arrest and claimed I was provoked and wasted the PC."

"How un-PC and unfair!"

"Yeah, it never was explained how the patrol car just burst into flames. I read a fascinating article once about spontaneous combustion."

Eliot turned up the volume of his gag as loud Latino music had invaded their space. "The bike was laid to rest in true style with full burial rites: half of it in my bin, half of it still padlocked to a post outside. It'd acquired a terminal illness: two punctures, snapped handlebars, saddle fallen off, non-functioning brakes, one pedal missing and the mischievous wrath of two friends. They decided to donate it to medical research without my permission and took a hacksaw to it, lovingly done apparently."

"Not very sporting though."

"Well, I got my own back on one of them – a radical-spirited young lady named Diane – a few months later by taking her on a trip to Dundee in a mate's car. One way; I left her there!"

"Worse than hell!"

BOOZE, HASH TART, PARTIES

"You drink a lot, you know," Gordon verbally spanked Eliot like a parental prude.

"Huh, you can talk!"

"Well, there are other ways of achieving a similar state, but they're not the methods favoured by my contemporaries, it would seem," Gordon said rather pompously then continued, even though he'd lost Eliot. "Yes, the product of the vine has allowed me access on many occasions to the depths of the soul, stripping away mortality to help me make that step. But in St Andrews, drinking beer was a relatively new concept for me, despite my times in old England, and was fun I have to admit. But wine remains the noble drug of artists and revolutionaries, in a certain way of thinking. And I never was a great fan of whisky, much to the disbelief of Scots acquaintances long buried and newly forged."

"Well, wine offers elegant inebriation; beer leads to contretemps with gardens, hedges and streams, from my experience." Gordon didn't say anything, despite Eliot's blatant leading words, but obligingly gave off an air that needed clarification. "At university, I thought I'd share some of my knowledge and experience on drinking matters and became president of the wine society *and* the ale society..."

"How very public spirited of you," Gordon added cheekily.

"Yes; one offered the possibility of introducing some civilised appreciation to a more discerning audience, but not by much; the other riotous piss-ups with um-pah band and knees-ups. The culture of alcohol was endemic; all part of the freedom-let-your-hair-down thing, I guess. We and rival societies held ubiquitous wine and cheese events which were eagerly sought out - £2.50 for a head of red steam with rubber cheddar and Day-Glo Leicester thrown in. Not bad, huh?"

"Quite."

"The beer society's answer to this was ale and crisp evenings, attended by the highest social order. Twelve pints of William McTaggart's Old Plop and seven bags of toasted thrush, sweet and sour badger or eel and chives flavoured crisps," Eliot spat out as he munched on the contents of a bag of such nibbles, although no doubt an altogether less exotic flavour. "One such soirée celebrated the democratic right of members to vote for a new committee at the AGM. Foolishly, we allowed Phil 'Animal' Jones to sort out the drinking requirements, who ordered a sizeable barrel of deep coloured and menacing beer. The casualties were high on that forgettable and forgotten malty night. Even Michael and Rachel, usually moderate and restrained, were almost lost forever, submerged in sticky brew."

He then attempted to impersonate various uni pals to render a more concrete setting to the narration. Unfortunately, his Rachel wasn't very convincing: "Good job it wasn't very deep," Rachel explained the next day.

"I couldn't wait till I got home, I had to piss there and then. But the bank, and my legs weren't up to it..." Michael continued the episode but was cut off. (More evocative, even if Eliot's Michael sounded just like him).

"Neither were mine when I tried to fish him out, so in I went too."

"But there's only about two centimetres of water in the burn at the moment," I added.

"Yeah, but enough to get soaked if you fall in twice."

"Dick-head here slipped back down the bank just after I managed to pull him out," Rachel clarified, who always was the more macho of the couple.

"And what about you. Safe and sound?" Michael tried to change the subject, obviously humiliated once again by his domineering girlfriend.

"Oh fine," I gloated, "apart from the curious discovery of a pile of flags outside this morning."

"Flags?"

"Off a golf course. The culprits have taken them back now, anonymously."

"Who?"

"Andrew and Neil. Some sort of a challenge; they brought them back in Neil's car."

"He drove?"

"Kind of. I liked his explanation though: 'Who'd have thought you could get fourteen green-flags in a Chevette?'"

"I don't know what a Chevette looks like but I don't think it matters!" Gordon laughed. His out-pouring friend went on:

"Other extraordinary booze delights included a range of stomach-crunching student cocktails, the *crème de la crème* (in overdone French accent as if clearing phlegm from his throat) being the 'Pan-galactic Gargle Blaster'. Various spirits (gin, vodka, Bacardi etc.), a bottle of Special Brew, a green element, topped up with cider and served with a straw, of course."

"Of course."

"Guaranteed stomach ulcer and unpleasant following day," Eliot confirmed, adopting the style of a cheesy radio ad as he recalled the pain felt one long Saturday AM/PM. "But I was a willing Guinea pig the previous night. Bargain at £5."

"In deep contrast," Gordon heavily emphasised *deep*, "I used to indulge in moments of pure decadence with other tutors and postgrads, or so thought those lucky few participants who I treated to a Margaux 1965. Mind you, '65 was a lousy year but I didn't tell them that – 'something I picked up from the *château* on my travels.' But for special people I had the '61; you can probably guess what I did with that!" Eliot had guessed, as personified by his enlightened expression. He took back the reigns of the memory flashbacks: "The Student Union was always well frequented, especially after 12.30 am on a Friday night cum Saturday morning. Then it was the most well, or best perhaps, frequented place, as it was more difficult to get a drink anywhere else. Without going to a club, I mean."

Eliot juggled clumsily but playfully with his words but didn't drop any. "The civilised Scottish licensing hours were extended to a hedonist extreme in the union on that particular day; the bar was open from 12 noon to 2 am, which was late in those days, remember. Unfortunately this opened up the challenge of a fourteen-hour session, a huge roller coaster of a drinking marathon. 'It's traditional' was the usual reply I received when I gave off an obviously sceptical signal; 'it's Friday after all, what else is there to do?'"

"Those were certainly strange times you were passing through." Gordon perplexed and amused.

"One particular Friday night, when we weren't engaged in the activity I just mentioned, a few of us had a little gathering... that expression reminds me of how a friend of mine, John, warned an elderly neighbour that they were holding a party. 'We're having a bit of a get-together', which unfortunately for her translated as 'we're having around a hundred and fifty people in the house after the pubs close to make a lot of noise'. But that's another story... under the guise of a phallic tea party: bring your own witty penis-shaped parsnip etc. It was the final culinary masterpiece of the evening, however, which proved most interesting. Home made hash tart, delicately flavoured with choicest herbs. We were all possessed and, for some reason that wasn't worth trying to understand after the event, we all grabbed as many empty bottles as possible and smashed them on the road outside. Much to the *chagrin* of an unsuspecting taxi driver, the first vehicle to encounter our impromptu assault course, as his tyres screamed and the car swerved into and then through the wall in front of a harmless looking church. We also decided to borrow somebody's car – shouldn't have left it open – and drove it off the docks, which was perhaps a bit ahead of its time in terms of car crime."

"Certainly. You're more of a bad lad than I thought. Where did all that innocence go?" Gordon jested.

"I met you!"

"Perhaps it was never there. So, what was it, what you were smoking?"

"Strong stuff, that Venezuelan Purple; who knows what happens to the rational brain when it gets flowing? I haven't smoked anything like that for a while," Eliot concluded somewhat regretfully.

"Were all your parties like that?"

"No, usually tamer. Actually, my friends and I were very inventive and imaginative when it came to parties; so much so that people expected an 'improvement' with each eagerly anticipated spectacle, something wilder and more happening every time. They started off innocently enough – pyjamas I think – then a new layer was added – hell and evil in pyjamas, for example. Then we ran through the whole gambit and merged several *genres*." Eliot painted the word with as much Gallic feeling as he could. "Sheep shaggers in togas disguised as famous pop stars in drag, or *Oktoberfest* as a boy scout using mandatory black plastic bin-liners for decor. Whatever the theme, the drink was usually the same: some sort of 'punch' – good word – coloured and flavoured with raspberry foam, and spiked with cheap vodka and Pernod. I suppose the *apogée* was the sacrificial destruction of somebody's no-longer-required Amstrad tower hi-fi system, lovingly dragged up the stairs then butchered with hammers to the surprise of many of the guests. The pieces were subtly placed in the bin downstairs and left for the cleaners to tut over. This latter event put an end to the free-form party: Andrew Bernard grassed us to the Warden and I had to explain what'd happened that previous night: 'well, we had a party'."

KARATE, RONIN, KAGEMA

"No, not like that. Keep your knuckles forward and flat, tuck your fingers in tight otherwise you might break one. The knuckles are the hardest part." Gordon patiently demonstrated his punch once more, trying to slow it down so Eliot could see more clearly. He watched and mimicked.

"And the key is in the twist; that's where the real power comes from." Gordon quickly flicked his forearm over and back, each time halting the potential blow in front of Eliot's face, so that he could see, hear, feel and smell the grace and pure rushing force; then the sudden controlled stop and relax. He'd been teaching Eliot for several months now, who was eager to learn all he could from his lover, companion and now Master. Gordon reached out and searched through his Eastern library, those experiences and star signs traversed around 1815 or so in Japan. It was during the Eleventh Tokugawa Shōgun when he'd become a supporter and pupil of the samurai Saigo Takemoto, soaking up all he could of the ancient fighting arts in the short period he served at his side.

"Right, more stretching exercises: legs."

"More? They're still stiff from yesterday," Eliot whined.

"Good. You can't kick effectively if you're not supple." Gordon sat on the wooden floor of his lounge, Eliot reluctantly followed. Ten minutes on. "You must curl your toes up; strike with the ball of your foot." He demonstrated a straightforward frontal kick and held the pose, tree trunk-steady on the remaining leg, which was stuck to the floor with superglue.

"It'll come, and balance too," he added to encourage Eliot, who looked knackered and frustrated. "Samurai Takemoto was always tough when training, I used to drive him mad when I wasn't concentrating..." They rested a while on the ground as Gordon reminisced...

"I teamed up with Saigo after he'd become known as a *ronin*..."

"*Ronin*?"

"Masterless samurai or roaming warrior, although you didn't really choose to do this; it just happened. He decided to go independent; the term was normally used to signify one rejected or outcast. It was unheard of at the time; then again, Saigo liked to style himself as a bit of a go-getting revolutionary type. Quite a reputation too; homo, I mean!"

"Bit ahead of his time perhaps."

"Well, it was quite fashionable amongst all these misogynist, power-obsessed men. Anyway, he said he wasn't being paid enough by his *daimyo* – lord and master – but I wasn't convinced that was the only reason. Deep down, I didn't believe he could stand it any more; the supposed superiority his position represented and the resulting segregation from ordinary folk. The ones who were really paying for these feudal warriors, by forced taxation."

"So who was top dog in those days?"

"I assume you mean the Shōgun: Ienari, another in a long line of corrupt and incompetent rulers. Saigo, myself and the few others who'd made an unwritten pact, tried our utmost to subvert his government and the *Bakufu* led by Mizuno Tadanari. He was one dodgy bastard but managed to form a powerful group and shape policy by dishing out, and receiving, bribes. He also happened to be the nephew of Ienari's favourite concubine."

"Ha! As usual, hip action dictates events."

"Oh yes, there was plenty of that. Ienari apparently had over fifty children from his many concubines."

"Randy old sod. Sounds like everybody at the top was having fun at least."

"This inner circle was very debauched, by all accounts. And the *daimyos* weren't exactly setting an example either, living it up at everybody else's expense."

"Come on, you're telling me you weren't a tad, er, lavish?"

"Well, nobody's perfect. But it did all create flourishing business in the towns, you know; the places of entertainment were crowded..."

"Brothels?"

"Yes, but restaurants and theatres too. In the city of Yedo – the population here was over a million – the theatres were packed every day, much to the disgust of the ruling classes. Well, the vaguely moral ones who didn't like enjoying themselves. You can imagine what they thought of the 'illicit quarters', as taboo named them, which didn't officially exist. There was a big rise in *kagema* – male prostitutes – and some of them were hot too!"

"So much for Confucian ethics."

"That virtually died out with Matsudaira Sadanobu, who'd resigned as *hōsa* – the adviser and regent – long before I got there. Saigo was one of his apprentices; I met him only once. He was nearly sixty then; a substantial figure, I should say, but not over-weight. Looked like a cross between a wrestler and a philosopher, if you can picture that. Massive bushy eyebrows and a sour but comic face. He'd tried to introduce reforms to stamp out corruption but was too much of an idealist to beat Ienari, who he'd actually supported originally. Not very tolerant of other ideas either, which made him less popular. Tremendous with a sword, though; taught Saigo a trick or two. And I added to the technique, a few old Scots battlefield manoeuvres!"

NEW YEAR, ROSES, POSSE, DIVE

The grandly regal old woman – modelling pressed scarlet skirt and almost clashing jacket, leopardy top hat and matching dead scarf but blotched white and black instead, huge diamond stud silver earrings – weaved through the crowd in disgust on Princes Street. She held her head to the sky, trying to avoid smelling or touching any of the commoners who had the nerve to pass her by. Eliot smiled to himself; he adored colourful characters like her, the kind you just bump into at any time. He and Gordon powered on through the icy Edinburgh air and turned up Hanover Street. They'd been doing a bit of post-Xmas shopping – why bother before when everything was discounted to death afterwards? Most had already been ripped off in the mad panic to do the traditional thing and have the full complement of presents lovingly sealed and handed over on the Day ("It's not the same otherwise"). Eliot had bought new black jeans and a vibrant green shirt (he hadn't entered his red period yet). Gordon had settled for a pair of good-old DM boots – dark brown suede, or Nubeck to be precise, and black stitching for a change. They hit George Street and had a simultaneous but brief memory blackout: neither had paid any attention as to where exactly they'd parked the car. And it's a long road.

"Don't remember; down that way a bit I think," Gordon gesturing towards the Assembly Rooms.

"Yeah, you're right. Let's move it, it's fucking freezing," Eliot complained.

"Ignore it – you won't really feel it if you try." He knew what Gordon meant and let his mind meld with his, to surf the same frequency. The car was duly recovered, started, unparked and joined in the Hogmanay spirit with all the other cars not really going anywhere.

"Shit!" Gordon slightly irritated but not much. Eliot put on a tape – the Stone Roses obligingly played 'I wanna be adored'. The guys sang along, keen to get the party mood flowing; they had a long night ahead. The engine mumbled along with the bass line, the heating cooked up an indoor gig ambience, the band did the rest.

Later: the entire area around Parliament Square and down and up High Street was packed like granules of instant coffee in an overflowing jar. Dark roast and espresso strong of course, caffeine-esque buzz mounting.

"Wow. We should've invited a few more people," Susie shouted and let out a breath of warm air that rapidly cooled and expressed itself. The gang of party-heads all held hands, forming a hopefully unbreakable chain, as they slowly edged through the throng.

"We're best just staying put, I think. We'll never move through there," Ewan doubted.

"Aye, the view's fine from here."

"What, thousands of other people trying to move!" Eliot squeezed a half-bottle of whisky out of his pocket (well, half full) and took a satisfying slug, then offered it to Gordon.

"No, thanks. You know I don't like whisky," Gordon almost tutted.

"Sorry, forgot."

"No worries – I've got my own fuel," he replied as he presented his flask like a guilty schoolboy. "Armagnac. Vintage of course."

"*Bien sûr.* Very old?"

"Na, only 1942. I've none of the original collection left, the French era stuff."

"I'll have some of that then!" Gerald insisted having overheard. Gordon handed the flask over; plenty more where that came from, he thought.

"This is mad." Susie. "But brilliant."

By now the cold seemed less cold, as the swarm of bodies huddled in the streets raised the city centre's blood temperature. A few folk had climbed on top of postboxes and bus stops to get the more civilised, higher picture. One girl was really swinging and opened her shirt and bra and jiggled her breasts seductively at the two coppers, who were attempting to sensibly ask her to dismount, although without a sense of humour failure. A seriously pissed-up bloke – quite cute actually, Eliot thought – let out some incomprehensible vodka and coke alphabet and dived into the crowd from a bus stop roof.

"Ha, cool." Gordon. "Looks like fun. Are you game?" quietly to Eliot.

"Game? From there?"

"Oh no, much higher." Gordon pointed up to St Giles Cathedral.

"Fuck off mate, you're off ya heed!"

"Trust me; indulge me. Jumping gives you a real rush." Eliot looked at Gordon bemused, unsure of what he meant exactly. But then he smiled.

"After you, Master."

"You lot stay here. We'll be back in a minute," Gordon to the others, who nodded, confused. They broke free from the chain and plunged into the noisy herd.

"How do we get up there?" Eliot asked naïvely.

"Climb of course – follow me." Eliot was initially startled by the speed at which Gordon scaled the building, but not for long.

"Feel it," Gordon shouted down. Eliot closed his eyes and, before he was conscious of it, he'd joined Gordon up on the church. But he had *felt* it, the sheer effortless power that streamed from his mind.

"Come fly with me. You'll be OK." Gordon grabbed Eliot's hand and pulled him into the air with him. His head whirled in tune with the surge of blood and oxygen; he felt fabulous as he seemed to float for a moment, then dropped like a stone towards the hordes below, still tightly clasping Gordon's reassuring hand. The next second they were standing on the road in a small clearing, which had formed by panicking people evaporating out of the way. They walked away, leaving the disbelief languishing behind them.

"Wow," Eliot uttered.

"Wow indeed. Again?" Gordon

"Ha, you bet."

"But not here, not now. We could attract too much attention."

"Next time I want to film it – as part of my 'urban movie' – first a shot of you going off, then me following with the camera."

"You and your home videos."

"I'm serious; I've already written some of the screenplay."

"Why not? Anyway, let's find the others. This way." They found them easily enough.

"Shit, you just missed something unbelievable," Gerald blustered out, still awestruck, "two nutters just jumped off the cathedral straight into the crowd. Couldn't really see what happened from here, though. Did you hear anything?"

"No, we went off around the corner for a piss." Eliot.

"A snog more like!" Susie.

"Or a shag!" Ewan. The posse slowly pushed through to the other side of the High Street outside the City Chambers.

"Now where?"

"Party of course."

"Which one first?"

"Well, we could head down towards my place. Some friends are holding a very major fuck-off party," Gordon mooed. Agreed and already on the way.

LEATHER, CUT, PASTE

Eliot sharpened the focus on the camera to fully engrave the saucy features and contours of the leather and Velcro thong on film, to catch the kinky sensuality of the minimalist costume the guy was(n't) wearing.

"Interesting party!" Steve exclaimed, drooling with excitement.

"Yeah. I feel a bit overdressed," Gordon responded ruefully.

"Well, I wasn't told there was a theme," Steve quipped then motioned his head to a couple in the corner: "Eliot, make sure you get those two."

"You'd have thought there'd be more chains." Gordon.

"No, bit *passé*."

"But plenty of sexy black and silver though," Eliot remarked nonchalantly as he filmed.

"This beer's awful." Gordon grimaced the words out as he

forced the last swig down from an unrecognisable can.

"I'll go in search of vodka," Steve offered and plunged into the now throbbing pack.

"And this is part of your screenplay, huh?" Gordon to Eliot, who'd stopped recording for the moment.

"Not exactly, but what's wrong with a bit of free improvisation?"

"Nothing, but I thought it was about an artist?"

"It is, kind of. But you never know what might work as a parallel jump cut." He spotted a hefty waft of creative leather in the vicinity and fixed the lens on the clichéd bronze statue that waltzed past.

Eliot slowly tracked back from the stark and erotic photograph and kept moving until he settled on the unassuming artist, who'd taken this and all the other photos in the exhibition at the Gallery of Modern Art. He was talking to a journalist, but Eliot filled the screen only with his image alone, just to catch his lips jiggling but without recording any sound. The scene was the opening preview of Alistair McAlpine's latest collection entitled *men and women hiding*. Thirty or forty highly charged, mostly black and white (but not all – some bathed in strong red and yellow tints) pictures of people enjoying wearing leather clothing, whether it be shoes, jackets or something altogether more arousing. Eliot had decided to take his camera along, as he wanted to integrate it into his fledgling movie. He cut abruptly and twisted around to take in the moderate gathering of gallery staff, journos, dealers and general arty types. Gordon was standing with Jane, a work colleague of Eliot's, observing one of the works and sipping champagne (supplied by Gordon). Eliot began to roll the film again and approached them, as they studied the frozen images before their eyes. Gordon became aware they were being watched and deliberately played to the camera, so to speak.

"I find the contrast of the grey sky, the derelict building in the background and her cheerful face inspired."

"Bollocks!" Eliot responded.

"Spoken like a true professional," Jane remarked and sniggered.

"They're pretty good though, no?" Eliot now more serious.

"Aye, they are. Not exactly classic Bauhaus but there are similarities," Gordon continued. Jane didn't really follow but smiled anyway.

"Any bells ringing?" Eliot asked.

"Now that you mention it..."

The times they shared in Edinburgh and Paris were good and pure (relatively); Gordon was visited by a happiness not experienced since those far away belligerent days and years with Thomas. And then Eliot left; lured to London by a better job and a change of scenery. He wrote a few times and they chatted on the phone, told Gordon how he'd developed an interest in acquiring works of art, a passion which grew beyond mere professional curiosity. Gordon also visited him there once or twice; the two lifers had some laughs just like before. But Eliot moved to Manchester a few years on and they lost touch. Gordon heard no further news, until well, not so long ago.

MANCHESTER, BEN, DETECTIVE

"Gordon?" the voice on the phone asked, nervous and hurried.

"Yes."

"It's Ben, a friend of Eliot's in Manchester. He might've mentioned me?" he continued.

"No. But I've not heard anything from him since he moved there."

"Oh," he sounded surprised and embarrassed.

"Anyway, it doesn't matter – how can I help?" Gordon added to reassure Ben; and he had the tone of somebody who needed reassuring, help even.

"Took some doing to get your number; I only had a name and Edinburgh, from what Eliot's told me about you."

"Only bad things I hope."

"Ha." Pause. "I thought you'd want to know... Eliot had got into some trouble recently..."

"Trouble?" Gordon cut in.

"The serious kind. And now he's disappeared. I don't know where to – well, I may have an idea. Can you come here; I don't want to talk about it on the phone? I'd be grateful for your help; I think it's something you'd want to deal with, could handle better than me."

"Give me your address and number..."

Gordon took the first train he could catch from a less hectic than normal Waverley station and sat watching the calm countryside blur past (Edinburgh and environs had now faded from sight). Unlike his mind, which had moved to top speed, faster than the train as thoughts and ideas came and went. He was looking forward to this little mystery, this detective story. Gordon put on his long coat and trilby at Piccadilly station and hogged the shadows, trailing the crowds of arrivers.

"Jesus," Gordon said out loud, crossing between legions of buses no doubt going too fast and headed up to Piccadilly Gardens. He suddenly realised he hadn't been here for three hundred and fifty years: it couldn't be; he had to wrestle through a library of memories to fix on a date. But no, he didn't remember being in this city since the encounter with the Earl of Manchester; but then it wasn't a city, of course. How bizarre; and he thought *Edinburgh* had changed. Gordon had checked on a map how to orientate himself towards Chinatown and so took a left onto Portland Street. What was that monstrosity, a horrible hotel on top of a large boxed parade of shops or something? Nasty dirty concrete; no imagination. Ruined the whole appeal of potentially a grand European square, especially with those trams toot-tooting across. Pity about that bus station too. He almost spat out solid diesel fumes and then took a second, longer look up to the hotel. It was stalked by a run-down, possibly disused tower, which struck him as offering better visual appeal. The coloured or perhaps weather-stained dark glass windows were easier on the eye and smoothed out the practical-over-pretty design of the whole. Why hadn't they just let it do its own thing and stand free, instead of on top of that thing? That might've worked; what a mess it made of the focal point of Piccadilly. Gordon strolled on further, unfazed by the traffic din and stressed-out motorists. He peered into and up at another hotel as he passed – the Old Portland – which seemed to coax you in more effectively: cosy chairs, old-fashioned uniforms, top-hatted geezer at the door. Then the British Hotel – a kettle of fish of its own – magnificently kitsch wedding cake entrance hall seething with bright lights, loud and dark fabrics and huge fake chandeliers. On the roof he could just about see, craning his neck, some sort of stone-carved wagon wheels all in a line adorning the fascia, like fancy gun slots on a fort. They looked even odder when it got dark, illuminated by hundreds of Christmas tree lights, but Gordon didn't know that, of course. He was suddenly almost mown down by an aggressive pram being employed as a weapon by a grumpy mother; Gordon, unawares, had become acquainted with the original scally family. The picture was complete: mum and dad and two different-sized kids, all dosed up in matching grubby shell-suit trousers and crap baseball caps.

Gordon quickly crossed Portland Street and took a right into Charlotte Street. The Chinese Arch soon presented itself to his left and confirmed he was where he wanted to be. It lured him down the street on the left, and he decelerated his walking pace. Three solid rows of neon restaurants, aromatic supermarkets and Chinese-calligraphed offices formed a large square, all surrounding an inevitable car park. The Arch was dynamic and imposing and created an illustrious approach to the road he was strolling down.

"Excuse me, where's Faulkner Street?" he asked the pretty Chinese lady.

"You're on it," she responded cheerfully and in a taken-for-granted, nasal-twang Manchester accent, "but it carries on over the road past the Arch."

"Thanks." Gordon idled on a few metres. There it is, the Bay of Opportunity, he thought and entered the restaurant. Ben looked very different from what Gordon had pictured: strange how you could form an image of someone from their voice alone, and how wrong it proved to be when you met them. He could see why Eliot had got close to Ben, apart from his unusual looks: alluring East Asian iced with a dollop of Celt. He was intelligent and articulate and, despite the concern buried under his words, had a commendable sense of humour. He offered a glass of a zesty Riesling *spätlese trocken* made by a grower Gordon had visited in the Rheinpfalz.

"No doubt chosen by Eliot," he pitched in, smacking his lips and enjoying the cheek-puckering finish, "only he would suggest something this obscure for a Chinese restaurant." Ben smirked.

"It sells, actually," he defended Eliot's choice sternly. Gordon admired the loyalty in his tone.

"Good, deserves to." Pause. "Anyway, what can you tell me?"

"Where do I start? Well, we were having a bit of local trouble, a gangster called Kar-Wai, but that's no major deal. We can resolve that, I think. I doubt it has much to do with Eliot's disappearance, but could be a factor. Kar-Wai has tried to hit us but my family is stronger."

"Not sure I should get involved in that, although I can be quite persuasive. Perhaps I should visit this guy."

"It's OK, you don't need to."

"Up to you." Gordon had already decided to help out but didn't communicate these thoughts. Any friend of Eliot...

"The police were after Eliot as well. They did arrest him but he escaped."

"That's my boy!"

"They've been hassling me a lot. I've been in for questioning but gave them no useful information."

"What do you have for me?"

"It might be connected with two mates of ours; they're missing."

"Missing?"

"Presumed dead. But there's no evidence suggesting Eliot."

"What do you think?"

"Don't know. He did always have a mysterious side; I never fully understood him."

Gordon tried not to laugh, but Ben sensed he knew what he meant and creased his brow.

"Never mind. Anything else?"

"Yeah, as I said, something mysterious that was bothering him. Somebody mysterious; his past haunting him perhaps. I'm not sure, he didn't explain."

"Sounds like nothing," Gordon lied. So the Doctor had caught up with Eliot before me, he pondered, in this time at least – I'd met him once and I had that warning, that vision just a handful of years ago too. I must find Eliot.

"Any clues as to where he's gone?"

"Possibly – I didn't tell the cops this, but they'll probably find out eventually. He flew to Hong Kong. To pick up some merchandise." Gordon gave him a quizzing look that didn't require words.

"Pictures. A friend of ours received them a few weeks ago. She runs a gallery there." Ben gave him Charlie's card.

GORDON, BEN, PUB, PRAGUE

"Do you know where they lived?" Gordon asked.

"Damien in Chorlton, Mark in Cheetham Hill. Why?" Ben obliged.

"Oh, I might have a look around, for some evidence or clues. What are the addresses; do you have them?"

"Yeah, I've got Mark's in my diary. But I didn't really know Damien that well. Somewhere off Wilbraham Road, I think, which is very long by the way."

"Great." Gordon took another pensive swig of his beer.

"Want me to come? I know the area a bit."

"Uh, maybe. I don't want to implicate you in what I have in mind, make you an accessory."

"What do you have in mind?"

"Well, I'm not going to search for the kind of 'evidence' the police have no doubt already combed for. Something much simpler, something to plant perhaps. Maybe on the premises of your gangster 'friend'." Ben smiled.

"I see. Good idea; life would be more comfortable around here with Kar-Wai behind bars."

"At the same time we'd be giving the police what they want – the possibility of solving a messy, clueless case."

"Perhaps we could add a little more petrol on the fire." Ben was obviously enjoying unravelling those possibilities.

"Like?" Gordon.

"Some other 'evidence'. Virtually all his money comes from trading in drugs; he's one of the biggest in the region. But clever though – Narcotics haven't managed to find much on him, of course."

"Of course."

"You know, the usual chain of command and network; he keeps himself well distanced from the street."

"Sounds like you know quite a lot about the business."

"Just enough to keep tabs on Kar-Wai. We're not involved in that, not interested. So, if we gave the cops a little helping hand, there'd be no repercussions on us."

"Everyone needs a little help every now and then!" They both chuckled and paused for a moment, finishing off their beers. "Another drink?" Gordon asked him, raising the tone of his voice. "This is getting more interesting by the minute." On returning from the bar, Gordon decided to change the subject back to Eliot.

"So, you and Eliot were pretty close then?"

"I guess so. We just seemed to... get on really well..." Ben stuttered, slightly embarrassed at Gordon's question.

"It's OK, you don't need to be shy with me."

"He's probably the nicest guy I've ever met..." Ben winced at what he said. "I hate that word – *nice*!"

"Well, sometimes it works. How about interesting, sexy, eccentric. On occasion deliciously evil too, wouldn't you say?"

"Er, not sure...."

"You really don't know, do you?"

"What?"

"About... his other side."

"Well, I did suspect something odd, or rather, different about him. Powerful... other-worldly... but I just couldn't believe..."

"Believe it." Gordon loitered on these two words, then laid it all on him in simple terms. Ben was astounded and turned on at the same time.

"It's difficult to take."

"Why? Let it go, destroy your perceptions."

"Why didn't Eliot... turn me into, er, one of you?"

"Dunno. Maybe he felt you weren't ready, or he ran out of time. Perhaps he didn't want to. Out of respect or whatever."

Ben wanted to add something but hesitated, then nervously asked: "Would you?"

"Do you realise what you're asking?" No reply. "Well, I can't deny I find you attractive and I sense a thrilling life-force coming from you. But I can't. Eliot 'found' you and didn't. I have to assume he had his reasons and respect his wishes. Maybe, but not now."

"Bring him back then. For me."

"For us." They both smiled an African sun and remained quiet for a moment.

"Oh yes, he gave me this just before he left. Rather, he left it for me at the restaurant. No note or explanation, but I s'pose it says everything unsaid." Gordon beamed and almost wept at once. Ben sensed his emotional disarray: "Yes. I gave him that when he left Edinburgh. It belonged to a very charming companion... long time ago... wonder where he is now?" Searching but rhetorical.

"I see. I don't know anything about its history but figured it symbolises powerful bonds between people close to one another... you should have it back then," Ben stated and went to remove it.

"No," Gordon snapped. "You hold on to it. It's best that way." The two of them both took deliberate and deliberating gulps of their drinks.

"He went on a big trip, you know, around the world sort of thing." Ben to de-intensify the air.

"No, but it doesn't surprise me. It's normal for us, but particularly for him. Never could stand still for very long."

"Yeah, too right!"

"Where did he go?"

"Oh, here and there. Across and around Europe a fair way; to the States."

"Did he tell you much about his travels?"

"So many questions!"

"Sorry, but it's useful for me to fill in a few blanks. Those missing years could be important, if we're to find him, save him."

Ben was glad Gordon used the term "we're"; he liked being considered part of the team by his new friend. He refreshed his mouth and throat with cool Sauvignon Blanc, as Gordon had bought a bottle of white without asking him what he wanted to drink. But good choice though, he thought, and continued: "Well, it's funny. He talked a lot about some of the places he went to, like Paris and Barcelona, and people he met, but hardly anything about others. I remember particularly his short visit to Prague – at first he said he only 'passed through' and didn't do much. But slowly he revealed more…" Ben adopted an intentionally dramatic posture and intonation, switching to story telling mode… "He stayed in the city centre…er, the First District?"

"Yes; it's called Praha 1."

"Anyway, he said between the Old Town and the Jewish quarter. It's a bit mysterious; he ran into somebody who, well, scared the living daylights out of him. He said he resembled an old friend…" Ben paused as he looked at Gordon's face once more. He must've thought a piece of the jigsaw had slotted into place, "… maybe from Edinburgh, now that I think about it. You weren't in Prague then, were you?"

"No, not for a long time."

"Hmm. But he did say he was mistaken. One day he was strolling around a quiet residential area where there were some offices too – you know, tall old buildings with several storeys. Suddenly someone he recognised appeared at a doorway, called out 'Eliot' and beckoned him in. He followed him up a majestic, sweeping staircase almost to the top where he met a middle-aged woman, who said he was expected and had an appointment. He entered a small, sparse office with nothing more than a desk, two chairs and a filing cabinet, and was told to wait. When Eliot asked 'who for?', he was told 'Dr M.' At least, I think that's what he said; the story was a bit vague and I can't remember all the details."

But Gordon found it a little difficult to believe, or it entered his mind in this way, as in contrast Ben was in fact being quite precise. Never mind, he thought, you're so suspicious, and added: "Doesn't surprise me. The last time I saw him, in London, he seemed to be experiencing more and more problems. Vivid hallucinations, dreams, whatever. I don't know if it was just his imagination, or perhaps he was smoking too much weed!"

Ben laughed in a 'sounds familiar' way, then completed Eliot's tale: "He definitely said he sat in the office for a while, but nobody came. When he tried to find the woman he'd met at the top of the stairs, she'd vanished."

KAR-WAI, SORTED, AU REVOIR

Gordon switched off and stood absolutely still, his soles velcroed to the dusty and uneven concrete floor. Somebody had opened the door above the cellar – or storeroom or whatever it was used for – and was noisily plodding down the loose wooden steps. Just an unlucky coincidence, Gordon thought; I couldn't have been heard, I didn't make a sound. He'd easily forced the door at the back of the building, hidden until he'd climbed down a rubbish-strewn bank, and closed it carefully behind him to conceal the unwelcome entry. Shit, this won't work if I have to make one of his men disappear; Gordon's mind worked overtime to calculate the best move. But he's bound to see me if I budge even one centimetre. Too late – Kar-Wai's unsuspecting henchman (or perhaps cook for all he knew) jumped back in fright when he saw Gordon, who now accelerated upon him.

"Don't worry, you won't remember this," he joked then sucked out the guy's consciousness. He passed out. Gordon caught him before he fell to the floor.

"Perfect." Gordon arranged the scene to make it look like the bloke had fallen down the steps and knocked himself out. He'd already ensured that he wouldn't recall seeing him; those events no longer existed in the guy's memory banks.

Gordon almost floated up two or three flights of stairs in the old warehouse building owned by Kar-Wai and occasionally used for meetings or beatings. Fortunately, and as he'd sensed before entering, there weren't many people around; apart from the 'fall guy' down below, Gordon had only seen one other, who certainly hadn't noticed him as he gracefully stalked around. A kitchen; ideal, Gordon thought as he penetrated said room. He placed the items and substance he'd brought along for the job in a steel-doored cupboard at floor level. Not too well hidden but not too easy to find. Our detective-provocateur turned into air.

"Greater Manchester police." Presumably a copper, as Gordon stood calmly in a nearby phone box.

"A tip – get your CID friends to check out Mr Kar-Wai's premises on Tariff Street, near the station. It might help solve those two local murders. Dodgy chef, you know."

Back at The Bay, Gordon placed another prawn dumpling in his mouth and sized up the rest of the dim sum selection in front of them.

"They were raided last night, according to my spies," Ben confirmed.

"Let's hope they're decent detectives, huh!"

"So, you're leaving when? Tomorrow?"

"Yep; 11am flight."

"Can I come? I want to help."

"No, I don't want to put you in danger. And... don't know if and when I'll be back. Depends on many things, many variables." Then much less dramatic: "But thanks anyway."

HONG KONG, NOODLES, OZ

As the aircraft autographed the lonely sky, Gordon realised he'd never been to Hong Kong before, or even the mainland. How odd, why hadn't I explored the Far East, he thought? Hardly due to lack of time. That all too brief trip to Japan was all I could boast in my psychological passport, a welcome escape from Europe before my adventures in America. Mind you, I did flirt with the Chinese border to crow-fly to Vladivostok, if that counts. Gordon wondered if Eliot was still in Hong Kong – he remembered the fascination he held for Chinese art and culture, martial arts and food – as he savoured a thick, fruity red wine. He surveyed his fellow passengers; a veritable microcosm of international faces, each wearing a different identity kit but many a similar expression: angst or stress. It was obvious some business people were feeling obliged to maximise the time available on this fairly long flight: reports to finish for the boss, memos, plans, ideas, meetings. Gordon could see frowning faces ageing by the minute and on this occasion, for a change, he sympathised. Who could say what might happen at the end of this journey, wherever it may be? Perhaps his timeless face would begin to wither; perhaps his mortal genes would be kicked back into operation. And now it didn't seem to matter any more: after aeons of living, deep down Gordon didn't care how the situation would resolve itself. Perhaps the inevitable appeared more appealing than the evitable; the key was that he found Eliot, that they could be together again, even if only for a few hours or minutes.

Gordon closed his eyes and smiled warmly, then reopened them and scanned the passenger profile again. An Asian woman (hard to tell if Chinese or from somewhere else – her complicated, attractive face didn't readily betray her birthplace) across the aisle looked like the only other one enjoying herself, as she chatted to a... no, she wasn't, she was singing to herself. Yes, she was wearing slim-line headphones and was wired to something quite dramatic and emotional, opera or blues perhaps. Some old guy a few rows down, although probably younger than he appeared, coughed again and forced his cigarette-browned fingers through his remaining hair, as if it might help him think and relax. He was wearing a dull but smart-ish dark navy blazer with once-fashionable gold cuff buttons, a washed-out yellowy beige shirt, handkerchief to almost match stuffed in the blazer breast pocket, and a blue and pale yellow (again desperate to match) striped tie, which sat embarrassed, the wrong way round. His face and all those around soon faded from colour to black and white, as Gordon wandered off from the scene into the deepest buried nooks and crannies of his mind.

"He wouldn't tell me specific details, he just said Australia," Charlie explained over dinner. They'd arranged to meet at the restaurant at 8pm, it was now 9.20 and they'd feasted comprehensively. Exotic flavours lingered on Gordon's taste buds as he sipped refreshing, delicate Chinese tea. She was impressively direct, with an ordered brain; he listened further.

"He said he couldn't tell me, things could get dangerous. I suspect he's in Sydney."

"Why Sydney?" Gordon didn't let Charlie answer: "Hang on though, thinking about it, makes sense I suppose; yeah, that would be my guess too."

"Most of the cut and thrust of the art world is there." He found her use of words amusing.

"Amongst others," he added. She obviously got the joke as a knowing smile stretched across her face.

"So, Sydney; that narrows it down." Sarcastic, then asked: "Any contacts, any leads you can give me?"

"Perhaps. Come to the gallery tomorrow." Unnecessarily obscure, Gordon thought.

SYDNEY, JOHN, FOR SALE, THE DOCTOR

Who would've thought it would end in Sydney? Anyway, no time to pontificate, I've got things to do. Eliot's mind is racing. His brief stopover in Hong Kong was fun; Charlie was on good form. She'd stored the crate of precious souls in the gallery warehouse, those ageless portraits concealed behind others. The crate is now in a warehouse (more like a garage actually) that Eliot has rented, which is where we find him checking the 'merchandise'. Or that's the plan, sort of – he's hoping to sell these for much more than mere money. No price could be placed on that collection; just the value of his life perhaps, immortality or damnation.

A few weeks later. John and Eliot are sitting comfortably outside a café on Campbell Parade overlooking übertrendy Bondi Bay, enjoying a light lunch. Eliot felt he needed a serious injection of reality to off-load too much mental activity.

"Phew, lighten up mate; all this heavy shit on your mind, it's not healthy!" John jokes.

"And highly dangerous," Eliot adds, laughing.

"So what now? You're here for good or just a stop-over on another world tour?"

"No idea. That decision might be beyond my control. Let's wait and see. Either here for good or..." John looks at him, confused. "... Anyway, forget it... what did that publisher say yesterday, about your new novel?"

"Looking good – I think they may go for it. I'll know in a few days."

"Needs time to get to grips with it, perhaps. It's pretty fucking weird, after all!"

Eliot watches passers-by and gazes out to sea; the waves turn up the volume so he doesn't hear John anymore, just sees his lips moving in a fox-trot. The hypnotic ocean helps to decelerate

Eliot's mind, dims the bright pictures to a fade. He feels a little more at ease with the world.

The hyperactivity is now going on around them rather than in Eliot's head: that night they are, predictably, out on the town. For some reason they're drinking cocktails – not usually Eliot's thing – but John suggested it for the hell of it. They're in the Great Atlantic Green Room in Paddington: noisy mixed crowd, live jazz of the frenetic and modern style. Seems to fit the mood.

"I told some friends to meet us here, then we'll take in some other bars," John almost shouts in Eliot's ear. They arrive, as if they heard him.

"This is Tim; Bob," he introduces.

"Pleased to meet you, guys. What you drinking? For some strange reason, we're on Margaritas." Eliot offers.

"Yeah why not, the same... spot the queens!" Tim joins them in mutual parody.

Next stop – the Volcano Bar back on Oxford Street. Much calmer, young, hip crowd; or at least until they came in. They sit down in one of the lounges tucked away in a corner. White wine is the consensus – tastes like Sauvignon – and gets the posse talking more.

"No, I can't tomorrow, I've got a meeting," Eliot turns Tim down for lunch, who didn't waste much time. "At midday, at the Museum of Contemporary Art... dinner would be good?"

"You're on. I'll meet you here, say 8.30?"

"Fine."

"Watch out for him," John jokes, "I hope you'll tell him about your interesting pet and the disease it gave you." Directed at Tim.

"Fuck off mate." Good sense of humour, Eliot thought. He'll probably want to know more about me than I should say... it transpires that Tim is a marine biologist and does have some interesting pets of the underwater kind, but alas, is disease-free.

The team end up at some dodgy haunt called the Cab Club;

John is a member, the drinks are cheap and it's open 24 hours at the weekend. Functional pleasure palace with half-hearted transvestites thrown in. Still, it was a laugh; or Eliot is trying to convince himself of that today, ie the following morning at 11.30. He's more than half an hour away from the Rocks, where the gallery is, physically and spiritually. He decides to change into his brave face; anything's better than the one he was wearing.

The director of the museum liked Eliot's proposals for an exhibition and asked him to 'develop the concept'. She's also interested in his 'secret' collection, from a black market point of view (she looked so honest as well, at the outset), and wants to introduce him to a colleague in a couple of weeks time, when in Sydney again. It's now two weeks later and, although you may've thought Eliot should be surprised, he's not in the slightest bit so, when the mysterious colleague reveals himself as he joins them in the restaurant. He smiles deliciously at Eliot, who laughs, resigned to fate.

"What now?" Eliot asks.

"Let's order dinner at least and discuss the possibilities," he calmly replies, "maybe a last supper of sorts." Very amusing, Eliot thinks.

"Dr Mabuse is a reasonable man, after all, as you know."

GORDON, TIM, JOHN, SEARCH

Gordon is strolling down Oxford Street with heavy feet, contemplating his next move. Charlie gave him some names – acquaintances at art galleries and dealers – but the trail is frosty up to now. He rang up a couple of them, visited a couple more, but no leads; nobody seems to know of a stranger in town who may have a small private collection. But I know he's here somewhere, I can feel him. In Hong Kong I wasn't sure but here, now... I can smell his sexy aroma and hear his dreams, Gordon thinks. Still, I've got more contacts to follow up and haven't tried the main galleries yet. Too obvious perhaps, or too foolish.

Gordon wanders into the Museum of Contemporary Art, which resonates with peaceful and airy aura. He rotates on the spot in order to engage some of the works; looks interesting but I don't have time for that.

"Who's the director in charge or head curator?" he asks a bored member of staff.

"Anne Reynolds; she's both I reckon. Her office is upstairs. Shall I buzz her?"

"No thanks, it's OK. I'll catch up with her another time." Gordon pretends to leave then sneaks back past the desk and up the stairs like a panther. Luckily, Reynold's door is made of glass, so he can get a good butcher's at her.

Later, outside. The gallery director comes out so Gordon follows, not too close but near enough to keep tabs. It's lunchtime; she goes into a café, now noticing her tail, as he intended. She sits, so does Gordon.

"Mrs Reynolds, could I have a quick word?"

"If you must. Why did you follow me in here?"

"I'm looking for a colleague of mine, Eliot Murphy; it's possible he might've been to see you?" Gordon makes up a surname.

"Eliot who? Never heard of him."

"He's probably trying to sell some rare pictures."

"Probably? You don't sound very sure; I find it difficult to believe you."

"Please just think about it for a moment."

"I'm very busy you know, I can't remember all those who might just turn up unannounced."

"Recently perhaps?"

"If it was recently I'd remember him. No, I'm sorry but your friend hasn't been to the gallery," Reynolds lies unconvincingly and picks up her handbag, opens it and pulls out a card. "Try a friend of mine; sounds more likely he'd go to somebody like him. But I think he's in Melbourne at the moment."

"Thanks," Gordon takes the card and leaves, not trusting her one iota but doesn't want to push it too far. Nevertheless, he does check out the address on the card the next day and, afterwards at random, pops into a small but plush office housing another dealer on the same street, just to be thorough.

"Melbourne? Oh, right," Gordon receives another off-putting answer, surprised that Reynold's story actually holds water. "Will he be back soon? Can anyone else help?"

"I'm afraid not. We're not a large company; Mr Smith handles such matters," comes the snooty reply. Gordon gets the impression there's a conspiracy forming before his eyes. Maybe I am in the wrong city, he ponders... no, trust your instincts; shit, after all this time!

A few weeks have elapsed. Gordon goes into Café Solo on Oxford Street for late lunch, coffee and thinking. It may've been pure luck that he chose this place at this time, or perhaps fate whispered in his ear. Either way, it seems so unlikely Gordon just goes with it. As the seafood soup is delivered with panache, he hears two people talking at the table next to him. Did he say Eliot? Gordon's mind tunes in to a stronger signal and he eavesdrops further.

"Yeah, he's really nice. Refreshing change from this lot."

"And cute no doubt?"

"Of course, but in a different way; not your normal fake-pretty."

"And Eliot, what kind of a name is that?"

"Dunno. Not sure where he's from – could be English, Irish or Scottish! He's been around."

"I bet."

"No, I mean well travelled."

"Excuse me, but did you say Eliot? Sorry for being nosy, but it's important," Gordon butts in. Tim and his friend give him a half-dirty, half-curious look. "My name's Gordon, I'm looking for an old pal called Eliot. I think he might be in Sydney." Gordon introduces himself and joins them at their request. The efficient waiter moves his soup with much fuss.

"I'm Tim, this is Veronica," Tim points first to himself then his lady friend, as if there might be confusion.

"So, he just arrived a few weeks ago, from Manchester..." Gordon reconfirms the facts he receives, the words he wants to hear.

"Have you known him long?" Veronica asks.

"Several years but we lost touch. A friend of his in Manchester contacted me, and I decided to try to track him down," Gordon answers without adding any revealing details.

"Why? I mean, coming all the way here; sounds a bit serious?"

"Not really. But it's important I find him quickly... personal reasons... too complicated to explain." Gordon transmits no further information and closes their minds so they lose the thread of the conversation, then continues; "So, do you know where he is today?"

"No," Tim responds vaguely, "but we're meeting him later tonight. He's got a dinner date somewhere first," he adds, obviously jealous of Gordon's potential presence in his new arrangement.

"Dinner, who with?"

"Don't know. Why don't you join us later and surprise him." Tone is a little less bitchy.

"I need to find him right away." Gordon realises he sounds rather dramatic and tries to lighten his questions. "It could be important, as I said."

Tim and Veronica become slightly suspicious but still believe Gordon is a genuine acquaintance; he seems to know Eliot very well.

"John might know." Veronica.

"John? Where can I find him?"

"He's probably at home finishing his novel. Deadline's way past!" Tim. Gordon remains silent waiting for further information as his expression demands. "He's a writer (you don't say, thinks Gordon, most novelists are), met Eliot before us. Lives quite near here."

Gordon demolished the soup – shame as it was tasty – and is now buzzing John's apartment. No answer. Buzzes again, and again.

"Shit," out loud, then decides to hang around. Nobody shows up, Gordon goes for a walk around to kill some time. Four hours later, a reply:

"Hello."

"Is that John?"

"Yes."

"I'm a mate of Eliot's from Britain; Gordon."

"Oh... right," John hesitates, surprised of course. "Come up. Second floor." Gordon pushes the door as it's released and bounds up the stairs to 22. He finds John very warm and charming. He explains the situation, to an extent; John seems laid-back.

"Yeah, he said he was meeting some people for dinner. Actually, he gave me the card with the restaurant's name and address. It's around here somewhere. Hang on a minute." Gordon tries to look patient, as John hunts around calmly, but feels time is dripping away. Unfortunately John's flat is a real mess: paper, newspapers, empty and unopened cigarette packets and used cups form a layer or two everywhere. He'll never find it amongst all that, Gordon thinks.

"Ah, here we are." He suddenly contradicts the stray mental words; "*le Grand Oeuf*," he reads off the card. "Quite good apparently. If you want to catch him, you're best taking a cab." Gordon grabs it, thanks John and mutters something about seeing him later. John looks slightly taken aback but certainly not bewildered.

END 1

"Champagne, I think; I mean the real French stuff?" Mabuse quizzes the waiter. "Preferably Charles Heidsieck, if you have it. I know it's my friend's favourite." He gestures to Eliot. Just what the doctor ordered, Eliot says to himself. Said fizz duly arrives. Eliot appears impressed by this restaurant, the name of which doesn't seem significant anymore or who else is here. He examines Mabuse's face, trying to record and describe it, but it's impossible. The features are so striking, yet Eliot cannot picture them, as if there's no face; every time he blinks or looks away briefly, the images erase themselves.

"Cheers, to your health!" M purrs.

They drink and talk; an amount of time passes. The Doctor suddenly gets up and draws two sparkling silver guns.

"*Adieu*," he proclaims before opening fire on Eliot, who feels the warm silver bullets tearing through his soul and the voices of other souls released gasping through the wounds. He seems to fall slowly to the ground then looks up for the last time at M, his face is now clear; Eliot is standing there looking down at himself, a vicious smile across his face.

Gordon hands the taxi driver a note and adds, "Keep the change." Here it is, *le Grand Oeuf*, he thinks, takes a deep breath and enters the restaurant. He senses fear, elation and released pain in the air. There's a body on the ground and somebody pointing a gun at it. Gordon seems to recognise them.

END 2

"Cheers, to your health!" M purrs.

They drink and talk; an amount of time passes. Eliot begins to feel a little strange inside, rather hollow, as if the energy is being slowly sucked out of him.

"I'm not interested in your pictures, they're not going to help you," M finally announces. He stares at Eliot, his face now very clear; so much fear and hate, joy and passion in those burning black eyes. Eliot tries to penetrate deeper into his eyes but they are empty; two barren, dark caves. The Doctor suddenly gets up and beckons to Eliot, who follows him into the toilet. There's a large mirror on the wall but neither of them throws a reflection. They walk through the melting glass shimmer. There are some stairs on the other side and they descend; can't see how far down they lead.

Gordon hands the taxi driver a note and adds, "Keep the change." Here it is, *le Grand Oeuf*, he thinks, takes a deep breath and enters the restaurant. It's not particularly busy, scattered handfuls of diners here and there. A lady brushes past him in a hurry on her way out; Gordon scans around for a few seconds. Eliot is not here.

END 3

"Cheers, to your health!" M purrs.

They drink and talk; an amount of time passes.

Gordon hands the taxi driver a note and adds, "Keep the change." Here it is, *le Grand Oeuf*, he thinks, takes a deep breath and enters the restaurant. It's not particularly busy, scattered handfuls of diners here and there. He scans around for a few seconds; his heart misses a beat or two then pounds, as he spots Eliot and a familiar (although he's never seen *this* face before) eating companion. He quietly approaches.

"Gordon!" Eliot is surprised, to say the least. "What the fuck..."

"Long story; but I'm here now." Gordon replies calmly, trying to conceal his excitement at seeing Eliot again.

"Indeed. How are you Roxburgh?" M states, matter of factly, and smiles; "Join us for a drink."

"You two are obviously acquainted?" Eliot says and asks at the same time, a touch confused, although he knows there's no reason to be. No response from anybody at the table. The gallery director nods politely to Gordon as he sits but says nothing. Gordon smiles back and thinks: 'Bitch'.

"So, this is a merry little gathering. What's the outcome to be?" Gordon business-like. Eliot exudes a lingering glance at him; he's relieved to perceive his presence, very glad he's found him.

M sits and ponders, looking from one to the other. Then: "I have to claim some of my debts; a deal's a deal."

"And my collection?" Eliot pitches in somewhat nervously.

"Perhaps."

"You did the same for me once. Or similar at least." Gordon adds.

"You know, Rox... Gordon..."

"Whatever."

"What's a name, after all?" Pause. "It really is good to see you both." Eliot and Gordon exchange mistrusting expressions. "I sense great loyalty between you two; a bond," he goes on. A few painful moments of silence and thinking scrape around the surface of the square clock on the wall. The hands reverberate in Eliot's spinning head.

The Doctor suddenly gets up and puts his briefcase on the table, which he opens and turns towards Eliot. Two silver automatics sit on top of piles of money. A lot of money.

"I'll pick up the pictures tomorrow. You can keep the guns; you may need them," M states finally and sits back down, taking the rest of the champagne out of the ice bucket and topping up the glasses. They all drink, at the same time. An hour later Eliot and Gordon leave the restaurant together, carrying the case, and step into the characterless air. But very still. They don't notice the few mortals who follow them out and along the road, although they should look familiar.

Bend Sinister:
The Gay Times Book of Short Stories 3
edited by Peter Burton

A deeply disturbing collection

"There is a long tradition of gay authors writing stories which are at once decidedly sinister and decidedly queer," writes Lambda-nominated editor Peter Burton in his introduction to *Bend Sinister*. "Gothic literature, in which sinister is an essential component, was, after all, virtually the invention of gay men."

Here 28 contributors demonstrate this affinity in work that ranges through horror and fantasy to crime and detection, including stories which are decidedly erotic.

An ideal gift for anyone who likes to be spooked, *Bend Sinister* includes famous authors such as Francis King, Neil Bartlett, Christopher Bram, Michael Wilcox and Richard Zimler, as well as the cream of GMP's own writers and many exciting new voices.

October 2002 UK £9.99 US $14.95
(when ordering direct, quote BEN427)